Dolphin Sands

The novel by

Laurence Durley

Inspired by
and dedicated to
a faraway friend
who knows who she is

ISBN : 979-8-6478-3804-9

**

Author's Note to his Readers

*The characters in this book
find themselves at times in challenging
and confronting situations,
but not everybody has the support they found
amongst their friends, family, or neighbours.*

*If you are in Australia and need to talk to someone, don't go it alone.
Please reach out for help.*

__Lifeline:__ 13 11 14 or <u>lifeline.org.au</u>

__Beyond Blue:__ 1300 22 4636 or <u>beyondblue.org.au</u>

__Kids Helpline:__ 1800 55 1800 or <u>kidshelpline.com.au</u>

__Headspace:__ 1800 650 890 or <u>headspace.org.au</u>

Dolphin Sands

Chapter 1

Some weeks before my 70th birthday party, in the depths of my marital misery, I made the decision not to end my life altogether, but to end the life I was living. I would simply walk away from a situation I could no longer endure, instead of walking away from life itself. The change would be just as radical, hard though it might be, but my wife wouldn't get the insurance.

So the day after my party, I had one last chance at my local train station to reconsider my choice. Step in front of the train, or step onto the train? No contest. I stepped aboard with a backpack containing one total change of all-purpose clothing, my laptop, a hard drive with everything that mattered copied onto it, my mobile, and my key documents.

Halfway to Melbourne Airport I phoned my wife. I told her I'd gone. I said my younger brother was going to come round and pick up the rest of my stuff. He didn't know that yet, so I phoned him too. He's a good guy. He didn't say 'what the fuck' more than about six or seven times.

I got the plane to Tasmania. Some might say, are you sure that's better than the step-in-front choice? But that seemed to be the most English-like viable option. I come from England, London actually. It's a national characteristic that we seek for viable options. Take Brexit for example.

I guess what made the whole thing easier was that we were about to move out of our rather grand house anyway, and we'd sold it, and the solicitors had been instructed to split the money 50/50. But we'd not really settled on what was going to happen next. Still, I guess the implication would have been obvious to anyone, except her. The biggest change was in the timing. But I could tell from her voice she wasn't pleased – something said along the lines of 'I wished you'd stepped in front of that train instead of getting on it.'

I had in mind a place to go to. I planned to rent for as short a time as possible, see if I liked the area, then I would buy. I had a good pile of cash in the bank, in my own account, which in Tasmania would buy a pretty reasonable house, so long as it was in the back of beyond.

I picked up a rental car in Hobart and drove for a couple of hours. In the early evening I arrived at Swansea (half way down the east coast, to save you looking it up). It looked pretty ordinary. I thought, this should do. I headed for the Victoria Inn. That looked pretty ordinary too. Not out of place at all. I was born near Victoria – the one in London – so it had a homely sound to it. The Inn got a lot of five star ratings on a Russian tourism website. It had its own bottle shop. I needed a bottle.

The young woman on the desk was beyond pretty. She looked probably mid twenties, I'd guess Malaysian origin, not very tall. They didn't have many lights in the reception area because her smile lit up the room on its own. As soon as she spoke, I thought, maybe her folks are Malaysian but she's a whole lot more Australian than me. I glanced at her name badge, which she wore in such a place on her uniform shirt that I couldn't dwell on it long without getting my face slapped. I thought, staff should have their names tattooed on their foreheads, and that way it would save all-round embarrassment. I mean, you wouldn't pin a name badge to a guy's trouser fly, would you? Anyway, I filed away the name 'Colette' for future reference, in case I started a new career as a movie director and needed a leading lady. She could lead me anywhere. I heard a voice from home saying, Petrus, for god's sake, act your age.

I explained that I was new to Tasmania, looking for somewhere to live, and I needed a hotel room for a few nights to begin with. She said it was fine to book open-ended, just give 24 hours notice of leaving. I thought, perhaps I should have left home on the same terms, but I'm no good at long goodbyes. I dealt with the paperwork and payment. Colette didn't seem to notice that my parents had deployed their weak sense of humour in naming me.

I walked up the stairs. Lifts are bad for your health. Anyway, they didn't appear to have one.

The room was ok. The walls were bare brick. I could see why it appealed to the Russians. The view of the car park was handy so that I could check whether any young Tasmanians were stealing the wheels off the car in the night. I remembered that someone I knew once told me about how on a really wet night, he heard sounds outside of a car wheel being changed, went back to sleep feeling sorry for the poor bastard in the rain, then found his car up on bricks with no wheels when he went to drive to work. Then again, that was South London, and this was East Tasmania. But boys will be boys the world over.

It was getting dark, so I turned on the lights. They made little difference to the gloomy room. Still, the wifi worked, though I couldn't tell whether the hotel management were busy stealing my passwords. I checked my emails on the laptop. There was one from my brother, who had been round to the house and brought away the PC before anyone wiped it or guessed the password, and several others written in an increasingly threatening manner from my wife's solicitors. But actually, there was little or nothing they could really threaten me with. I was home free. Free of home.

I checked the real estate site for the three properties I'd got my eye on. One had 'sold' on it already. Still, it was my third choice. I would arrange to see the other two the following afternoon. And if those didn't work out, they weren't the only ones for sale in Tasmania.

I put away the laptop and went back down to the lobby. The bottle shop was off to one side, and was depressingly small, but I consoled myself that, for now, I only needed one bottle anyway. I chose a cheap red. To my surprise, Colette appeared at the till to take my payment.

"So when you've finished on reception they move you in here to sell the alcohol? Are you old enough?"

She just smiled, giggled a little but not enough to make me feel other than stupid. "Actually, I cover the shop and reception at the same time. And I'm old enough to have three kids, so I guess I'm old enough to be behind this till."

"Really? Three kids? Well you must have been busy in your teens." Immediately I wished I'd been typing that in an email, so that I could have deleted it before clicking on 'send'.

Colette was unfazed, riveted me with her smile, and said with no self-consciousness at all, "I'm thirty-seven. I didn't start early. My daughter is eight and the twins are three."

I couldn't think of a response apart from "Congratulations," and looked for an escape hatch in the floor. No dice. The doorway was the only way out. Before I'd walked past the reception desk, she had materialised behind it again, and wished me goodnight.

The bed didn't look too inviting but I was beyond tired, so I showered quickly and tucked myself in. I fell asleep wishing it was young Colette who had done the tucking. Or not so young. The downside of being 70 is that everyone looks very, very young. The upside of being 70 is that you can get away with anything.

In the morning I half expected Colette to be serving breakfast, but she was nowhere to be seen, apart from at the local school where she was dropping off her daughter, but I hadn't got that worked out. The breakfast was so bad that she probably wouldn't have been seen dead serving it anyway. Cold scrambled egg is close to the worst thing in the world. The prize winner in that category is refrigerated scrambled egg, and these eggs were front row contenders. The tea seemed to have been lovingly distilled from last night's washing up water. At an adjacent table, four Russian guys seemed to be delighted with it. I resolved that I would find out why so many Russians were congregating here as soon as I had improved my Russian language skills. But I knew no Russian. I would be on that case for some time, I thought.

At least there were some bananas in edible condition, so I helped myself to a couple and returned to my room. I called the real estate agency and explained my interest in the two properties. They were within fifteen minutes' drive of each other, so I arranged to view both of them that afternoon.

The properties were at opposite ends of Dolphin Sands, and were at opposite ends of the price scale too. Dolphin Sands is a narrow strip of land behind Nine Mile Beach, where piecemeal development has straddled the main road running its length. The local council had sat late into the night to deliberate the naming of this road, and had finally come up with 'Dolphin Sands Road'. To be fair, at the western end the name changes to 'Cambria Drive' for some reason, and it was in that road that the more expensive of the two properties was situated. The cheaper property, almost half the price, was at the east end of Dolphin Sands Road, close geographically to the town of Coles Bay, but due to a substantial unbridged inlet between the tip of Dolphin Sands and the town, it was a 50 minute drive from the property to the town around the inlet, despite the two being within easy view of each other.

The agent, Jilly, suggested starting with the cheaper property first, and I arrived a little late to find her waiting at the gate. She must have been new to the business in those parts, as she was wearing high heeled shoes which almost prevented her from walking along the unmade road to the house. For a moment I debated whether to offer her a piggyback carry.

The first problem with the property was that it was on the side of the main road furthest from the beach itself. I had known that from the photos and the map, but the distances were significantly greater when seen on the ground. The second problem was that it was much smaller than it had appeared on the agent's website. Properties always do, but this seemed a prime example of the inverse Tardis effect, whereby the inside of a house looks significantly smaller than the outside. The internal layout seemed odd and wasted space. It was quite light and airy, but at the same time cramped, which seemed a pity when the plot was ten acres.

I suggested to Jilly that we should move on to the second property and I followed her car, which wasn't too difficult as she drove with a town-dweller's caution.

On the website I had seen that this was a modern house, built as if on stilts to take advantage of the sea views afforded by its beachside location. But on the ground, it seemed even more contemporary in style. The steel lattice on which it stood was flimsy-looking at first glance, but closer inspection revealed a clever design that seemed proof against any reasonable storm event. Almost all the habitable parts were on top of the frame, but one room, together with its own bathroom, was at ground level. "The servant's quarters I presume," I said jovially to Jilly.

"Oh no, any member of the family could use this space," she replied, not having had her sense of humour transplant yet. "For instance, an older member of the family might have difficulty with the steps up to the main house." And she looked at me as if to say,

I'm not sure someone of your age is suited to a house on stilts.

"Well, let's see how a young lady in high heels manages those steps. After you!" I responded with my sweetest smile. I walked up behind her admiring the view, which took in the whole sweep of the coast if you looked in the right direction.

I have always been quick to make up my mind, and I decided to put in an offer for the house within seconds of entering the upper part. Floor to ceiling windows gave a magnificent view of the bay. The deck around two sides of the house was deeply shaded. The bedrooms could be used flexibly for other purposes if preferred. An outdoor entertainment area in the yard was shaded from the sun by a sloping roof. I struggled to find something wrong which I could use to negotiate the price, which was very slightly more than I could reasonably afford. I made some adverse comments about the state of the yard, which clearly needed a lot of work, and I said that the yellow colour of the exterior would absorb too much sunlight in the summer and would have to be repainted in white. Jilly made appropriate notes. I asked for a few minutes to sit and think about it, and settled on a bench on the deck.

I could hear the sea. The view really was superb. No other house was visible from this point. It was easily big enough for my needs, indeed the ground floor room would probably be superfluous most of the time. Reluctantly I peeled myself off the bench.

I found Jilly sitting on the sofa with her shoes off. I could understand why. "I'll call you in the morning to make an offer," I told her. "Once you have locked up, is there any objection to me sitting out here on the deck for a while? I'll be sure to close the road gate when I leave."

"Of course, that's fine. I look forward to your call in the morning. About 10am perhaps?" And she locked the entry door and carefully navigated the steps in her stockinged feet, replacing her shoes at the bottom and wobbling her way back to her car.

I returned to the bench and sat quietly for almost an hour, reflecting on the last few days' events. I felt calm here. It felt right. It felt meant-to-be. And it felt like a new beginning, with infinite possibilities. As the sun set behind the house, I returned to my car and made my way back to the dreary confines of the hotel. Yet perhaps I would see Colette, which would make it that much less dreary. But it seemed to be her day off. After the evening meal I consoled myself with the remaining half of the bottle of wine.

Chapter 2

At 10am I made the call. I offered all I could afford. Jilly said she'd call back after consulting the owner. She did. I went to the office. I came away a house owner, with only the legal stuff to be completed over the next couple of weeks. And I came away with the key, on a temporary rental basis pending the formalisation of the purchase.

The house was partly furnished for rental already, having been occupied by occasional Airbnb renters for some months. Fortunately no wild parties, it seemed, judging by the condition of the place. So I could move in right away with my backpack of stuff, pending delivery of my belongings from the former marital home. I called my brother on the mobile and told him I'd made the purchase, so he could get the stuff trucked across the water as soon as possible. He seemed surprised at the speed of my progress. He said "what the fuck" a few times more. The thing is, when you hit 70, you stop hanging around. The sound of the clock ticking gets a whole lot louder. And I'd been planning this for months.

After lunch I went to the hotel reception desk and there was Colette, back on duty, with her smile fully functional. She asked "How are you today, Mr Stone?" in a way that made it sound like she really wanted to know.

"I'm very, very good," I replied. The size of my own smile probably conveyed that anyway. Indeed I felt very, very good; first because I was talking to a beautiful young woman, second because I'd just bought a beachside house. Or maybe the other way round. No, the first way round was right. I explained what had happened and said I'd be checking out right away, and would be happy to pay in lieu of the 24 hours' notice she'd stipulated.

Colette looked around to check no managers were snooping and said "Don't bother, we'll pretend you told me yesterday."

"You mean, when you weren't here? Well, thank you, that's very kind."

"So where is the house, Mr Stone? In the town or further out?"

"Call me Petrus. I can only call you Colette as I don't know the rest. And yes, it's out on Cambria Drive."

"That must be number 135, the yellow place. I think you will be very happy there, congratulations."

"You know it? I guess it's a small town and everyone knows everything."

For some reason she hesitated for a moment. "Yes, I have seen it often. I remember when they were building it, and wondering quite what it would turn out to be. Anyway, thank you for staying at the Victoria Inn, Mr Stone, and do enjoy the rest of the day."

It looked like we were going to part on formal terms.

"There's one more thing – I think a bottle of champagne will be required at the house tonight – I'll meet you in the bottle shop."

"Fine, Mr Stone, I'll be there in just a minute, if you care to be making your selection."

The little shop had only three varieties of champagne and I chose the mid-priced one. I'd be drinking it alone, so no need to impress anyone. As I took it to the cash desk, Colette materialised on the other side.

"Thank you, Mr Stone," she said.

"Petrus," I attempted to correct her.

She ignored me. "Will Mrs Stone be joining you at the house tonight?" she enquired.

I thought, how does she know about Mrs Stone? And then I remembered my wedding ring, still on my finger due to the physical difficulty of removing it after almost twenty years. I'd need to work on that little problem soon.

"You're very observant, young Colette."

"I notice people's hands a lot. You know, they're in front of me signing things or making payments and stuff. I sometimes think I remember hands more than faces."

"Ah. I see what you mean. Anyway, no, I shall be living on my own in the house. If Mrs Stone ever arrived there, I would leap off the balcony and run to the sea."

Colette giggled. She smiled readily and she laughed easily. Yet she had three kids and presumably a husband. I wondered what the secret of her happiness was.

"It will be a big house for one person," she said.

"I have a lot of stuff on its way from Melbourne," I told her, "and I'm sure I'll have a girlfriend or two with me before long."

Colette giggled again, holding her hand to her mouth as if she might get fired if anyone saw her being happy with a customer. I was unsure whether her giggle was because I'd said something risqué, or whether the notion of someone my age having a girlfriend, or two, was a joke in itself. I hoped the former was correct.

"Maybe I will be back for more champagne in due course," I said, "but I guess for now it's goodbye and thank you for your help over the last couple of days."

"You're welcome, Mr Stone." Colette bestowed a last radiant smile on me, and carrying my backpack, I headed out to the car park.

My hire car was nothing more exciting than a Golf, but the car beside it was clearly something radically more exotic. On closer examination I realised it was a Tesla electric supercar, but with two child seats incongruously in the back. I hoped those kids would be well strapped in for the ride. Perhaps it belonged to one of the Russians, perhaps an oligarch on tour. With his kids. No, not likely. Maybe the hotel owner.

It took only ten minutes to drive to the yellow house. It took no more time than that again to unpack my backpack and arrange all my property, such that it was. There was wifi and it worked. There was a washing machine and that seemed to work too. A change of clothing was going to be good. Something in the fridge and pantry was going to be good too. A trip back to town before the shops shut would be the next task.

Morris' Store is one of two supermarkets in town, and it sells just about everything. This being an area with a long history, the supermarket has a museum room. This is not something you'd encounter in a Melbourne supermarket. I stocked up on groceries and then wandered round the hardware section, picking up things like scissors and some basic tools.

Starting from scratch makes you realise the little things in a household that are important. But I was also going to be very careful about not filling this house up like the last one. I once had a friend in London, Lila, who unlike me seemed to go through life with almost no possessions. She travelled light. She had come lightly into my life and then moved lightly on. I thought, now that I'm a free man, maybe I'll see whether Google will tell me where in the world she is now. Hitherto, she'd been on my mind from time to time, indeed more often than that on the bad days, but getting in touch wouldn't have been an option. But right now, Lila Eyon would have to wait.

Back at the house I realised that the up-on-stilts design had a downside – everything I had just bought had to be humped up the staircase. Well, I thought, this will do me a world of good on the fitness front. Currently I was sporting an unfitness front, which I tried to conceal by never tucking in my shirts, but even that wasn't hiding the size of my beer belly. It seemed to be particularly cruel to have one, as I rarely drank beer. Still, a few weeks of climbing those stairs would transform it into a single birth size from its current twins configuration. My heart surgeon would probably approve.

I stashed my purchases, and the pantry and fridge took on a different look. For my first dinner in the new house, I had selected a tuna and pasta frozen meal, which looked like it would go well with the modest champagne. I had also purchased some candles just in case the power went out, and I pushed one into the neck of the empty bottle of red wine that I had brought away from the hotel as a souvenir of Colette. Pathetic really, but that's the way I've always been. I keep stuff.

The late summer evening was warm enough for me to eat at the little table on the terrace, and it was sheltered enough there for the candle to burn, so in a little while, that's what I did. A candlelight champagne supper for one. For now, it didn't feel lonely. It felt good. I felt free.

Chapter 3

The following morning I woke early, because I hadn't thought to lower the blinds anywhere in the house, and the generous windows admitted a considerable amount of light as soon as there was any to admit. I had a quick breakfast and decided I would check out the land that I'd bought without having really looked at it at all.

Don't ask me what kind of trees and bushes were on the land, but they were scrubby kinds of things growing from what amounted to a flat sand dune. There were some proper trees but not many. A large area around the house itself had been cleared leaving a stony, sandy surface. No hint of grass anywhere. Lawnmower definitely not required, which was just as well as there wasn't one in either of the small sheds.

I briefly checked out the covered outdoor entertaining area. There was power and light. Good for wild parties with music.

Wearing a tee shirt, shorts and trainers, I strolled towards the beach along a lightly worn path between the bushes. As I emerged, the full sweep of the beach could be seen almost disappearing in the sea haze. I had previously calculated that it would take at least three hours to walk its length. I resolved that one day I would do it. But not today.

Not far from where I stood, to my right, a family group was playing in the sand. Two small boys were making sandcastles with a notable lack of success, supervised by a woman who must have been their grandmother. A young girl played in the shallows nearby. The grandmother must have seen me emerge from my property, and as I walked in their direction on the soft sand, she smiled. She was from some kind of Asian background, but her sun-hat and sunglasses made me unsure whether she was from Vietnam or Thailand or neither. In fact, to be honest, I probably wouldn't have known in any event, nor did I particularly care, except that when she spoke to me, it was evident that her English was not of the best. Fair enough, I thought, I couldn't speak a word of any Asian language to save my life.

The lady made a gesture in the direction of the yellow house.

"You!" she said. "You new here!"

I nodded. "I have just moved in," I said, not quite resisting the temptation to speak like a robot.

She pointed towards the neighbouring house, an imposing residence which I could glimpse between the trees from one end of my balcony, but here was completely hidden by the rise and by the low trees and bushes. "Me here!" She made a gesture towards the children. "All here!"

I was about to say something very English like "So glad to make your acquaintance, Madam," when I heard a shriek from the sea. I spun round and saw the young girl retreating backwards from something in the water, then fall into the sea in panic. The grandmother cried out in alarm, but seemed frozen to the spot. I ran as best I could towards the child and splashed into the water in my only pair of trainers. My mind was torn between anxiety about the trainers and anxiety about the child, but the latter won, and I grabbed her under her armpits as she flailed about, and dragged her from the water. A small jellyfish watched us with apparent disinterest from the shallows nearby. At least, it seemed disinterested, although I cannot quite think how it would seem otherwise.

"Come, you're ok now," I said to the child once her legs were beneath her. The grandmother had now recovered herself and was talking at a considerable rate in her own language. It seemed that the poor child was getting little sympathy despite shedding tears of fright. Grandmother took her arm with little delicacy, rounded up the boys, and they all retreated through the bushes towards their house.

"No need to thank me, I'll be here all week," I said more to myself than to Grandmother. I pulled off the sodden trainers and headed barefoot back to the yellow house, thinking that my first foray onto the beach hadn't gone that well. Still, the shoes would probably dry out in the sun on the deck before I needed them later in the day.

A mug of coffee restored my spirits, and I settled down with the laptop to send off what seemed like a hundred emails to all those needing to be notified of my new address and circumstances. Lunchtime slipped past, enlivened only by a cheese and pickle sandwich. More emails sped on their way. Some could be duplicates of others, but most had to be prepared one at a time. My eyes and fingers grew tired. As the afternoon drifted towards evening, I'd had enough, and fell victim to the calling of the deck facing the sea. I would probably have dozed off there were it not for the hardness of the wooden bench. I resolved to find something more comfortable on which to relax out there, in the fullness of time.

As I watched the sky transform itself into its evening colours above the sea, and the sea respond in kind, I was aware of two people walking up my land from the shore. This, I thought, would not do. I've just paid an arm and a leg for this plot and it's not going to be a handy route to the road from the sea for all and sundry. I put on my almost-dry trainers and went down the steps two at a time, although after the first pair of steps, one at a time seemed to be a better idea.

Walking towards them through the open space beneath the house, I realised that these were not strangers. Or rather, there was one stranger and one familiar (and rather lovely) figure. It was Colette, and from the way she held his hand, the other person was Mr Colette.

I thought, Ok, one or two comments were a bit risqué, but bringing the husband round to beat me to a pulp seemed to be taking things a bit far. However, the ever-sunny smile on Colette's face was reassuring, as was the hand held out by her husband as he approached.

"Good evening!" he said, affably enough – warmly even. "I'm Doctor Cheung – Ezra Cheung. I'm here to thank you for saving my daughter's life. And my wife tells me she has already met you, and she would like to thank you too."

Sundry things fell into place. No wonder Colette was familiar with the house. She lived next door.

"Very pleased to meet you, Doctor. And pleased to renew my acquaintance with Colette – er, Mrs Cheung. As for your daughter, it certainly wasn't a matter of lifesaving. She just panicked for a moment when she saw a jellyfish and then fell into the shallows. I'm sure her grandmother would have managed without me."

"Well, I did rather feel that the account we received from

Colette's mother was on the dramatic side," replied the Doctor, "but we remain grateful. And we'd like to take the opportunity to welcome our new neighbour."

I did a quick calculation and realised there was probably just enough champagne left in the fridge to go round. "Please, do come up and help me finish the champagne that Mrs Cheung so kindly helped me to select yesterday at the hotel. I think there's a glass each to be had from it."

"That is most kind," Dr Cheung responded. "It would be interesting to see the inside of the house, having watched it appear here, but we must not be long. The twins' bedtime is approaching."

I was optimistic about the glass each. The house seemed to have only one glass amongst its rental equipment. The rest had probably been stolen or broken by the Airbnb guests. Colette had the glass, Dr Cheung had a mug, and I had another mug and an embarrassed demeanour.

They admired the house and I explained how the rest of my belongings would be arriving from Melbourne before long. I noticed that Colette did not smile quite as much as she usually did now that her husband was with her. She was in fact rather quiet and reserved, which I took to be a cultural thing, deference to her husband and so forth. It was a pity that my wife hadn't seen things that way, I thought, and then unthought it right away in case anyone was reading my mind.

"Have you signed on with either of the local medical practices?" asked Dr Cheung as he finished his mug of champagne.

"Not yet," I replied, "but I'll be sure to sign on to yours."

"Whatever you think best, Mr Stone. I'd be happy to advise you on weight loss and getting fit if you cared to consult me."

Bloody hell, I thought, that's not appropriate in front of Colette, as she probably hadn't noticed my shape. Then I thought, get real, Petrus. It would have been the first thing she noticed.

"Thank you, I look forward to it," I replied, thinking something akin to the opposite.

I accompanied them back to the yard and invited them to cut straight across to their own house rather than going via the beach. They did so, and at the boundary Colette turned and waved. I

15

waved back, and climbed those mountainous steps again.

As I busied myself microwaving my supper, I thought, how come Colette works as a hotel receptionist and bottle shop cashier when she's living in a luxury house with an evidently well to do doctor as a husband?

Before I turned in for the night there was a short email from my brother saying that my stuff should arrive on Wednesday; it was currently Friday. All I had to do was to think where it was all going to go. Obviously the big stuff like bookcases and my desk would have to be brought upstairs by the removal guys first, and the boxes, which were legion, could somehow be wedged in around them until I could unpack them at my leisure. I wished now that I'd spent more time throwing stuff out back in Melbourne instead of paying to have it brought here and then throwing it out. So many wishes.

Saturday late morning saw me back at the hotel for wine, having done a further shop at the store. Colette was there, happily, as it would have been easier and cheaper to have bought wine elsewhere, but I needed a dose of her smile. I thought, I bet half of her husband's patients would recover more quickly on a short course of Colette than on whatever drugs he was pumping into them. As before, she sincerely asked after my health and happiness, and I mentioned the problem I was about to have with the hire car. I had to return it to Hobart on Monday but then I needed some tips on how to get back to Dolphin Sands without it.

"Monday? I have to drive to Hobart and back on Monday for my husband. Perhaps I could drive you back?"

"For your husband or with your husband? Well, whichever, I'd be very glad if you could give me a ride, a ride back." I doubted whether she would react to the initial accidental double meaning but I made sure by correcting it, which only served to emphasise it.

"I will have to ask Ezra if it's ok, but I'm sure he would be fine about it. If there is a problem, I will let you know somehow. Otherwise, wait for me at the bus stop opposite the visitor information centre on Elizabeth Street at 2pm." And she took my payment for the wine. "See you on Monday, Mr Stone."

I spent the weekend dealing with a lot of admin stuff on the laptop, and in having a detailed look at the house and the property.

I was at a loss concerning what to do with the land. I didn't have enough left in the bank to employ someone to landscape it, and I didn't fancy my chances of doing much with it myself. Maybe the best option would be to buy something to kill stuff growing near the house, and let the rest run wild. I was in two minds about how I should allocate the bedrooms, but the obvious thing was to simply claim the largest for myself, make the smaller one the guest room, and the one facing inland could be a TV room or a study, or both.

As for the room at ground level, it had its own shower and toilet, and a small sink in the corner of the bedroom itself. It had an unusually high ceiling, as it sat below the main house on its stilts, and I quickly realised that a loft bed could be installed so that the whole room would be usable for living in, with the bed raised above it. For a long term guest, it would be ideal.

I also spent time scanning the car ads on the internet, looking for something passable for sale locally, and bookmarked four which seemed worth considering. I didn't need much, just a runabout capable of occasional trips as far as Hobart, but normally just into town and back.

So the weekend passed, and I was in bed and asleep by 10pm on the Sunday night, ready for an early start on Monday. I was very curious to discover more about Colette on the drive back from Hobart – but ready for a bit less discovery if her husband was indeed with her.

Chapter 4

The drive to Hobart took almost two hours, partly because I'm not the world's fastest driver, and partly because that's how long it takes. I had started later than planned, having lingered over coffee on the deck admiring the morning view, and by the time I had done battle with the hire company's paperwork in their offices, there wasn't a great deal of time left to be a tourist. I got the feeling that if I wasn't at the appointed spot at the appointed time, I might find myself walking home, so I just strolled around the Marine Museum and the Art Gallery briefly, grabbed a light lunch in the Gallery cafe, then headed for the rendezvous spot in Elizabeth Street. As 2pm approached I began scanning the approaching cars, trying to guess which one might be driven by Colette. Holden Commodore – maybe. Ford Escape SUV – might suit the kids. VW Tiguan – a bit small. Tesla Model S – no way. Except it was pulling up. And the window was lowering. And a beautiful young lady at the wheel was smiling just like Colette and saying, "Hop in, Mr Stone!"

I hopped with as much aplomb as I could in order to impress the others at the bus stop. Then as the car swished ahead, I turned to Colette and said "Please tell me you didn't just steal this and we're going to be arrested any minute."

Colette, needless to say, giggled, while deftly circumnavigating a bus which had suddenly stopped. "Don't be silly, it's mine. Ezra gave it to me when he bought his new BMW. I'm surprised you didn't notice it in the hotel car park."

"I did, but I didn't expect it to be yours. I thought it must belong to the hotel owner."

"Well, he does seem to wish it was his, but it's all mine. It's even got personalised plates. CC2020. That's my name, Colette Cheung."

"I know that. But I didn't associate the plates with you."

"Because I'm a receptionist and cashier, I suppose, and a woman."

"Because I didn't think you were wealthy enough. Doesn't mean that I didn't think you could one day be wealthy enough." I paused, confused by the double negative. I had no real idea what I had just said. I had even less idea when we reached the foot of the Tasman Bridge and Colette encouraged the Tesla to cruise up as if there was no slope to it at all. Once clear of the city, the car sat on 110km with little noise and no effort, and the kilometres fell away behind us.

After a while, I reopened the subject of the car, and said, "Let me put it another way. Ezra, or Ezra and yourself, have two exotic cars, a substantial home overlooking the sea, and three children, but you yourself work in relatively low paid jobs although outwardly there seems to be no need."

"Not all my work is low paid. I do two afternoons a week in the pharmacy."

This was news, perhaps because in the short time I had been in Dolphin Sands I'd not needed to visit the pharmacy. "I didn't think shop work paid much," I ventured.

"It's not shop work. I'm a qualified pharmacist. The hotel stuff is just for pin money."

I digested these facts with initial difficulty. But then I thought, her age was no debar to any of this. She was perfectly of an age to have qualified as a pharmacist, to have married a doctor, to have had three children, and to live a very comfortable life in financial terms. Perhaps because she looked a lot younger than her age, and because she was a very beautiful young woman, I made a slew of assumptions that had no real basis. I even wondered whether my attitude was also influenced by the fact that her family came from Malaysia. Could anything good come out of Malaysia? Of course it could, and had.

"But you must get exhausted. I guess your mother helps with the kids, but even so, with all those jobs I hope you get some good holidays."

"Not really. I go back to Malaysia every few years, but always with the kids, so it's not much of a break. Ezra thinks that if I want a break from the kids, then I'm not a good mother. And he says the only way we have become quite wealthy is by earning all the time and by spending carefully."

"Like buying a Tesla when a Toyota would do."

"Ezra likes cars."

"I like your car, I have to say. Is it true that if you doze off it will drive itself?"

"I don't use all that stuff. I just drive it like a normal car."

"And very well, if I might say so." I instantly regretted the patronising tone, but Colette made no comment.

The car was so quiet that dozing off would have been a strong temptation if I was driving it. As a passenger, it was irresistible. Soon I was sleeping like a baby. We were almost at Swansea when Colette woke me.

"Mr Stone! You have to wake now! We are nearly home." And in a few minutes, we had reached the gate to the yellow house property.

"Colette, thank you so much for driving me back – you have no idea how much time and trouble that has saved me."

The natural thing to have done in the situation would have been to lean over and kiss her cheek, but Colette's demeanour signalled strongly that any such thing would be distinctly unwelcome. She conveyed that at the same time as giving me a smile which would easily have recharged the Tesla in moments. I stepped out from the low car with as much grace as I could muster, and waved her off as she turned it expertly in the space near the gate.

"See you soon!" she called out of the window as the car glided away.

"I hope so!" I called after her, but she was already almost at her own drive.

Back in the house, for the first time I was conscious that I was the only person in it.

I did not see her again until Wednesday. My stuff from Melbourne arrived first thing on a substantial truck, which lumbered slowly down the track from the gate and drew up beside the steps. The two guys in the truck looked at their instructions on a clipboard, looked at the steps, and then looked at me. "Furnishing items to first floor," the older one read, "remainder to be stacked in ground floor room. Existing furniture to be removed and delivered to landlord's storage."

I groaned inwardly and wondered what my brother had been thinking of. Both I and, it seemed, the removal men doubted my ability to get the contents of the boxes upstairs myself. Still, at least that would keep the main part of the house tidy with all the junk hidden downstairs.

In the space of about four hours and with the consumption of several beers, the truck was unloaded, then refilled with the rental furniture, and with a couple more beers apiece taken to ease their journey, they were gone in a cloud of sandy dust. I went upstairs to survey the scene.

My wife was moving into a much smaller apartment and had been perfectly happy for me to take the bulk of the furniture. That is, she was as perfectly happy as she ever was about anything, but that didn't really amount to a whole lot of joy. Consequently I now had beds for the two upstairs bedrooms, three easy chairs, a dining table with half a dozen chairs around it, and a sofa for the third room. I also had several bookcases and my glass topped desk, which miraculously had survived the journey undamaged. I had been able to encourage the delivery guys to put the beds in the bedrooms and the sofa in the sofa room, not to mention the dining furniture in the dining area, but the bookcases were in a huddle at the side of the lounge room. I would need to work out where they could live. The problem with an open plan house with lots of windows is that there's little blank wall space for bookcases to occupy. I sat in one of the easy chairs, temporarily overwhelmed by the task in front of me.

Out of the blue, there was a voice calling me. "Mr Stone! Hi! It's Colette. Can I come in?"

I almost fell over trying to leap up from the low chair. "Come on in," I called, and Colette made her way slowly into the room, taking in the sight of the new furniture and slight state of chaos.

"I just got back from my morning shift at the hotel and I saw the van leaving. I brought you some leftover sandwiches from the hotel lunch, just in case you needed something."

"Colette, that is so sweet of you."

"And I didn't know if you needed any help. Where are all the boxes? There are always boxes."

"In the room on the ground floor. It's piled high. It'll take me weeks to sort out. I should've thrown most of it away before I left Melbourne, but that was quite sudden."

Colette busied herself in the kitchen for a few moments and

then put two plates of lunch on the newly delivered dining table. "We can christen the table," she said, "that's if you don't mind."

Without thinking, I said "I'd christen this table with you any time you like."

From the silly grin on my face she could tell exactly what I meant. The smile left her face and the room grew dark. "That's man talk," she said in a voice that conveyed not anger but disappointment. And she turned away to the table and faced the door, as if debating whether to go.

I was aghast at my juvenile stupidity. "Colette, please forgive me. That was a stupid thing to say. You have my respect. You really do. No more man talk, I promise. I really am sorry."

She paused, then walked back into the kitchen. She returned with two glasses of lemonade, gave me one, and sat down at the table. I sat opposite her. Still without smiling, she looked at me as if studying the contents of my mind and measuring the degree of my contrition, and the nature of my future intentions. I made sure she read copious amounts of contrition, and the most innocent of future intentions. And from that moment, I meant it. Time to grow up. Time for respect.

Finally she seemed to have made up her mind, and asked, "So what happened with your wife? I mean, you really could do with some help around here."

"Her? She'd be bossing me around to hell and back at this point. Endless complaints, constantly accusing me of stuff, daily unpleasantness – I'm much happier struggling on my own, thank you."

"You were married for long?"

"About 20 years. Marry in haste, repent at leisure. We dated for a week and then got engaged. Crazy."

Colette looked surprised. "That's weird," she said, "Ezra proposed to me a week after we met too. I can't believe you were the same."

I thought, who could blame him. I said, "At least you haven't repented at leisure."

"No." But for a moment, Colette looked out across the bay, as if looking for something lost long ago. "He's very kind to me."

"Well, he certainly gives you nice cars. But he seems to make you work so hard."

Colette said "Yeah, work." She looked at me with one of her direct looks and said, "I got fired this morning from the hotel. Ezra won't be pleased. I've not told him yet."

I was sorry to hear that, but relieved I would no longer feel compelled to patronise the hotel bottle shop. "What happened?" I asked.

"Officially it's because I was undercharging customers."

"Like me? I hope I didn't get you into trouble."

"No, not you." Colette was an unconvincing fibber. "But I think the real reason may have been that the owner kept asking me to take him for a ride in the Tesla. I finally agreed, but we'd hardly got out of the car park when he put his hand on my leg. My thigh. High up. Bastard. But fortunately we had a straight clear road ahead, so I slammed down the accelerator and he got pinned to the back of his seat so strong he had to let go of my leg. Then I slammed on the brakes, and I can tell you, the Tesla stops pretty smartly. That nearly put him through the windscreen, seatbelt notwithstanding. Then I told him to get out, and he had to walk back. Then an hour later, I got fired."

Colette looked down at the table, pursing her lips. Then she looked up at me, caught the look on my face, and burst into giggles.

Colette glanced at her phone to check the time and the messages, then said "I'm not expected home till about five, as I was supposed to be doing an afternoon shift. So I can help till then. What's first?"

"You are beyond kind. I really would appreciate a hand. I need to slide these bookcases to somewhere better first of all. They're quite light, I'm sure we can do it between us."

Colette was not tall and was sensibly slim, but she was nonetheless blessed with a mother's wiry strength, and in no time the shelves were manoeuvred to the few places it was possible to locate them. My desk had been left in the lounge, but fortunately it had industrial wheels, and it was simply a matter of trundling it into the sofa room, which I had decided would also be my study. Having it in a general purpose room would help to motivate me to keep it tidy.

"Now what?" asked Colette.

"I guess we need to bite the bullet and see what the downstairs room looks like. Then it's a matter of bringing stuff up a box or two at a time, unpacking or throwing away, then the next box, and so forth for the next few weeks."

"Now I've been fired I guess I'll have more time than I otherwise would to come over and help."

"I'd be more than grateful. But one glance in that room might put you right off."

Colette skipped down the steps, I trudged. I opened the door downstairs. I made a gesture of mock horror and closed it again quickly. Colette giggled, which was what I was hoping for. I reopened it and I led the way in.

The delivery crew had stacked the boxes into the space with remarkable intelligence, largest on the bottom, smaller ones above, and had left corridors between the stacks so that it was possible to some extent to pick and choose which ones we wanted. But the sheer number was daunting. I have always been a hoarder.

"This might seem odd," I told Colette, "but what I would really like would be to get the audio and video equipment in first. Then I'll have music to listen to while I work upstairs and I can slump in front of a movie or whatever at the end of the day."

I picked out the relevant boxes one by one and we carried them upstairs. I noticed Colette did not shrink from picking up the heaviest rather than the lightest. I didn't want to seem to be a wuss, so I also went for the heaviest. It developed into something of a competition but I suspect she won. By the time she had to leave, all the tech stuff was upstairs.

"You've been amazing, Colette. I can't thank you enough. I do hope you don't get into too much trouble with Ezra over getting fired," I said as she walked with me towards the property boundary.

"I'm sure it will be ok," she replied, but with a trace of apprehension in her voice. "I'll come over again when I can. Maybe tomorrow for a while, but I have a pharmacy shift in the afternoon."

I watched her walking across her own property, then strolled back to the house, and went upstairs to begin installing the hifi and

24

tv.

It was about an hour later that I heard a knock on the door. I thought, I must get a wireless doorbell with the push at the bottom so I can get longer warning of arrivals. There at the door stood Ezra Cheung.

"Ezra! Come in. Colette will have told you what's being going on here. She's been most helpful."

"I heard indeed. She is a very hard working young woman."

And one who needs a holiday, I thought.

"I believe you heard she lost her job at the hotel," he continued. "She will be needing to find another job."

I found it very hard not to make a comment that Ezra would not have appreciated, but for the moment I said nothing other than to invite him in for a beer.

"No thank you, I am due at the evening surgery very shortly. But I wanted to make a suggestion."

"Oh? Please do."

"I think you would find plenty for Colette to do here in the coming weeks."

"I would indeed. She is as hard working as she is intelligent. A great asset to any organisation, or to an elderly man trying to get his affairs in order."

"Perhaps you would be prepared to employ her."

I was completely taken unawares by that. My first thought was, is he her husband or her pimp? I'd imagined that she would pop over from time to time in a neighbourly fashion to give me a bit of a hand, but paying her had not been uppermost in my mind. But then I thought, why expect a person of working age to do hard work just to be nice? I wished she had made the suggestion herself rather than having this conversation with her agent, I mean her husband, but at the end of the day, it wasn't a bad idea.

"I'm sure we could come to an arrangement. Colette and I could sort something out when she has a moment to spare."

"I think she would prefer me to speak on her behalf. It's always difficult to talk about money when seeking employment. Tell me, you are retired I believe?"

"Semi. I used to be a recording engineer, now I'm a writer."

"Ah. That's very interesting. A writer. Well, maybe we could agree on something nominal – perhaps $20 an hour. Flexible hours according to your need and her varying availability. For as long as you need her or until she finds a proper job again. Whatever duties you think appropriate. Perhaps some general housekeeping as well as the initial sorting out of all your, er, stuff."

I did a rapid calculation. I actually received two pensions, and my income as a writer was quite closely related to the effort I put into writing. With Colette acting as some kind of housekeeper I'd have more time to write, and my writing was successful enough to bring in rather more than the hourly $20 I would be paying her.

"That's fine," I told him. "But of course, you will want to discuss it with Colette first."

"I'm sure she will be very happy," replied Ezra. I thought, she'll do as she's told, that's what I'm sure of. Still, I'll be more fun than the hotel manager. At least she'll be sure I won't be putting my hands where they're not wanted. She knows I'm not going to risk that look on her face again.

"Well, I must keep going," said Ezra as he turned to the door. "Oh, by the way, what sort of writing do you do?"

"I write short stories mainly. Mostly erotic ones. Don't worry, Colette won't feature in them."

He gave me a very direct look. "You are an older gentleman, so I am sure that I need not say that I would not wish to think that Colette would be involved in any, er, research for your writing."

I looked him straight in the eye back. "Of course not. You have my word. She has my respect." I wasn't sure if he had understood the implied insult.

He just turned and closed the door behind him as he left.

Chapter 5

Getting all my tech stuff set up occupied me for most of the following day. Colette was unexpectedly busy at home in the morning and had her shift at the pharmacy in the afternoon, but was booked to come here the next day, Friday, from 10am to 5pm. I looked forward to her company, and her help, but I also looked forward to just having anyone reasonably congenial in the house. I was still getting used to being on my own, and living a fair distance from anyone I knew.

"So what's first?" she asked when she arrived at exactly 10am.

"First is helping me pick up my new car. Well, not new new, new to me new. Do you know Old Spring Bay Road? It's in a street just off there. Hopefully driving me around is part of the deal?"

"Of course," replied Colette. She hesitated, then added, "I just want you to know I'm not very happy about this whole 'deal' thing, Mr Stone. I would have been entirely happy to give you some help without payment having to be brought into it, but Ezra..."

Her voice trailed off. I said, "Hey Colette, don't worry about it, you need the money and I've got it. I don't expect people to do me favours."

"I'm not sure we exactly need the money."

"Whatever. It's not a problem. Now, where's that beautiful car of yours?"

We walked across to her property where the Tesla was parked in the curved drive in front of the house, and in a few minutes we were at our destination. I gave Colette the house key and she drove back to the house while I completed the transaction. I was now the owner of a blue Toyota FJ Cruiser as well as a yellow house. Colette looked down from the deck as I arrived and parked the Cruiser under the house.

"That looks practical and kind of fun too," she commented as I came in. "Here, coffee and biscuits."

I couldn't help noticing that in the time I'd been away, Colette had totally sorted the kitchen and I could hear the washing machine doing something soapy to my dirty clothes. Well, I guess she'd had plenty of time as her journey home probably took seconds. But then the thought of Colette picking up my discarded clothes from the bedroom floor, underwear included, made me wish I had done it myself. I thought, not only will Colette help keep this place shipshape, she'll provide the motivation for me to keep it that way. I'm enough of a 'New Man' to not expect any kind of slavery from a woman. Probably unlike Dr Ezra, I added to myself.

We sat opposite each other at the table, and she gave me one of her happy smiles, and said, "Ok, Mr Stone, what's the plan?"

I'd been thinking about that, and suggested that we should first undertake the relatively straightforward task of bringing up the books from downstairs, and filling the bookcases, which were looking a bit sad in their empty state. Coffee finished, we started the task, filling the shelves in a semi-haphazard manner to begin with. Books of a similar nature seemed to have been put into the same boxes, but only by unpacking all of them could the overall best sorting plan be determined. I made some notes on a crude plan of the bookcase layout, and showed it to Colette.

"Perhaps we could try to sort them like that."

"But I won't know which is which."

"It's quite straightforward. For instance, all the biographies together, all the travel books, novels, poetry, and so forth."

"I never read, so I might not be good at identifying them correctly."

"Ah. Perhaps Ezra doesn't give you time off for reading quietly."

"No. That doesn't happen. Anyway, let's have a go and we'll see what happens."

We had a go. Between us it happened, although to this day I'm occasionally finding books in completely the wrong place, which reminds me of Colette every time. We took a break for an extended lunch, and I dozed in the sofa room for a little while because I had lunched too well. Meanwhile Colette made an interesting mixture of the novels and biographies, clearly not so good at distinguishing fact from fiction. Then there seemed to only be time to have a 4pm afternoon tea, after which just half an hour was left of Colette's allotted time.

"Let's have a look downstairs and see if we can decide what to do next time," I suggested, "and then maybe you could slip away a few minutes early and go home after ten minutes on the beach."

We identified kitchen and crockery as the next group of boxes to be taken up. Without being sexist, but simply acknowledging my incompetence, I strongly expected Colette would be better in the kitchen department than she had been with the books, though I could not fault her work ethic. She went on her sunny way towards the beach. Any beach-goers would find the afternoon down there to have brightened for a few minutes.

I took another look around the downstairs room. Colette would not be back until Monday. Perhaps there was something I could tinker with meanwhile, otherwise I would have to write, if only to earn Colette's keep. My eye lighted on a trunk which had emerged from beneath the books when we took them up.

It was one of those travel trunks, made of plywood but faced with metal sheet on the outside and decorative paper lining within. It was not very big, and I was confident I could manage it up the stairs. I was pretty sure it contained papers from long ago, but I decided to check, and undid the three unsecured locks.

As soon as I saw inside, I remembered it was a box containing everything that Lila Eyon had left behind when she said farewell to me in London. It was 27 years ago, before I worked full time in recording, and even longer before I became a writer.

We had worked on separate floors of a dreary concrete building, but my job involved occasional visits to her office. I remembered going to her desk for the first time one sunlit morning, and as I had approached I could not help but see that she was writing in a notebook.

As I glanced down at it for the briefest moment, I could not make out the words, but from the way the writing was set out on the page it seemed like poetry. Lila had looked up at me, and I had quickly looked away from the page and brought my attention to her face, and her smile had simply melted me. It was a deeper, more contemplative smile than Colette's simple happy radiance.

I had thought, she is a poet, a beautiful, beautiful poet.

She stood to show me some papers, and the sun from the

window behind her shone through her light blue dress, the delicate material allowing me to make out the beauty of the slim shape within, and my fascination became tinged with desire. And the blue of her eyes and the red-gold colour of her hair haunted me and drew me in, and there was nothing I could do to resist.

Then she had invited me to a bar one evening. Later she denied it was an invitation, just a passing comment, but fortunately that is how I saw it, as I would never have had the courage to ask her out on my own initiative. I remembered how we had talked and talked, about our past and our plans, sitting on opposite sides of a table as I recall it, but leaning in to catch each other's words against the loud music. And her hand lay irresistibly on the table, and reckless from the alcohol I had covered it with my own, and she had not moved away.

We had become silent in the moment, and then, or perhaps later, it was so many years ago, I had said to her "How long have we got?" and she had replied, "Perhaps until December," and so the days from mid August counted down remorselessly from that moment.

We had taken a taxi back to her flat, and she had sweetly invited me to stay the night. She offered me the choice of her spare room or her own bed, and I had said something stupidly polite like "your bed would be nice."

We had undressed with the light very low, and the music of the Divinyls very loud, and I had caressed her body as if exploring a foreign land for the first time. She had needed to give me very little encouragement with my erection, but simply gently decorated it with a condom and invited me into her. Then the music and the drink and the excitement and the unfamiliar room made me come way too soon, yet Lila allowed no trace of disappointment to escape her. We had slept at first in each others' arms, then turned away to search for our dreams in a deeper sleep.

I often wonder, and worry, about the workings of my memory. The past comes back to me in tiny slices, photographs rather than movies. So much now is lost to me that I should have remembered forever. But among those slices there were treasured moments from the months that followed. Turning back towards Lila after leaving her room, and seeing her dressing, in lacy underwear and stockings, and looking as if she had stepped from the pages of Vogue. Driving to Wales, and my eyes filling with tears as we came to the sea in the evening light, where villagers were drawing in fishing boats from the water. Lila walking across heather-covered countryside naked to the waist. She kneeling beside me on my bed, her hair cascading over my abdomen as she leaned down to me and took me between her precious lips and into her mouth as I brought my hand to her breast. Spending time with my two young children from my first failed marriage, she so patient and level with them, they clearly adoring her from the outset.

I remembered Lila's phone call late one evening, asking me to drive over and bring her to my flat for the night, and finding her wearing nothing but an overcoat, her long black overcoat, entirely naked beneath it, and when we arrived she simply wanted to sleep, which with difficulty I finally did. And our short holiday in Switzerland, from which I had treasured photographs, very occasionally taken out of this very trunk for a sentimental viewing.

And finally I remembered our long drawn out parting, our last lovemaking, the slow wrenching and splitting and separating over weeks, caused not by any action of our own but by the action of our parents, mine having brought me into the world too soon, hers bringing her too late. She was twenty-six, sixteen years younger than me, and it was too much. She had the restlessness of youth and I had ties and responsibilities and commitments I could not cast aside, even for her. We were at different times in our lives. The separation culminated in the drive to the airport, where I held her in my arms too briefly as I said goodbye, and I watched from the departure lounge window until I saw her climb the staircase to the plane door and disappear for years to come.

I carried the trunk up the stairs to the dining table, and took out the contents one item at a time. There were printouts of emails from when we worked together. There were letters, many letters, over a period of about five years. In one was the news of her marriage, in another a photo of her newborn baby. Soon after those I lost touch, until I made a single phone call after my emigration to Australia. Then my wife said, it's her or me. There were movie tickets, an invoice from a hotel where we stayed, golden hair discarded from her brush, lipstick stained tissues, underwear found tangled in sheets.

I closed the trunk and left it in the corner beside my desk. Suddenly, I needed to find Lila. I needed to apologise for losing touch, maybe apologise also for the person I had been then, but who was probably not much different from the person I now am. Google would be my friend, Facebook would be my trusty assistant.

It took me a few hours of trawling the internet but finally I found Lila's now grown-up daughter. She had mangled her first name for anonymity and had used her second name but not her surname as part of her Facebook identity. But she was remarkably casual about privacy settings, and I was able to read everything. There was a photo she had taken on her mother's house deck. That might be useful, I thought. I would have expected her mother to have been amongst her Facebook friends, which were legion, but I couldn't see her there.

From the old letters I knew her mother's new surname was Moone. but that brought up nothing on Facebook. I tried the 'white pages' site. Lila Moone was listed at three addresses. Two corresponded with addresses on the letters, and there were phone numbers. The last one seemed to have no connection with the first two, the address being a long way from the others, but I decided to check it out on Google Street View. Eureka, it was clearly the same house that Lila's daughter had included in the photo.

My hand hovered over the phone. The trouble was, I knew nothing of her circumstances now. What if I dialled the number and her husband answered? Should I tell the truth straightforwardly or should I concoct an elaborate lie? Perhaps I could pretend to be a florist checking that Lila was home before delivering flowers. Perhaps I should pretend to be returning a phone call from her about some dry cleaning.

I tried Facebook once more. This time, on a whim, I tried searching for her full name, which in the old days she never used, Lila-Rose Moone. Bingo, there was a match. She was hiding in full sight. There was no photo of this particular Lila, but there was a photo showing a tree in her garden, and in the background was the same house again. Home run.

It's such an easy thing to click on the button to contact

someone on Facebook. One tiny movement of one finger. But I hesitated. Part of me was telling me loud and clear that this was going to be one of life's pivotal moments. Another part was telling me that there might simply be no response, and that I would be left wondering forever, or would have to risk the phone call.

I ate my evening meal facing the windows that looked out at the wide ocean view. Then I went back to my laptop, and clicked the "Add Friend" button.

I made myself a hot chocolate, something I rarely drink, but when I was in the supermarket I'd picked it up as a potential source of comfort. And right now I thought I might need comfort.

There was a ping from the laptop. There was a message on Facebook. "Say hi to your new Facebook friend, Lila-Rose."

My hands shook a little. I needed to get a grip and type. I replied, "Well that was a quick response! For some years, on and off, I've been trying to find you to check that you are still alive and well and hopefully happy, So here's the big question - are you alive, are you well, and are you happy?" I hadn't thought this through in advance at all. Something had made me think that planning my response would be tempting fate, that it would be presumptuous, that it would assume a reply was going to come. And now it had. I hoped my reply struck the right note, conveyed the right tone.

A response was being typed. On the screen, the little activity dots were dancing. I tried to breathe normally. The reply appeared. It began, "When i saw the name i thought could it really finally be you! Have also searched on & off over the years..."

My life pivoted.

I need to cut a long story short. We switched to email, and each sent a long summary of life over the last twenty years or so. I explained my second marriage, its failure, my new life in Tasmania, and brought her up to date with how my children in London had grown up, married, and had children of their own. Lila's email described how her husband was now Deputy Principal of the school he had taught in since they were married. Her daughter was an air hostess. Lila made a living as a writer too, writing mainly for women's magazines about interior design and decor and similar topics.

After the emails, as the days went by and the pile of boxes and crates in the downstairs room diminished with Colette's ongoing assistance, I exchanged messages with Lila several times a day, and the years that had passed fell away. We seemed to be carrying on very much from the point where we had said goodbye – old friends chatting easily and comfortably about everything and nothing. Photos were exchanged, and links to music or movies. The tone was of an older man exchanging messages with a married woman – there was no reference to our former status as lovers.

But neither of us suggested talking on the phone, or video calling. Just the typed words seemed to work, and we were both writers, so perhaps it came naturally. And neither of us wanted to rock a very comfortable boat.

And then Lila phoned me out of the blue, which completely capsized it.

Chapter 6

My name is Lila Moone. I will explain how my marriage ended. It was sudden, it was traumatic, and I did not see it coming.

But I am kidding myself. I had seen it coming for months. And I ignored the signs. I was kidding myself then too.

My husband, Brian, was Deputy Principal at the school. He worked late often. Even when we were newly-weds twenty three years ago, and he was a junior teacher, he worked late often. I was proud of his hard work, and admired how he would not come home until the next day's lessons were fully prepared. Now, of course, I wonder.

So it was not the working late that first gave me misgivings. Over the years, the cynicism that breeds in schoolteachers gradually warped him, and the bounce went out of his stride. The jokes came less often. The complaints about pupils and other teachers were more frequent when he came home. He ceased to be a happy man. Our sex life turned from unexciting, to undemanding, to under once a month. This also did not give me misgivings. I thought this was how marriages went.

One evening, not long ago, out of the blue I received a Facebook friend request from a man who had been my lover in the months before I met Brian, I think about twenty-seven years ago. Brian was well aware of my friend Petrus. He would sometimes ask, "Have you ever heard from that lover of yours, that guy Petrus Stone? The guy whose parents had a sense of humour, and a smattering of Latin? Petrus Stone, god."

Always I would truthfully respond that I hadn't heard. I didn't mention that I looked for him online from time to time, and that occasionally I would dream that he was in the shower with me, and that I pleasured him with oral sex. But as soon as I did hear from him, I told Brian. He seemed oddly pleased. This gave me misgivings, which I ignored.

For some weeks before that, I had become conscious that Brian's cynical demeanour was gradually falling away from him. He complained less. He carried himself better, losing the middle-aged slump in his shoulders. He showered more often and stopped wearing the same shirt two days running. These signs I also ignored.

He did not mind that I was messaging Petrus several times a day, as we caught up with years of old news. He did not seem to notice that my own demeanour was, well, happier. This I found harder to ignore.

Finally, there came a day when something happened that I could not ignore. I came home early to our home near Brisbane from a trip to Sydney. I had been meeting the new features editor of the magazine for which I most often wrote. His pregnant wife's waters broke unexpectedly, and he brought our meeting to an early conclusion and went home. I caught a much earlier flight, and the traffic from the airport was unexpectedly light.

Arriving home, I went straight through to our bedroom at the far end of the house to change out of my best clothes. I was surprised that the door was closed. I could have sworn that, as usual, I had left it open to air the room when I left that morning. I opened it and stopped dead. A girl I recognised as one of Brian's year twelve pupils was on our bed, on her hands and knees, naked. Brian was behind her, and his head was thrown back in the ecstasy of climax, his erection invisible within his pupil's body. His hands gripped her hips. Her eyes were tight shut. They actually didn't notice me there for fully twenty seconds. Then they noticed, because I stepped briskly across the room and pushed them over, hard. The girl landed on her side on the bed. Brian went right off the edge of the mattress and ended up on the floor. I slammed the door and ran back up the house, got back in the car, and drove straight back to the airport.

I parked on one of the upper floors of the departures car park, where there were few cars and fewer people. I turned off the ignition, leaned forward on the steering wheel, and sobbed until my skirt was wet with tears and nasal mucus. I felt like being sick. I opened the car door and retched.

I had no idea what to do next.

I pulled myself back from the edge of hysteria. Devastation turned to anger. Anger turned to action. My chosen action was flight, not fight. I knew I could never return to that house and that man. I thought, where to then? I thought, Petrus once said twenty or more years ago that if I ever needed him, he'd be there for me. Nobody I knew had any knowledge of him. He could help me and keep me safe from my friends. At times like this, friends could be as hard to handle as enemies. My hands were almost too shaky to hold the phone, but I managed to dial the number he had given me in his first email.

The phone rang several times, and then I heard his voice.

Chapter 7

On the day Lila phoned me, I had spent all of the morning writing. Colette had busied herself around the house cleaning and tidying. Because she had spent so much time in the preceding months alongside me, going through everything I owned, keeping some stuff and throwing out most, she could now be relied upon to put things away either in the right place or in a good place. From time to time I had to ask her where a certain thing might be, but she invariably went straight to it. Perhaps this is part of a pharmacist's skill. When you take in a prescription, regardless of how obscure the drug, the pharmacist goes straight to it on the shelves. But by observation, I have determined that it's not just a matter of alphabetical order. It is something more complex, and something secret.

But to return to the writing. When I write erotic stories, I have to do so on the basis of personal experience. The storyline can be completely fictitious, although it helps to have visited any location involved. But the sexual activity, and the woman involved, has to come from memory. Of course the performance of both parties tends to be optimised on the page. Being unable to maintain an erection, or coming within seconds, doesn't on the whole make for an erotic experience for the reader.

It was a problem for me therefore that I had led a celibate life for a great many years. My wife had developed certain problems with sexual activity early in our marriage, which were not her fault, but nevertheless they caused her to regard me with disinterest at best and revulsion at worst. As the years went by, the revulsion tended to be the dominant emotion. I had coped with this by regarding sex as unimportant, so although I had teetered on the edge of affairs on a few occasions, I had not fallen. But my wife's intuitions were sharp and she usually knew about the teetering, and could identify with whom I teetered. The object of my lust was invariably banned from the house and from my email address book. Consequently I was short of practice and my memories were becoming distant.

Apart from a couple of tawdry flings before my marriage, the person who most recently figured in my sexual memory was Lila. I had rarely 'had sex' with Lila – to me, it had been more about making love. Our sexuality had been firmly grounded in our relationship, which had not made it boring and unadventurous, because our relationship had been far from that. But I could not write about her with erotic intent without writing about the context, about the relationship itself. This however had proved to be popular with my readers, who perhaps had tired of the weird and the kinky, the unlikely and the biologically impossible, and were themselves trying to buck the trend and seek for more meaning in their sex lives. I liked to think it was the romantic's erotica.

The stories tended to revolve around a fictional reunion between myself and Lila. When we had started exchanging messages, translating the unreality of the messages into the real world, where I presumed we would continue as lovers as well as friends, had become the subject of a great deal of my thinking.

To meet Lila in that real world seemed to be a far-off dream. Consequently our meetings in my stories were often dreamlike and unreal. Sometimes the opposite was the case – I imagined how difficult it would be to transition from the exchange of messages through to actually meeting, talking face to face, the sudden revelation of what the years had done to us, conversation inhibited because we had completely lost touch with the detail of each other's life.

So it was on this particular morning. I sat staring at the screen, waiting for words to come. Colette came in to the study quietly with my morning coffee and a couple of biscuits, then left without speaking. She tended to avoid me when I was writing, partly because she realised I would prefer not to be disturbed, but partly because her husband had warned her never to look at what I might be writing on the screen, for fear that she might be outraged. Or perhaps he thought she might be unduly interested.

The first sentence arrived. This was always crucial. The rest usually flowed almost without pause once the first sentence was down, or ideally the first paragraph.

I wrote, '*Their cottage was so close to the beach that the sound of the ocean was a constant background, even on these cooler days when the windows were tight shut. They had rented it for a few weeks.'*

Then more words began to arrive in a rush. That was somehow the way it worked. They arrived on their own. *"She had arrived first and made sure that there was plenty of food to hand, and wine, and good things for breakfast and for afternoon tea. She remembered his love of croissants for a breakfast treat and rich, dark fruit cake in the afternoon."*

I liked that. Treats for me. Somehow Lila's name was not attached to the story this time. The 'he and she' mechanism sometimes seemed to be best, but 'he and she' were clearly myself and Lila in my imagination.

"When he arrived on the following day she was more than taken aback by his appearance. He had aged from his middle years to his later years since last she had seen him, decades before. He was clearly exhausted by the journey. After a light evening meal she had suggested that he should go early to bed, and he was more than grateful."

The shock of seeing a former friend who had become old regularly haunted my thoughts. I had experienced it most recently a few months before I had left Melbourne. A friend originally from my teens and his wife came to stay for a week, the first time I had seen them in almost twenty years. My friend looked older but still himself. His wife, his beautiful wife, had changed much more. Time is so unkind to women. But if I ever met Lila again, while she would be no more than middle aged, barely so in my view, I would be classified by the newspapers as 'elderly' if they were to report on my being knocked down by a bus. I had last seen her not long after I had turned 43. From that age to seventy was a big jump.

She had taken him to the second bedroom, made sure that he had all he needed, and then she had taken his hand, squeezed it gently, and kissed his cheek. He had lowered his head as if in shame. Then he had raised his eyes to her, and she took him in her arms, holding him close to her, feeling him breathing against her, and kissed him as a sister might, on his lips but lovingly rather than passionately. And then as she drew away, she saw that his eyes were still closed, so she held him a moment at his shoulders until he recovered, and he looked around him almost bewildered.

"Sleep now," she said, and closed the door behind her as she left him to undress.

Was I suggesting a degree of confusion in myself, and pity in Lila? There was no reason to think that an impossible scenario. But would it really be something like that? I very much hoped it wouldn't.

Her sleep in her own bed was light, as might a mother sleep, half listening for the cry of her child.

There. Lila sees me as a child. That's pretty depressing.

More words came. *She let him rest till mid morning, then quietly carried in a tray with what she somehow recalled was his favourite breakfast. He was still asleep but woke as she entered. It seemed to take him a moment or two to realise where he was. She opened the heavy curtains a little, admitting the light of a grey day and a little more of the sound of the ocean, decorated with the occasional cry of a wheeling sea bird. She made sure he was comfortable sitting up in bed, fussed a little with his pillow, and then sat down on the wooden chair in the corner. But then she went as if to stand again, saying "Perhaps you want to be on your own?" and he replied quietly "No, please, it is good to have you here. You are making such a fuss of me," he added appreciatively as he realised the care that was on display on the tray over his lap.*

They sat in companionable silence for a little while, and then she said "Perhaps you would like a walk by the sea in a little while?" and he nodded as he cleared the last morsel of croissant from the plate. "At least your appetite is good," she smiled. She rose and took away the tray, and left him to shower and dress.

Again, a middle aged woman is performing almost a carer role for this elderly man. How is this going to turn erotic?

Later, they made their way down to the very edge of the sea as the tide receded and revealed the great swathe of smooth, firm sand. The beach seemed to extend as far as the eye could see. The incoming waves broke in long, long lines of foam. The sky was a mass of low clouds of every shade of grey, with pinkish overtones here and there where the sun tried to break through, and in the distance a glimpse of blue sky promised better to come. They walked quite slowly, arm in arm, and spoke little as the roar of the ocean demanded all their attention. They stopped when he spotted

41

a child's plastic bracelet glittering in the sand - he bent to pick it up, saying "Some little girl will be missing this treasure," and she was aware of his slow movement. Having retrieved it, he did not seem to know what he should do next, so she gently took it from him and tucked it in the pocket of his jacket saying "We will find a good place to leave it where it might be found."

'He did not seem to know what he should do next.' This is me I'm writing about. Doddering, confused. God.

About two-thirds of the way along the beach, he stopped and said "Perhaps we should turn round. We have come such a long way." And his eyes met hers, and she thought, "Yes, we have come so far, you and I, from where we began, to this place and this time," and he seemed to catch her thought, and maybe she detected a tear at the corner of his eye; but perhaps it was the wind that brought it there.

I liked that a little more. When I feel emotional as I write, I know it's working.

At the cottage they ate a sandwich and salad lunch which they prepared together, side by side in the kitchen; his task was mainly to butter the bread, but she did not wish him to feel unrequired. At the end of their lunch she saw again the tiredness in his eyes and suggested he should settle himself with a book in a comfortable chair in the lounge while she tidied the kitchen. "Are you sure you don't need me to help with that?" he asked, but did not argue, and when she had cleared everything away, she walked quietly through and saw the book unopened on his lap, and smiled at his sleeping. She took the chair opposite, facing him, and soon dozed herself.

Thank god they are both taking a nanna nap, I thought as I stared at the screen, waiting for more inspiration. I could hear Colette putting lunch together. Food. I let that thought lead me.

Later, she brought in tea and he said "I seem to wake only for meals that I haven't contributed to," but she assured him it had taken no effort to prepare, apart from the time it took to bake the cake. They both chuckled at this fiction. The afternoon grew dark as the sun set, and they stood at the bay window looking out to the sea and the reddening sky, he standing behind her with his hands on her shoulders. After some minutes she turned to him, and they kissed gently but with intimacy, and he held her in his arms until she said that they should turn on the lights, and he reluctantly released her.

At last, some intimacy. And on more level terms. In many of the erotic stories by others I had read, that kiss would lead forthwith to athletic sex on the carpet. This was not my way.

She had prepared a vegetable lasagne before his arrival, which only needed final reheating, so there was little to do in the kitchen, but she asked him to open a bottle of red wine, and he wrestled briefly but finally successfully with the cork, commenting on how rare it was to see one these days. She said "If you check the label, you will see that this one has been waiting for us for some years," and he saw that the wine was from the year of their parting, and was of not inconsiderable quality. It was for that reason that they made sure not a drop remained after the meal. The wine eased their conversation, which inevitably circled from the past to the present, but never to the future. No wine in the world could help them see what might lie ahead.

Whenever I had Lila in my mind, thoughts of her kindness and consideration and little loving gestures returned to me. She had been a lover on so many levels.

Afterwards they sat on the sofa close together and talked on into the night. Finally, they fell silent, and she turned to him and said "How would you feel about us sleeping together tonight?"

He replied, "That would be good. So good. But your bed or mine?"

She chuckled and said, "I think my double bed would be more suitable than the single one in your room. And we'll take things as they come, ok?"

Finally, some real erotic content is arriving. As always when writing it, if I didn't get at least a slight erection, there was something wrong, and I'd reach for the delete key. But what would actually happen in this scenario? Would there be sudden passion? Probably not.

The words wouldn't come. I relaxed and tried to run the scenario like a movie in my head. I began to type again.

Later they lay together in her bed under a single sheet, having undressed discreetly and slipped into the bed unwatched by the other. They lay with their backs to each other, suddenly strangers.

After some moments, he turned onto his back, and she did so also and looked across at him. He lay on the bed as if washed there by the sea from the wreck of his life, driven onto the rocks by the repeated errors of his own navigation. He still looked a little weary, his expression calm but somehow wistful. She turned onto her side to face him. "Turn to me," she said. He did so.

I re-read the paragraph. The sentence beginning 'He lay on the bed as if washed there by the sea...' was one of the best I had ever written, though I said so, aloud, myself. That one sentence completely summarised me and my life and everything. But how depressing.

"It has been so long," he said, "could you take my hands?" And so they lay there with their hands intertwined, and after a little while she began to stroke his hands with hers and he responded in kind, and he said "I think I will need you to guide me - I feel so inexperienced now, and clumsy."

She smiled and took one of his hands in hers, laid it on her breast, and said "Here we are ageless, with no expectations, no demands, no judgements, only infinite patience and love." And she moved her hand with his, caressing herself but feeling his touch. Soon he needed no further guidance there, and she withdrew her hand. Then he moved his hand to her other breast and she closed her eyes as his confidence returned, as did his ability to arouse her. Then came a moment when her need for him drove her to take his hand once more, and with fingers interlocked she slid them between her legs, turning on her back. Once more she guided him with her own hand, and felt her own wetness there, and gently pressed his finger into her, and left him to find his own way. He searched her, found her, caressed her, and then her arousal took hold of her, and she raised her hips as she came, and called his name, and he said "My love," and leaned over her and kissed her with a passion that denied his age.

'A passion that denied his age'. Let's hope I could manage that in real life.

Once more she covered his hand with hers and stilled his movements because her arousal was becoming almost more than she could bear, despite her climax. She turned herself onto her side, and gazed at him with the intensity of fire. "I think it is high

44

time it was your turn," she said, sliding her hand down his tummy. But he gently lifted it away and said, "Tonight was for you, my long lost friend. Perhaps tomorrow will be for me, or for both of us. My hands have been reawakened, and they need to wander for a while yet on their voyage of rediscovery." And so they did, until they knew every part of her with deep and intimate knowledge. Then their eyes closed as the sound of the great ocean waves spirited them away to their dreams.

Yes, I thought, that is love-making, erotic, but love-making, where one's partner's pleasure is of equal or greater importance than one's own.

In the morning, he woke first and was the one to make breakfast as best he could. When she had finished and he had left the room to allow her to shower and dress, she turned back the sheet and saw that on the downy place between her legs, the child's bracelet had been carefully laid, twinkling in the morning sun, reminding her of his eyes, the sea, the sand, and their love.

I felt driven to write that, but had no real idea what it was about. But it felt right. It felt like the kind of crazy but loving gesture I might make, if given the chance to be crazy and loving again.

Colette tapped gently on the door. "There's lunch ready if you want it now."

The story needed polishing but my appetite needed attention first. I went through to the kitchen, still feeling an inner arousal, and yearning for physical contact, to be hugged, held, connected with another human being. Colette was already sitting in her usual spot at the table, and instead of going around to mine opposite her, I found myself on the same side, almost behind her chair. In my head, the alarm bells rang so loud that I was surprised that Colette didn't hear them too. Perhaps she did. She turned in the chair and looked at me with some surprise. "Mr Stone?" she said in a puzzled voice, frowning a little.

I thought, I want to stand behind her, put my hands on her shoulders, and I want her to cross her arms over her breasts and lay her hands over mine. Just that. Just that human gesture of affection. And then I thought, this is Colette who is younger than my daughter, who I know is very fond of me but who has zero

45

interest in any physical contact whatsoever. With Colette, it would be one strike and you're out. Even that stupid comment when she first came here nearly ended things. It has to be possible to have a relationship with a young and attractive woman without getting involved, without sexual overtones creeping into the picture. It has to be possible to have an appreciative friendship, even at some levels an intimate friendship, with a woman, without desire corrupting something beautiful and simple.

"Sorry, I'm just taking in the view of the sea before I sit down with my back to it. Sometimes it seems almost disrespectful to appear to ignore it."

"Would you like to swap sides?" Colette asked quickly. "Or you could sit here next to me, you don't have to sit opposite, and then we can both admire the view. I mean, you've paid enough for it, you should be able to enjoy it whenever you want."

"Maybe I'll do that, I'll bring my plate over here." And so we sat side by side, with an appropriate distance between us, but it felt how friends might sit, just naturally and companionably.

After lunch, Colette cleared away the plates and restored the kitchen to its pristine appearance. I returned to the study with the intention of revising the story, but I felt tired after my creative efforts and I slumped onto the sofa instead. In moments sleep washed over me, and I did not wake when Colette quietly left, having put a teabag in a mug, a little milk in a jug beside it, and an oversized portion of fruit cake on a plate beside the jug.

It was only the phone which woke me, late in the afternoon.

I fished it from my pocket almost still asleep. I answered it on about the sixth ring. I could not immediately identify the caller. I heard the words "Petrus, it's me, Lila. I need urgent help."

"Lila – I didn't recognise you, I'm sorry. I've just been having a nap and my brain is barely working. Are you ok? You sound upset. You sound awful. Sorry, that came out wrong. Where are you?"

"I'm at Brisbane Airport. I need somewhere to hide, now."

"Who from? What's happened? Never mind, just get here somehow."

"I want somewhere to hide from... everything. Have you got a spare room I could use for a few days?" Then I heard her sort of

46

wail, childlike. "Petrus, I need to hide. Hide me, please, please."

"Ok, of course, come here, I'll fix everything, you can hide. Look, if I drive to Hobart Airport right now, and you get on a plane, we'll be together in no time, and I'll bring you back here, and we'll hide together. Have you got money?"

"All I've got is my credit card and my phone, more or less. But that's enough. I'm in the car park. I'll walk over to the terminal and see what I can arrange, then I'll call you again."

"OK, I'm going to start driving just in case you arrange something quick."

"No, don't do that, I doubt whether I can get a flight till the morning now. Just stay put till you hear from me. Please, don't walk away from your phone. I need you to be there."

"I'm here for you, Lila. I'm here. Take a deep breath, know that I'm thinking of you, make a plan, and everything will be ok."

I waited for about half an hour at the dining table with the phone literally in my hand, and with pen and paper in front of me to take notes. Lila rang again.

"Petrus, I'll be on the 6.30am Jetstar flight that gets to Hobart at 10.15am your time. Meet me at the airport. I'm sorry, I'm totally disrupting you, but I just need to be on my own and I know I can be on my own with you."

"It's no problem, Lila. There will be a big hug waiting for you at the airport, and then you can tell me everything."

"Petrus, when I see you, please don't even touch me. Please."

I was totally taken aback. "Are you physically ok? You've not been attacked or something?"

"No, I did the attacking. Look, I can't talk. See you in the morning. I'm going to find a motel or I might just sleep in the car. Keep your phone by you, ok? I'm so sorry about this..." As she rang off, I could hear her crying.

I thought, thank heavens that the house is looking immaculate. Lila used to be a big fan of immaculate. The spare bedroom was fully functional, bed made, and I just needed to find the niceties such as towels and stuff like that. In the morning I could go first thing to the store and get other things she might need – toothbrush, shampoo, maybe even something like a cheap track suit so she could change into clean clothes. Underwear? If I got the size wrong I would be in dead trouble. Still, in for a penny – I would take a guess and hope for the best.

I went to bed early, put on two alarms, but slept badly. I hoped Lila was sleeping at all, wherever she was.

Chapter 8

I moved the car to long-term parking and slept in it. Or barely slept. Maybe dozed for a little while. I needed to be sure to check in on time for the early morning flight. There was nothing I could do about my appearance, apart from wearing the dark glasses I kept in the car. I found a sturdy shopping bag in the boot and cleared anything useful from the car into it. That was all my luggage on the plane.

On the flight, I drank coffee and declined food. I wasn't ready to do something so life-affirming as to eat.

There was no call from Brian. There was nothing he could say. There was nothing he could say that I would accept as true. I now suspected everything and everybody. I did not find it at all hard to believe that he might have been screwing his students for years. Did those regular training conferences he supposedly attended in beachside locations really exist? I even wondered what our daughter might have known. I trusted nobody. I would trust nobody. I did not even trust Petrus to turn up on time to collect me at Hobart. I was right.

I hung around the gate for half an hour. Eventually I could see him coming across the arrivals concourse, or rather, I saw a quite elderly man, who I realised was Petrus when he was a few metres away. I was shocked at how old he looked. He moved like the age he was. He was slightly bowed and he carried a little more weight than was healthy at his waist. He was clearly trying to hide both those defects but it wasn't really working. I thought, that portrait photo he sent me must have been taken a few years back. Then I remembered that the photo I'd sent wasn't exactly recent either.

I realised he was looking at me and not liking what he saw either. I snapped at him. "No need to stare, you're not a fucking oil painting yourself, mate."

Petrus blinked, and looked shocked. I thought, Christ, that's the first thing I've said to him face to face for twenty-seven years. I've just kicked a sick puppy. Oh god.

He spoke very quietly. "Look at every oil painting in every gallery in the world, and you won't find one that loves you." He paused, then added, "I'm looking at you with concern, nothing else, because something terrible has happened to you, and with the best will in the world I can only say you look awful. And I care about that."

There was a bench right beside us. I sat down on it heavily, almost fell onto it, and the tears and sobs came again unstoppably.

Petrus sat down beside me, but left a space between us. He said nothing for something like a minute. Then he said, "Lila, you said don't touch you, so I'm not. But I've never wanted to hug someone more in my whole life." And he stood up to make it clear that he wasn't asking to do that.

He rummaged in a shopping bag he was carrying. "Here, packet of tissues. Use them when you're ready." Between sobs I took them and started cleaning myself up as best I could.

"I'm sorry I was late, I wanted to get some stuff for your arrival and I didn't leave enough time for the journey," Petrus told me.

"I think I would have preferred punctuality than stuff, but thank you anyway. Oh god, I'm sounding like such a shit again."

"Lila, don't worry. For twenty-four hours you can be as big a shit as you like. After that, maybe it will be my turn." He gave me a slight grin. That grin made him look a bit more like I remembered him.

"If you are ready, let's get going. I'm still not the world's fastest driver, and getting home for lunch would be better than getting home for tea."

As we drove out of the car park in his SUV, he said "Let's leave the talking till we get home. These days I need to concentrate to avoid getting lost, or arrested, or both."

"Don't bet on the talking even then," I told him. "I may need time."

"Don't worry. Where we are going, time is about all we've got."

His mobile rang on the handsfree. He said, "Shit, I forgot about Colette."

He answered it and a young woman's voice was on the other end. "Hi Mr Stone, it's Colette. I was worried that you're not here. Is everything ok?"

"It's fine. I've had to go urgently to Hobart to collect a friend who is coming to stay for a few days."

"Ah yes, I remember when we first met, you said you would have a girlfriend or two staying before long."

"No, Colette, this is just a friend. Now could you finish cleaning anything that needs cleaning, make sure the guest room is looking nice, leave some sort of light lunch, vegetarian, for two people, and then you can go as soon as you are ready. I'll pay you for the unexpected short day."

"Ok, Mr Stone, I'll get that done." I was sure I could hear a giggle as she rang off.

"That was Colette," Petrus said, superfluously.

"Yes. But I didn't listen." I might not have listened but of course I'd heard.

He had told me a fair bit about Colette in his messages, but possibly not all. I trusted nobody.

We didn't talk. Petrus had taken the hint. Despite myself I fell asleep and didn't wake until the SUV was bumping over the drive down to the house.

Petrus had said it was a yellow house, and it certainly was. The designer had taken leave of his senses when it came to the colour scheme. It had to be a 'he'. No woman would have done that. I know about this stuff. It's what I do.

Petrus parked under the house between the stilts and came quickly round to the passenger side, and helped me out as if I was his grandmother. He took my arm briefly, not my hand. I was suddenly very conscious that it was the first time he had touched me in all those years, and I was also conscious that I had told him not to, but it was meant as a courtesy, and I had been unkind enough to him already to last a few months.

I could hear the sound of the sea at the end of the yard. That was about the only sound I wanted to hear right now.

I could tell Petrus was keen to show me the house, so I resisted the temptation to walk down to the beach, and possibly to keep walking into the sea until the waves closed over my head.

"Ok, Petrus, show me the house but keep it brief. I'm exhausted." I realised I was answering a question he had not asked.

51

He showed me the downstairs room and its ensuite bathroom, and the handy sink in the corner. He explained he was going to order a loft bed to go in there maybe even that day. Currently it was almost empty.

We climbed the steps to the main part of the house. As I took stock of things I thought, this is pretty ideal as a place to hide. There was a great expanse of sea and sky beyond the huge windows, and no other human habitation to be seen. The house seemed quiet, and there were plenty of books, largely in cogent order on the shelves. I could see some stray novels among the biographies, but I could re-sort everything very quickly when I felt more like myself. I wondered which self I was going to feel more like. All my anchors had been dragged loose. My ship was in full sail in a storm. I could end up anywhere. I did not know who I might become.

Petrus showed me the guest room. "I don't know how long you are planning to stay," he said, "but if you think you'd prefer the privacy of the downstairs room, I could get it sorted out in a few days. It would be no trouble."

"I have no plan. I might go tomorrow. I might stay. I need to get my bearings. I'm sorry, I'm not ready to talk. Just bear with me. I'll be in a better state tomorrow."

"There's some lunch here – sandwiches and stuff. Salad I guess. Do you fancy some?"

"I'll nibble on a lettuce leaf. Is this what Colette put together? Hmm."

An image of Petrus and an imaginary Colette naked and entwined flashed across my mind. I pushed it away. I pushed them over.

I actually ate one sandwich and a little salad, sitting alone at the dining table, looking out across the bay as Petrus hovered and fussed.

"Don't hover, don't fuss," I said. "Come, sit with me," I added as I realised I was being at least potentially offensive again.

Petrus sat with his sandwich, opposite me with his back to the view. I said, "You've got your back to the view."

"No," he said, "I don't think I have."

It was a nice thing to say. It annoyed me intensely. I said

nothing rather than say the wrong thing.

Lunch finished, I said to Petrus that I'd like to take a shower and then have a lie-down on the guest bed. He showed me the things he had bought, and actually he had chosen well. I was embarrassed by the accuracy with which he had guessed my size. I inwardly forgave him for being late at the airport due to his shopping trip.

"Petrus – this is going to sound weird, but could you leave me on my own while I shower and stuff? Maybe you could go for a walk on the beach for an hour. Or go and see Colette." I shouldn't have said that.

"I don't ever go and see her. But the beach will be good at this time. Are you sure you have everything? I'll be sure to be an hour, don't worry, it's not a problem. I'll have my phone with me."

I thought, I can trust him. Then I thought, I trust nobody. And I thought, I trust nobody, but given time, I might trust Petrus. Maybe.

The shower was good. I had so much to wash away. No blood, not any more, but sweat and tears. And images I could not stop flashing in my head over and over again. Brian's semen on the carpet. Brian's semen on her thighs. I washed and washed but there was no relief. He had fucked her and in doing so he had fucked me. Suddenly I heard myself howl like a dog in pain. Thank god Petrus was by the beach, though I could believe the sea heard me and roared back its anger.

I dried myself, blocked the thought that the feminine way the towels were arranged on the rail was Colette's doing, and put on the t-shirt and tracksuit trousers Petrus had bought. I lay on the bed. I slept. And I slept. And I slept.

Chapter 9

When I got back to the house after an hour on the beach, there was complete silence. I walked through the foyer, into the lounge area, and through to the hallway leading to the guest room, the toilet, and the bathroom. The guest room door was closed. Lila must be asleep.

It was pretty clear from her behaviour that Lila had been significantly traumatised by some event. She had been clear that she had not been attacked, otherwise I would have expected rape to be the event. She said she had attacked someone else. Well, maybe the problem was a murder, which would explain her desire to hide. I thought, hiding a murderer is a criminal offence. Would I go to jail for her? Yes, in a heartbeat, despite what she had said when we met.

I scanned the news for her home suburb online. No reports of violence, domestic or otherwise, that would fit the circumstances. That at least was a kind of relief.

I made myself some afternoon tea, and debated for a moment whether to wake Lila. No way. Whatever had happened, she needed sleep.

I went quietly into my study, and tried to write. I thought of Lila in the shower. This was a guilty thought. Right now, she was in trauma-induced sleep, and having a sexual fantasy about her, let alone writing it down, would be highly inappropriate.

Having my lover from 27 years ago sleeping only a few steps away was kind of confusing, especially when she'd made that comment about me not being an oil painting. She was probably right, but it wasn't the best way to begin a reunion. She, on the other hand, was looking in damn fine shape. She'd obviously changed over the period, but as Shakespeare would have put it, 'into something rich and strange'.

But never mind all that, she was a friend in need, and any other thoughts would have to go on the back burner indefinitely. Or, quite likely, permanently.

The afternoon slipped away, and it was time for an evening meal. I looked in the fridge to see if by some miracle Colette had left me a surprise. The surprise was, there was nothing worth eating. I'd asked her to prepare lunch, and that's exactly what she had done. But I tried the freezer. In there was a frozen vegan lasagne and a frozen meaty lasagne. Clearly she had indeed thought ahead, and had shot down to the shops and back in that car of hers in less than no time.

I went as quietly as possible to the guest room door. There was still silence within. It still seemed best not to wake Lila. I imagined that before much longer she would need to wake for a pee. Then I'd offer the meal. Meanwhile, I popped mine in the microwave. In a little while I was sitting at the dining room table, positioned so that I could see Lila immediately if she reappeared, and I was enjoying the fruits of Colette's foresight together with a glass of cheap red wine.

The evening passed by. I read erotic stories online, always happy to keep up with others' take on the genre, especially as I was arrogant enough (and still am) to believe myself to be a better author than most of them. I went to the Ikea website and looked at what I could order for the room downstairs. But then I thought, Lila's the one who does interior design and suchlike. She should choose what goes into that room. I'm the one who writes erotic stories. I should decide what goes on in that room. Wait, that's not appropriate either. If that becomes her room, it's not for me to even go in there, let alone think erotic thoughts about it.

Now I too needed to sleep. Jumping up at dawn to go to the shops, driving to Hobart and back, and then being insulted by Lila had all taken its toll on me. The problem was that the toilet and bathroom could only be accessed from the hall outside the guest room, and the toilet itself was separated from that room by a possibly un-soundproof internal wall.

I had often wondered in the past at the different customs surrounding the use of shared toilet facilities in the night. There are two schools of thought. One is that having used the toilet, one should lower the lid and leave it unflushed to avoid disturbing others. The other school of thought, to which I had always subscribed, was that leaving the toilet unflushed was a disgusting thing to do, and would be confronting to the next user, so it was better to risk a disturbance than a health hazard. So I used it, flushed it, cleaned my teeth at the bathroom sink, and went quietly back past the guest room door to my own adjacent room. I rummaged some pyjamas from the bottom of the chest of drawers. Normally I slept naked. But I had to be careful not to confront Lila in that state in the morning, for fear of her referring not only to an oil painting, but to something horrific by Francis Bacon.

As I drifted rapidly towards sleep, I heard the sound of the guest room door being opened, and then the toilet door closing. I was asleep before it reopened. I was therefore unable to evaluate whether Lila was a night flusher or not.

In the morning Lila woke before me. I was deeply asleep until I heard a certain amount of clatter from the kitchen, which told me that someone was in unfamiliar territory and trying to find the means to make breakfast. I dragged myself from the bed and put on some trainers over my unsightly feet. I visited the toilet – which was in flushed condition – gave myself a perfunctory hands and face wash, and made my way to the dining area beside the kitchen.

"Who decided where to put everything in this kitchen?" demanded Lila. She looked semi-wrecked but not as wrecked as yesterday. "It looks like it was arranged by a committee. I can't find anything."

"Good morning, Lila – I trust you slept well," I said with pointed politeness. "The kitchen was a joint effort between Colette and myself. It has since suffered because neither of us can quite remember where each item should rightfully be. I am sorry that you have a problem with it. What in particular were you looking for?"

"Bread, plate, butter knife, spoon for marmalade. Mug. Coffee. In short, everything that a normal human being needs for breakfast."

"I've got a plan. You sit at the table, facing me. I will make your breakfast. While you watch, take note of what is coming from where. Tomorrow, if you are still here, you can do it yourself based on this morning's lesson."

Lila remained grumpy but sat down. "Perhaps I won't be here. I might just go to the motel I saw on the way in."

"You really, really don't want to do that. It's like a Russian gaol. I've stayed there. I know." I paused, then added, "And I really, really don't want you to do that. I'm glad you are here, actually, even if you are currently behaving like the guest from hell. That's ok because I gave you 24 hours to be shitty. You've got an hour left, I believe."

"Oh fuck off." Lila got up and strode to the front door. She opened it, then turned back and said, "Petrus, it's about time you learned that not everything is a joke, ok?"

I heard her clatter down the metal staircase, and I went to the windows facing the beach. Lila walked briskly down the yard, then disappeared among the scrubby bushes which line the shore. I saw her re-emerge on the beach itself, and I watched her make her way down to the water's edge, where the usual gentle swell brought small waves foaming lightly over the sand. She stopped and stood still for some moments, then I saw her squat down and put her face in her hands. Even without fetching my old binoculars I could tell she was sobbing salt tears into the ocean.

I turned round one of the dining chairs to face the windows, and sat down to keep an eye on her. After about a quarter of an hour, she stood up, but stayed at the water's edge. Another ten minutes passed, and she turned round and walked slowly back across the beach towards the house. I turned on the kettle and the toaster.

When Lila came through the door, I had her breakfast ready on the table. "I made your breakfast," I said unnecessarily.

Lila slumped down onto a dining chair facing me, and said, "Petrus, I'm sorry. You've made more than my breakfast, you've made my day. I'm looking forward to this. Maybe afterwards we can sit in the lounge and we'll have a long talk. I think I'm ready now. That's if you're ready to listen."

"Good, let's do that. I'll leave you in peace and I'll get dressed."

When I emerged from the bedroom looking reasonably clean, dressed and tidy, I saw that Lila had finished her breakfast, cleared the table, and was just finishing handwashing the stuff she'd used. I joined her in the kitchen. I said "Lila, there's just one problem."

"Oh?"

"I forgot to have breakfast. But I'll make myself a coffee and award myself an extra biscuit and that will be fine. I'll join you in the lounge area shortly. You want another coffee?"

I took our coffees into the lounge with a generous plate of biscuits and we sat opposite each other in the easy chairs.

"Welcome back, Lila. That chair you are sitting in came from London would you believe. You've sat in it a good few times there, in the good old days."

"Kind of looks like it's been around a bit. Maybe it needs the cover washed." But Lila smiled either with affection for the chair or perhaps even affection for me. The latter was perhaps less likely at this point.

"So, tell me everything. When you are ready. Or just the bits you want to tell. Whatever. I'm here."

So the whole story came out. She started at the end, with the traumatic scene in the bedroom. Then she worked backwards, trying to trace the course of the betrayal, trying to assess who apart from Brian had betrayed her, and attempting to guess who she could now trust. I listened in silence. There wasn't any need to ask questions because she poured out the details, cleaned out every corner of her defiled mind, unburdened herself of all that had threatened to crush her spirit to nothing. She cried a little at times, but she had few tears left. What had happened to her had undermined all her memories, devalued her past, and left her unable to cope with the thought of the future. Up to the moment when she had entered that bedroom, despite everything, she had loved Brian. As soon as she had opened the door, her love for him was shot dead at point blank range.

Finally, she came to a stop.

I wasn't sure where to begin. When we first got back in touch, I had been aware of the pivotal moment as I clicked the Facebook button. Now everything might pivot again on the words that I would say next.

"Lila, I think we are going to have to take this moment by moment. If there was a way I could magic all this away, Christ, I'd do it this instant, but there's no quick fix for this. I just hope that you can, in time, learn to trust again, and if you want to start that process with me, I'm here. But I know it will be a process, maybe even a long process. I'm ready for that, ok?'

"Thank you, Petrus. You know, I can't think of anyone I am close to who isn't involved, who might have been party to my betrayal, apart from you. You could not possibly have known. You don't deserve my mistrust. And you didn't deserve my anger."

"Hey, don't worry. Don't forget what 'Petrus' means in Latin. The rock. I can strive to be that for you, if you want. Up to you."

Lila's eyes filled with tears again, but she smiled just a little.

"There's also the practical side, Lila. And maybe dealing with all that will be a diversion while you gently approach the emotional side. There's a thousand things you need to decide. Let's start with here. Do you want to stay here for the time being?"

"Yes. Would that be ok? Is that going to complicate things with Colette?"

"Lila, Colette is just a good friend, and good friends don't give rise to complications. I know we seem close, but there's nothing even physical between us, let alone sexual. You know me, yes, I have this thing about younger women, maybe all men do, but I know that if I ever made any kind of pass at her, she'd be out of here just like that. She's out of bounds. Let me put it this way – she's never appeared in one of my stories, not even anonymously. I can't put it more clearly than that!"

"You see, straight away I'm thinking, can I trust Petrus over that? And yet it's not my business even. God, I'm so confused."

"Lila, think back. Make a mental list of the times I have proven untrustworthy. Have I ever betrayed you? What's my track record? Have you any logical reason to mistrust me?"

"It's not logical, that's the trouble. But no, right now I can't think of anything. You've always been straight with me. A bit too much information sometimes, actually."

"Well, if you think of anything in the past, or worry about anything in the future, I want to hear about it right away and we'll talk it through. Believe me, I understand. You know how I'm the possessive type at an emotional level. I curb it, mostly, at the logical level. But possessiveness, jealousy, they're all about trust issues. So I know a bit about what you are going through. But only a little bit. The rest I can barely imagine."

"So how is it going to work, me staying here? You need your privacy. I guess I need mine. When it comes down to it, it's not actually that big, as houses go."

"Ok, how's this for an idea. Together we could set up the downstairs room as a self-contained space for you, your own private space. There's the shower and toilet, there's a sink, we could put in a microwave or a mini oven or whatever so you'd only need the kitchen for serious cooking. You could write down there. You could come and go as you pleased. But up here would be yours whenever you wanted too. No need to knock before entering. Even if Colette is here." And I risked a knowing wink. Lila smiled, not for long, but she smiled.

"Petrus, that sounds just perfect, but are you sure? It seems like a massive intrusion still."

"It's nothing, honestly. It will feel good for you and me to be on our own, but together." I saw a slight look pass across her face, just briefly. "We'll be companionable, ok? Just that."

"I'll pay you rent or something."

"Don't worry about that, at least not at this point. Let's stick to the essentials. Later on we'll go to Ikea online and start picking stuff. That's your area. But there's something else which seems to me to be top priority, apart from me needing another coffee"

"What's that? You need a pee too?" I was glad that she seemed to be getting at least something of her sense of humour back.

"Your dear daughter, Emily. Assume for a moment that she knows nothing about her father bedding schoolgirls. In fact, that's a pretty fair assumption. I don't know her at all, but I would expect any daughter of any father to be pretty disgusted at that, and she would be far more likely to tell you than to connive with him. Or maybe she did know, but couldn't work out what to do about it, how to tell you. What is she, twenty-four? She's still a kid. Anyway, I think you should phone her before the day is out, tell her what has happened but maybe spare her the details, tell her where you are, and see if she's up to trying to sort out things at the house. You know, your clothes for a start."

"So you don't like my t-shirt and track bottoms?"

"I love them, but you'll need to change out of them eventually. We could pick up some cheap stuff in the town, but when we meet the local celebrities, you'll need something a trifle more formal."

Lila sat and thought for a minute, then said, "Maybe I should tackle that right away. Could you take your next coffee out onto the deck and I'll phone her on my mobile?"

"Sure. Can I just suggest you approach it like the mother of a young woman who will probably be pretty devastated about what she is about to hear, and if you get some feeling she saw it coming or knew something, remember what you were like at that age. Like I said, compared to us, she's a kid."

I thought, there's also the matter of the kid on the bed with Brian, even though she was apparently eighteen. Now was not the time to raise that concern with Lila, but down the track she would have to consider whether she had a moral obligation to report what was probably an offence. But after what happened, Brian would now be anticipating a knock on the door from a police person, which would inhibit any future activities of that sort he might have in mind.

As Lila fished out her mobile from her jacket pocket, I took my coffee down to the entertainment area in the yard, and sat where I could see the stairs and the door so I would be ready when she came out. It was quite a long wait.

Chapter 10

My conversation with Emily will probably haunt me forever. She had no idea what had happened, what had been going on. She thought I was at home. She hadn't spoken with Brian in the last couple of weeks. When I told her I'd left him, and said I'd caught him in our bed with someone else, sparing her any more detail than that, her voice became smaller and smaller, and then she said, "Mum, can I call you back in a few minutes?" The phone went dead immediately, but not so immediately that I didn't catch the first sob as she burst into tears.

At that point I felt a total shit for breaking the news on the phone, but then I reflected that there wasn't much else I could do. She needed to know as soon as possible, she needed to know from me, and there was no practical way of getting back to Brisbane quickly enough, and then back here.

Emily called me back after about ten minutes, and although she had a post-tears voice, she was displaying the iron grip on herself that I'd occasionally seen in other crisis situations.

"Mum, are you saying that you are down in Tassie with one change of clothes? Who is this guy that you are with? How long are you staying down there? Just tell me the rest, the practical stuff, and tell me what I need to do here."

Suddenly it was as if she was the grown-up and I was the kid, and I nearly started crying again myself.

I explained about Petrus. I felt I should tell the truth because there had been too much lying and there was no shame in the truth anyway. Petrus had been my lover before I had moved in with her father. Her father had known I was back in touch with Petrus. No, he wasn't my lover now, and I explained that he was significantly older than me. I didn't spell out that time had moved on, surreptitiously corrupting our bodies to put us beyond a reunion other than as friends. I also didn't explain that right now the idea of so much as touching a man made me feel almost physically sick.

I said that I would probably be here for some weeks while I regrouped, and asked her to tell nobody where I was. I could bear anything except the sympathy of friends. And I didn't know who my friends were any more.

I asked her to put herself in my place if she could. Whatever she thought I needed, I probably did. Emily is very clothes conscious and I could leave that side to her. I told her it was vital to get hold of my laptop, and a couple of portable disk drives I used. I suggested she should start by being straightforward about it, to phone her Dad and just tell him she knew, and was coming for my stuff. Any problem, use her emergency key to get in during school hours. I don't think Brian would remember that key so he might not have changed the locks.

As I spoke, I thought that maybe I was putting way too much on Emily. But then I thought, she's old enough to be having kids already if she wanted.. This wasn't as hard as that. And there was a tone in Emily's voice on the other end of the line which made me think that she was growing up as we spoke.

At the end of the call, Emily said, "Mum, I love you and I'll make sure we get this all sorted out, and it will all be good. I'll call you as soon as I have something to say." That brought the tears back, and I just sat on the bed in the guest room for at least twenty minutes until I felt ready to go and find Petrus. As I went slowly down the steps, I thought, I doubt whether there's anyone on the planet more right for me to be with at this moment than him. He would have left me alone for the rest of the day to make that call. He is a good man. There is such a thing as a good man.

He was waiting in the outdoor entertainment area for me, sitting on a bench at a table, doing nothing but wait. He stood up as I approached. "Do you want to sit, or do you want to walk, or do you want to do your own thing?" he asked, with nothing in his voice that suggested which he thought I should do.

"Let's walk. I can tell you about the phone call while we're walking. By the sea?"

When we got to the sand we turned left, towards the longest arm of the beach. He told me it could well take us as much as three hours to get to the end. I said "OK, I'll race you," and we couldn't help laughing. I recounted what had happened when I phoned Emily.

"Sounds like you now have two people on your trusted list – Emily and me. That's a start. And it also sounds like she's going to be more than helpful in sorting out stuff in Brisbane without you having to go back there for the time being."

"Yup. She's great. One day I hope you meet her. She's kind of... different... but you'd get along fine."

In the distance, a young couple walked ahead of us, with an energetic dog who was chasing the ball they threw as they walked. Petrus said, "It might be good to have a dog, one that could be trusted to keep to the property, a guard dog, but not fierce. One that might bark at an intruder, prior to licking him into submission."

"You do need company, Petrus. I guess Colette will be coming in less often now that everything is sorted out. I could imagine you spending days here without needing to interact with another human being, and that's not good."

Petrus was silent for about a minute. Then he said, "You could be right. Once you go, it will be kind of quiet here. But hey, you've only just arrived and we're already talking about you going. And anyway, maybe you'll be downstairs for days and I won't see you. And that will be fine. I mean, that's the whole idea."

"I'll need clean clothes, Petrus. I'll need to come upstairs and use the laundry."

"I'll hide when you do. Or maybe you could just put a basket outside your door, and Colette can collect it on her way in and do your laundry and iron it and everything, and return it downstairs."

"You'd really like a domestic slave, wouldn't you! I thought Colette was supposed to do kind of lighter stuff than that."

"To be honest I'm not altogether sure what she's supposed to be doing now. Maybe she's currently my dog substitute. But with less cuddles and tummy rubs."

"I knew it. You've been obsessing over giving Colette a tummy rub."

"And her giving me a face slap in return."

"I should hope so. Dirty old man." But I spoke with affection.

Chapter 11

After she had described her phone call with Emily, Lila and I walked mostly in silence for about half an hour, sometimes quite separately, she by the edge of the sea, me higher up. We had a lot, individually, to think about. Eventually I sat down on a hump of sand and grass, watching Lila walking on, lost in her thoughts. She moved well. She still had a graceful manner of walking, and carried herself well, unlike me. I had inherited my mother's slight stoop, which didn't help me to look as young as I wanted to look. In any event, that was starting to be a losing battle.

Lila turned to look for me, and seeing me sitting down some way back, she put her hands on her hips in mock exasperation. Then she walked back towards me.

She reached my perch, and held out her hand. "Come on," she said, "time to head back, if you are not up for going further." She was teasing a little, and that was good.

As a writer, writing about the interactions between men and women at a physical and sexual level in detail, I play with scenarios. So when I saw her hand outstretched, I automatically played forward the scenario, picturing her pulling me up and me taking her very naturally in my arms as she continued to hold my hand. That, I thought, would be way too premature, even if she initiated it. So I ignored the hand and got to my feet with as much athleticism as I could muster, as if saying that I didn't need her help. She just smiled, and turned in the direction from which we had come.

As we neared the yellow house property, I glanced towards the property next door. I had seen on the Google satellite picture that it was set further back from the sea than my house, with a deeper band of trees screening it from the ocean, which to my mind was missing the point of having a beach-front house. And there were also trees screening it from my house. I had often wondered who lived there, and it only then occurred to me that I should ask Colette, my neighbour on the other side of my property, what she knew. She was something of a gossip, and if anyone knew, it would be she. "Never tell me a secret," she once warned me. "I can't keep secrets to myself." Well, at least that was honest.

"How about if I fix us both some lunch?" suggested Lila when we got back to the house.

I didn't argue. I'm pretty useless in the kitchen. My idea of lunch is some meat out of a packet between two slices of buttered bread. Maybe a banana to follow if I'm really trying to eat healthy. Lila's idea of lunch is much more saWalter, salady, grainy, nutty, all that kind of thing. She had some difficulty finding anything in the kitchen that she would consider putting in her mouth, but before long she had performed a miracle not much different from the feeding of the five thousand, and we sat opposite each other at the table.

"So what's next?" I asked. I suspected that it was best to keep things moving forward, even though, when it came down to it, Lila's disaster was only forty-eight hours ago.

"I guess deliveries from Ikea will take a few days to get down here, so perhaps we'd better order today whatever is required."

"Sure, that'll be fun. Next best thing to sex is spending money." There I go again, inserting foot into mouth at the first opportunity.

"I've not checked our bank account but I bet Brian was doing both. I can't believe those girls were purely interested in his physique." I was relieved Lila made light of it, but within seconds I was taken aback when she turned away from the table to try to hide her sudden tears.

"Lila, I'm so sorry, that was a crass remark of mine. I'll get the tissues. And cry all you want, you've got reason."

I put the box of tissues within reach, fought the instinct to hug her with great difficulty, and returned to my seat. In a minute or two she recovered, said "Bugger!" and then "Not your fault. You can't keep tiptoeing around me. Life goes on and all that crap."

"What was that phrase you used in London a few times? 'One door closes, another slams in your face'. That's a good saying."

Lila smiled a brief rueful smile, and finished her lunch.

After I had first ensured that there was nothing incriminating on the PC screen, Lila joined me in my study after lunch and we selected the items we'd need to furnish the downstairs room. I explained my idea about the loft bed, and Lila thought that was both a practical and a fun idea. "Takes me back to childhood bunk beds," she said. "And Petrus – don't even think of asking whether I will be able to manage to climb the ladder."

"The thought never crossed my mind," I fibbed.

Lila chose a comfy chair, a small dining table with chairs that kind of folded into it, and desk add-ons for the loft bed. She also selected a compact wardrobe and a chest of drawers. I encouraged her to have two of those for her storage needs, and we did a bit of measuring and worked out that it would all fit. After that she picked out various soft furnishing and bedding items, and all in all professed herself satisfied with the outcome. She offered to contribute to the cost, but I pointed out that we had no idea how long she would be staying, and I needed to set that room up anyway. And I was glad of her professional advice on the décor, which she had freely given.

We also visited an appliances site and chose things like a kettle, toaster and microwave. Overall, Lila would be quite well set up to lead an independent and private life downstairs, for however long she wanted to stay. But we both shied away from any talk of the future beyond the coming week.

That task completed, and after afternoon tea, I suggested that Lila might want to doze, or read, or walk; she decided to find a book from the slightly confused shelves, and I settled down in the study to write.

Words did not come. The restraint I was exercising in my real life relationships, for once behaving myself, seemed to be feeding forward into my writing. An erotic story where the protagonist exercises some willpower and doesn't lay hands, or any other body part, on the heroine, is an erotic story which seriously doesn't work. After nearly an hour, I gave up, and went out to the lounge to see how Lila was getting on.

I was glad to see her fast asleep in the easy chair, a book closed on her lap. For some moments I watched her, then quietly eased myself into the chair opposite. I am one of the world's great sleepers – I can doze off in less than a minute, given half a chance. On this occasion, it might have taken two, as I continued to just gaze on Lila's face for that length of time, but then I was off and dreaming. For the first time in twenty-seven years, Lila and I slept together.

Chapter 12

There are three events I particularly recall from the first week that I stayed with Petrus in the yellow house. The first, meeting Colette. The second, the arrival of the downstairs room furniture. The third, Petrus' cardiac episode when we were setting it up.

It was on Monday, the day after we had ordered the stuff for the downstairs room, that Colette arrived soon after breakfast to carry out whatever her current duties were. When I say 'after breakfast' I mean after my breakfast. Petrus was still in bed. He's a late riser, given the option. I'm an early riser, and there's something in my body clock that makes it not an option.

I heard a tap on the door, and I saw it open as I sat at the table mulling over the last few day's events. In came a young woman, quite petite, very good looking, but with apprehension written all across her features. She stopped dead when she saw me at the table.

"Oh, I'm very sorry. Is it ok for me to come in?" she asked.

"Of course, please do. You must be Colette."

"That's me. And you must be Mr Stone' friend. Not a girlfriend. He told me."

"Exactly. Not a girlfriend. My name's Lila Moone."

"Pleased to meet you, Mrs Moone."

"Call me Lila."

"Mrs Moone – are you the Lila Moone who writes in 'The Decorator' magazine every month? Maybe that's someone else."

"That's me. You are just about the first person who has recognised me." To be honest, I was more than flattered by this, and having begun with an illogical dislike for this young woman, I had instantly grown to like her.

"I read all your articles – they are so good! I've tried out several of your décor ideas at home and they work really well."

"That's a relief. Nothing worse than recommending stuff that people turn out to hate. Maybe you could show me one day?"

"Sure, I'll see if that would be ok with Ezra. Ezra is my husband."

"I'm sure he wouldn't mind me visiting, if you invited me."

"I'd need to check. We always check stuff together."

I wondered whether it really was any kind of two way process. In his messages Petrus had indicated that Ezra Cheung wasn't the most likely person to win a "New Man" award.

"Perhaps I could take your breakfast things if you have finished, Mrs Moone."

"I'm happy to deal with them myself, but if you are going to be doing stuff in the kitchen, go for it."

"I'll do a bit if kitchen tidying first, then make Mr Petrus' coffee."

"And you take it in?"

"Oh no, I just leave it on the table and tap on his door to make sure he is awake. Then he comes out, and he drinks his coffee, and we talk about what needs to be done."

Colette busied herself in the kitchen, and as she had described, she made coffee for Petrus, and knocked on his door. Then she stood in the middle of the lounge area, looking around.

"Have you lost something?" I asked her.

"No, I'm kind of looking for something that actually needs doing, but not really finding it."

"You could help me, if that's allowed under your contract."

"Oh, there's no contract. It's all informal. I just do stuff to help in any way I can." She had taken my light-hearted remark too seriously.

"What I had in mind was this. I've arrived here rather suddenly with more or less nothing, and in particular, nothing to wear. Petrus did his best to find me some basics, but I need to improve on that as soon as possible. It might be a week or more till some of my own things arrive. So – maybe you could take me into town and show me where I can find the things I need. We can have a girlies' shopping trip."

"Of course! I'd love to help with that. But Swansea isn't the best place really. I'd suggest going to Launceston, but that's more than an hour and a half away."

I tried to think of anything that would detain me at the house for about six hours or so, and failed.

"If you are up for it, so am I. But it's going beyond the scope of the job, isn't it?"

"Well, I'll say nothing if you say nothing."

We drove in Colette's agile car in style, leaving a note for Petrus propped on his coffee cup. It felt a little bit like 'Thelma and Louise'. Colette seemed more than happy to break out a bit, without permission either from Petrus or Ezra, and I was more than happy to spend some hours in the company of someone who had no connection with anything to do with me, and who could therefore be trusted.

We drove, we parked, we shopped, we lunched, we shopped, we drove, and finally we were home, both of us giggling like naughty schoolgirls. That's the phrase that sprang to mind at the time, and it didn't jar. Around Colette it was impossible to feel miserable about anything. She just radiated happiness and it was infectious. We talked about all sorts of stuff but I couldn't bring myself simply to ask, 'Why are you so happy?'

Colette parked outside her own house and helped me carry my shopping bags across from her property to the yellow house. Petrus was waiting at the top of the steps, arms folded in mock annoyance.

"So what's all this about?" he demanded. "I hope you two realise I've been forced to make my own breakfast, my own lunch, and almost my own afternoon tea?"

We took the hint and I made the tea while Colette cut a generous slice of rich fruit cake for Petrus, a treat we had bought for him on our trip. We sat at the table and he beamed at the two of us, clearly pleased that we'd hit it off. Had we not, our arrangements would have been a little difficult. We regaled him with the details of our lunch, with descriptions of the shops we'd patronised, and with my account of Colette's driving, which had been safe but fast. I like fast. I suppose I like safe if necessary. Then I took the bags into the guest room and changed into the various outfits we had bought, putting on a one-woman fashion show in which Petrus took a considerable interest.

Finally Colette checked the enormous watch which she always wore, gasped, and said she'd have to run else Ezra would be looking for her. Apparently spending more than a few minutes in the company of his three children stressed him more than somewhat – it was her mother's evening off. I saw her to the door, and impulsively kissed her cheek.

"Thanks so much, Colette. After that, I feel like a new woman."

I heard Petrus mutter something like "So do I," but I wasn't quite sure.

For the next couple of days I did very little. I read, I walked, I went into Swansea with Petrus to do a supermarket shop, and when Colette came to the house for a half day shift, I helped her thoroughly clean the empty downstairs room in preparation for the arrival of the furniture.

Just as we finished, my phone rang and I saw that Emily was the caller. I left Colette to put away the cleaning gear and sat myself down in the entertainment area in the yard.

"How's everything?" Emily asked.

"I'm ok. Petrus has been incredibly supportive, and I've made a new friend, a girl friend, his assistant Colette. I'm slowly rediscovering fun. What's happened at your end?"

"Not fun." Emily sounded reproving, and I realised I had been a bit insensitive. "Dad has been a weird combination of helpful and obstructive. He seems to realise one minute that he's wrecked everything, then next minute he says it's all your fault because you started having an affair with Petrus."

"Fuck him. I am not having an affair with Petrus. I wasn't having an affair with Petrus. You can't have an affair with someone with a messenger app. I've not so much as kissed him on the cheek since I've been here. I don't even touch him. I don't want any man to touch me right now. And for god's sake, he's seventy. So anything your father says about Petrus is a load of balls. He's just trying to justify what he did by blaming me. And for all I know he's been doing it for years."

There was a pause. Then Emily said, "Ok mum, but really I don't want to know. He's my father, and I don't want to lose him altogether, even though he's crossed every line in the book. You're my mother and I accept you haven't crossed any lines, even if maybe you've walked up to one or two and had a good look."

"Em, ok, let's leave all that and stick to practical stuff. Have you been able to lay hands on my PC and some clothes and whatever?"

"Yes. I got one of my friends to hire a van, and he's bigger than Dad, and Dad decided not to make any problems over what we took. Basically we've got just about everything we could find that was undeniably yours. Maybe Dad hid some of your underwear as a souvenir, but that's about all that could be missing."

"Em, you are an absolute star. That is going to make things so much easier. Where's the stuff now?"

"It's filling up the spare room at my flat. And until we put it in there, I didn't think of it as a spare room, I thought of it as my study. So let me know what to do next, please."

"How's your cash flow? Can you get a removal company to ship it down here? Obviously I'll transfer the money to your account as soon as you let me know what you've spent."

"Willingly, and I'll do it right away. But where are you going to put it?"

"We've sorted out a kind of separate living area here that I can use and be reasonably independent in for the time being. It's very quiet, very peaceful here. Did I tell you that Petrus writes too? So he understands what I need in order to work. At least for the time being, I think it's going to work out ok. Once I'm settled, come down and see me. A couple of days in Tassie won't kill you."

"It might. I'll see. But mum, I do love you and yes, I do want to see you and make sure you are ok."

"I'm ok. Or I will be. I'm a bit up and down I guess, but there's so much here to distract me, practicalities of one kind and another, so that's good. Let me know when the stuff is on its way and how much to transfer."

We said our goodbyes. Things were falling into place. I waited with baited breath for something to go wrong.

The Ikea stuff for the downstairs room arrived a couple of days later on a delivery truck, late in the afternoon. The number of boxes looked daunting. Petrus said, "We don't have to do it all at once. Let's start in the morning with the loft bed. Once that's in place you could start at least sleeping down here right away, if you prefer."

After breakfast next day, we made a start. Colette was with us, but she proved to be not well versed in the joys of furniture

72

assembly. However, her contribution was essential when an extra pair of hands was required to hold partly assembled bits in place. The loft bed had to be assembled on its side, and then heaved up onto its feet. Colette did her best to help with that, but with her relatively small stature, Petrus and I had to do the last push on our own. Colette and I gave ourselves a round of applause as if we'd just launched an ocean liner. Petrus did not applaud. He suddenly sat down on the floor. He turned to Colette and simply said, "Nitrolingual spray, bedside table."

For a split second, Colette looked at him uncomprehendingly. I had no idea what was going on. Then she said, "Got it," ran out of the room, and I heard her going up the steps two at a time.

"Sorry, Lila, I think I just overdid it."

"Shit, are you ok?"

"Right now, no. Shortly, probably ok."

Colette was already back down the stairs with a small bottle about the size of a perfume bottle. She was in trained medical practitioner mode, quite a different person. She said "Mrs Moone, help me get him with his back against that wall." We supported him either side and more or less slid him to the wall so he could lean back against it.

"Mr Stone, have you been using viagra or anything like it?"

I thought, really?

"No," said Petrus, understanding at once the medical reason for the question.

Colette pulled the lid off the bottle revealing a spray cap beneath. "Mr Stone, have you used this recently?"

"No, never."

"OK, I'll prime it." At once Colette turned away and sprayed five shots into the air.

"Mr Stone, I need to spray this under your tongue. Don't breathe it in. Try not to swallow for as long as you can. Ready?"

Petrus nodded, opened his mouth, and lifted his tongue. Colette sprayed one shot. "Close your mouth. Try to relax. Don't talk."

I confess I am not good at this sort of thing. I realised I was shivering.

Colette said, "Mrs Moone, if he is still in pain in five minutes, administer another spray under his tongue like I just did. I will phone Ezra."

She stepped outside, presumably so that Petrus wouldn't be agitated by hearing her conversation. I checked the time on my phone and tried to remember when five minutes would be up. Then I sat down on the floor next to Petrus, and took his hand. He turned his head to me and smiled faintly. "I think it's passing. Just a bit of angina. But that doesn't mean you have to let go of my hand." His voice was subdued, but a little sparkle was returning to his eyes.

"Don't push your luck, Petrus," I said. But I held onto it all the same.

After a couple of long minutes, Colette came back into the room. "How is he?"

"He says he thinks it's passing."

"Hey, I can talk," said Petrus. "I think it's passing."

"That's what I said," I protested.

Just for a moment, Colette looked as if she might lower her professional poise and giggle, but she restrained herself.

"Ezra is at home. My mum's with the kids, so he's coming across right now."

Ezra arrived almost as Colette finished speaking. I hadn't met him before but he ignored me for the time being, rightly concentrating on Petrus. He set down his small medical bag. He took Petrus' pulse and listened to his heart. He checked his blood pressure.

"Petrus, if we were in town I'd send for an ambulance and get you checked in hospital, but out here, that's not quite so easy. If I was seriously concerned I'd call in the air ambulance and they'd take you to Launceston. But I think you simply overdid things, and if you put your feet up for the rest of the day, you'll be fine."

He started putting his medical stuff back in his bag, then frowned and said, "I take it you've been taking all your tablets, every day?"

Petrus looked embarrassed. "Well, I have to admit that I did run out of ramace pills a couple of days ago, and I haven't got around to picking up some more."

"A couple of days?"

"Three. Maybe four."

"Petrus, that's very irresponsible. You've distressed your friend, not to mention my wife, and I've been brought over here when I could have been enjoying the company of my children."

I glanced at Colette. The expression on her face, unseen by Ezra, spoke volumes.

"I really am sorry," said Petrus, the colour returning to his face. "I shall drive down to the pharmacy this afternoon without fail."

"No driving till tomorrow, please," responded Ezra testily. "Perhaps your friend, Mrs..."

"Moone, Lila Moone."

"Perhaps Mrs Moone will deal with the matter on your behalf." For a moment, his voice became a shade more sympathetic. "If you feel any recurrence of the symptoms, use the spray once more, and call triple zero. They will assess whether to get you to the hospital and if so, how. Meanwhile, rest here for ten minutes before attempting the stairs. Once up there I suggest sofa or bed rest for the remainder of the day. And now, I will return to the children."

Petrus called after him "Thank you Ezra. I shall expect your bill!" But Ezra was probably out of earshot already.

Colette turned to us and said, "Perhaps a strong cup of tea all round would be good. I'll go upstairs and put the kettle on."

When we were on our own, I withdrew my hand. "Idiot," I said. Petrus grinned wryly. He looked at his hand. I read his mind. I was pretty sure he wasn't going to wash it for a week.

After the prescribed ten minutes, Petrus carefully ascended the steps with Colette and I either side of him, not that there was really room. The tea was more than welcome. Colette offered to collect the pills but I said I'd deal with that, and suggested she should take the rest of the day off, paid.

Apart from the interesting time I had driving Petrus' SUV to the pharmacy, which seemed to be about twice the size once I was behind the wheel, that was the end of the excitement that day. We had an early night. For the first time at the house, I slept with my bedroom door ajar, just in case.

Chapter 13

Over the following few days, Lila and I gradually got the rest of the furniture assembled. Needless to say, I took it pretty easy, and Lila wouldn't let me overdo things anyway. Colette helped once or twice, but her visits were now less frequent, simply because there was little left to do upstairs. I had never envisaged keeping her on as some kind of permanent housekeeper.

Once everything was complete and the empty boxes had been stashed in one of the sheds in the yard, Lila made up her mind how the various items should be arranged in the room. Fortunately the loft bed's location had been settled at the outset. The remaining furniture was quite easy to slide around. We stood and admired our handiwork. "I guess I should start moving my stuff from upstairs now," said Lila. "There's not much really, I can do that myself."

"And I imagine you'll be sleeping down here from now on?" I asked her.

"Might as well. Then you can run around up there in the mornings as nature intended, without me seeing your huge embarrassment."

"I had to stop doing that when Colette started helping in the mornings."

"But she's hardly over here now. You can be yourself. You are a free man, unencumbered by either of the two women in your life."

"Neither of you have ever been an encumbrance. And by the way, I've reached the age where my so-called huge embarrassment isn't quite so huge any more."

"Actually I was talking about your tummy. But as regards your penis, I noticed. You've not been quite so discreet with your bathrobe as you thought you were, after some of your showers."

"Blood hell, Lila, you've been peeking!"

"Couldn't help it. You should do the belt up tighter. If you can that is. Or put on underpants earlier. And don't wear just that robe in front of Colette, even if she is medically qualified."

Lila caught the look in my eye, and laughing, she ran out into the yard and towards the sea. I chased after her as best I could, but she was much fleeter of foot, and when I got to the beach she was nowhere to be seen.

I looked in each direction and she seemed to have vanished. Then without warning, her hands were over my eyes; she had crept out of the scrub, sneaking up on me from behind. "Guess who!" she said in a playful voice.

"I can't imagine. Let me feel." And I brought my hands behind me and settled them either side of her hips. "Yup, I'd know those hips anywhere. I used to get a firm hold on them when we were..."

"Petrus! That's enough. Get a grip."

"I have, and very nice it is too."

We released each other, and I turned to face her. Before I could say anything, she had taken both my hands, as we stood a pace apart.

"Those were the days, Petrus."

"Were?"

"Were. About the last thing I want now is involvement. Even with you. And I rather think too much time has passed. But friendship is not to be sneezed at."

"I'm not sneezing. Just a bit desperate after god knows how many years of celibacy."

"Not my fault, Petrus. And I'm sure not going to get involved with you out of pity."

"Ok. How about out of barely disguised lust? No? Oh well, you can't blame a guy for trying."

"No, Petrus, I don't blame you. Tell you what, let's go back to my place and make mad, passionate afternoon tea."

What made my day was that she released one hand, but kept hold of the other until we reached the downstairs room, where she gave it a tiny squeeze and relinquished it at last.

"There's one little thing we forgot," Lila. "Crockery and that sort of thing. I don't want to have to come upstairs every time I need to make a cuppa, because I haven't got anything to make it in."

"Walk this way, madam," I said, and that made an excuse to take her by the hand again. I led her across to the nearer of the two sheds, and opened it to reveal a number of substantial cardboard packing cases stacked inside. While Lila muttered about angina, I heaved a couple off the top, then dragged one outside that had been on the bottom.

"Here you go. Spare stuff. I will, just this once, allow you to carry it with me to your room."

We grasped it between us, somewhat awkwardly, and carried it across to Lila's room. I opened it with a flourish, and Lila looked inside. "God, there's enough crockery here to hold a banquet."

"One day I will throw a party for both the inhabitants of the town, and this stuff will then be very handy. Until then, use what you want from it."

Lila fished out the items she needed, including some storage jars. "Do you mind?" she asked, and went upstairs, returning with the jars filled with tea, coffee and sugar. She also had an almost empty carton of milk.

"What, no cake?" I protested.

"Not good for your angina. Be prepared to lead a slimmer life. After a few months, you'll get used to it."

And so we christened the room, not quite in the manner that I had fantasised about, but a tea christening is, well, not to be sneezed at – even without cake.

Later Lila busied herself bringing down her belongings from the guest room and stashing them in her chests of drawers and the wardrobe. Until her stuff arrived from Brisbane, there wasn't much to stash.

In the evening we ate our meal together, talking easily of nothing much, avoiding any mention of the future, even less of our past. Lila made coffee and we took it out onto the deck. The evening was unseasonably warm for so late in summer. The lapping of the sea along that great arc of sand was almost inaudible. Conversation lapsed. We sat in silence, watching the stars appearing.

Then the moon began to appear over the spur of land on the far side of the bay. It was full and bright, what we would have called a harvest moon when I was young in England. Its reflection on the sea was barely disturbed by the gentle waves. Lila was transfixed by the sight. I in turn was transfixed by Lila, her face so softly lit by the moonlight. She did not appear to realise that my eyes did not move from her, even as hers did not move from the face of the moon. Perhaps if she had been aware of my gaze, she would not have allowed the few tears that slipped from her eyes to fall.

I thought, yes – it is too soon. And I thought, no – it is not too late. It must never be too late.

Chapter 14

I don't know why I cried a little when I saw the moon rise. Perhaps it took me back to England, to a time when Petrus and I had driven from London to the far side of Wales. We came to the coast, at sunset, I think at a spot called Little Haven, and there was a small harbour, and lights on the little shipping vessels being drawn up by the fishermen and their families on the harbour edge, and for a moment we stopped in wonder at the beauty of the sight. Was there a moon? Perhaps. Nothing could have enhanced that vision more. It was Petrus' turn to allow some tears to fall that time. What a strange confusion of memories.

Suddenly I felt tired, weary from all the exertions of the past few days. I turned away from Petrus lest he should see the few tears before I could dab them away in the bathroom privately, and went indoors. Even his solicitude would be hard to bear in my still raw emotional state. I was living with my pain, coping, but the pain was still there. Perhaps it always would be.

He was sorting things out in the kitchen when I went back. I think he was confused by my sudden retreat to the house. But he seemed then to understand, and said "You look so tired now. Time for you to climb into bed. And I mean climb. It will keep you fit. Just don't forget where you are in the night."

Neither of us knew what to do next. It would have been very natural to have kissed, or at least for him to have kissed my cheek, but we kept our distance, following some instinct, and I went to the door, and simply said, "Goodnight Petrus. I'll have my mobile right beside me overnight, if you happened to feel unwell or something."

I wished I hadn't said "Or something." It sounded almost like an invitation. No invitation was intended.

"I'll be just fine. That episode the other day was just a bit of angina, it's of no consequence. It won't happen again." He smiled, perhaps a little sadly, and said "Sweet dreams."

Down in my new room, I looked round with some satisfaction. With the material available it wouldn't feature in a magazine article, but it was ok. It would serve very well as a bolt hole for the time being. I turned the lock on the door.

I used the little bathroom to prepare myself for bed, then climbed the ladder and slid beneath the duvet. We had attached a small clip-on light to the wooden rail of the bed and it was odd to look down on the room below in that dim light. I was about to turn it off and settle for sleep when I heard a notification beep from my phone. I checked it. It was a Facebook message, apparently from Petrus. My heart skipped a beat for a moment but then I thought, if there was a problem he would ring. I checked the message.

Hey Lila. You could be asleep I suppose.

> No, but almost. All well up there?

Yes, all is well because you are near. I suddenly realised that it's been a couple of weeks since I sent you a message.

> That's because we have been talking face to face.

Sometimes we say more in messages.

> Petrus, go to sleep, there is nothing more to be said, not tonight.

You know what I want to say.

> I know. Now is not the time. I have to sleep.

What are you wearing?

> Don't bother me with that old line. Nothing, since you ask.

Me neither. So we are naked, phone to phone.

> If you say so.

You are a cold and heartless woman. But I still love you.

> Good. Now sleep. Bye.

xx

Considering that it was a strange bed in a strange room, I slept very well. At least there was someone nearby who was not a stranger.

In the morning I drank my coffee black to avoid going upstairs to the fridge. I didn't open the door to the yard. The light coming in from the grey day outside did not have much impact on the room, which only had one window looking out towards the sea, but too low down to provide the view over the trees that was available upstairs. I turned on the ceiling light which helped somewhat, but it needed a better light fitting, and to change it would require an electrician with a big step ladder and a bill to match. I decided that I would make do.

At least the small desk beneath the loft bed was equipped with a desk lamp. I decided that I would spend some time researching for an article on curtain fabrics for teenagers' rooms. Then when I was sure that Petrus was at the morning coffee stage, I would go upstairs and get some breakfast. Clearly I needed to think some of the logistics through. A small fridge would be a good idea, but the room was filling up. I remembered the article I had written a few months before on the Japanese approach to room furnishing. The space between the furniture items was as important as the items themselves, I asserted. In my little haven in the yellow house, space was beginning to be at a premium.

I hated researching on my phone, which was all I had for the purpose. The sooner my laptop arrived the better. Eventually I gave up, a little before I judged it appropriate to go upstairs, and put on the cheap jacket I had bought in Launceston. Outside it was distinctly cooler than the night before, but there was a salty, sandy freshness in the air. I decided I would walk down to the beach for just ten minutes, simply because it was there, like Everest.

I looked along the sand towards the town, and was surprised to see Colette and her mother together with the two boys. I had never met them, so I walked over to where they were camped on the sand. Colette and her mother sat on beach towels while the boys were digging with great concentration and little success.

Colette jumped up as she saw me approach. "Mrs Moone! How are you? Have you moved into the new room?"

"I had my first night in there last night, and I slept very well, thank you. So these are the twins? And your mother?"

Introductions were performed although the boys barely raised their heads from their work. Colette's mother beamed and nodded but did not speak. Apparently her English was very limited. She had been waiting to emigrate from Malaysia for some years but had only recently qualified for entry. I wondered how Colette had managed before her arrival, as she had told me that she had been working in the pharmacy and the hotel for some years.

"You must be glad to be able to spend more time at home now that Petrus is well set up."

"No, not really." Colette was as discreet about herself as she was about other people, in other words, not discreet at all. "I'm not much of a mother for toddlers. Once they can hold a conversation and go to school, then I can relate a bit better. Soon I must see whether Petrus needs any more help now, because otherwise I'd better get another job before they drive me mad."

I had nothing but admiration for a woman who was prepared to admit her kids were a handful, while at the same time wondering why she had brought them into the world, by IVF as she had candidly told me on our trip to Launceston. I thought, I bet it was Ezra's idea.

"I rather think he has run out of things for you to do, but it's not for me to say. Good luck with your job hunting anyway! I guess round here there's not much available." And right that moment, an idea started to form in the back of my mind.

These days many businesses can actually be run from anywhere. You just need an internet connection, and off you go. Maybe I could start some kind of business related to interior design, run it from the downstairs room, and even employ one or two people like Colette if it started to take off. I wondered whether my landlord, Petrus, would permit that. I thought, if I blow in his ear, he'd permit anything. Then I thought, that was an unworthy thought. Yet quite probably true.

But that would be for the future. Right now, I needed my very late breakfast, or perhaps now, brunch. I took my leave of the family on the beach and headed back to the upper floor of the yellow house.

I was relieved to see that Petrus, having been left alone overnight for the first time in many days, was not only alive, but was up and dressed and boiling the kettle. He had evidently spotted me walking up the yard and had assumed, even hoped, that I would be coming upstairs.

We exchanged accounts of our night and morning adventures, such that they were. I said nothing about my vague plan to start a business, but I did tell him that he needed to make up his mind about Colette's further employment. Petrus said he had slept very well, safe in the knowledge that now he had the upstairs to himself, he could break wind whenever he liked and it wouldn't matter. I groaned. For a man of seventy, he had the mind of a schoolboy.

I had just finished my coffee and biscuits and was about to rummage in the kitchen for the means to make myself an early lunch, when my phone rang. It was Emily. I went out on the deck in case she had anything personal to discuss. Petrus was a good friend, but that didn't mean I felt comfortable talking about everything in front of him.

"Hi mum, just letting you know your stuff is on its way."

"Fantastic! I guess it will be here next week?"

"No mum, before that."

"This week? That's even better. I can't wait to have my laptop back, let alone the rest of my stuff."

"Actually mum, it will be there today."

"Today? How did you manage that?"

"Me and Ed hired a van and we've driven it down there via the boat. Only took a couple of days."

"My god! When will you get here?"

Then I heard the sound of a van tooting as it came slowly down the drive.

Chapter 15

The sound of a van coming down the drive, tooting annoyingly, and the sight of Lila suddenly running round the deck and leaping down the stairs seemed to be connected, in my estimation. I followed at a more mature pace.

I had seen photographs of Emily but of course had never met her, so as soon as I saw a young woman leap from the passenger side of the still-moving van and rush to embrace Lila, I put two and two together. The overall plot didn't take much to guess either. She and the driver of the van must have travelled all the way from Brisbane, and would now need to be accommodated for an unspecified period. I groaned inwardly at the sudden and unplanned loss of my isolation and privacy, while at the same time thinking that if nothing else, we'd be in for some fun.

Emily had 'fun' written all over her. She was casually dressed, but stylishly for all that, and considering the journey she looked remarkably different from her mother's wrecked appearance when she first arrived. But then, I thought, be fair, Emily is very happy and full of beans, but Lila had just been through a life-changing experience, and had looked it.

The van came to rest beside the stilts, and a very tall young man stepped out, looking like someone who had just driven a considerable distance, unlike Emily. She was still fully occupied in hugging her mother amid much verbal excitement.

I greeted him. "Hi! You must be... actually I haven't a clue, as we didn't know you were coming. Well, I'm Petrus."

"Oh, hi, I'm Ed. Just call me... Ed."

He seemed to be more than somewhat disoriented by the journey. Later I discovered that he was just as disoriented at almost all times.

I shook him by the hand. He looked up at the house. "Nice place," he said. "Nice colour."

I went to speak, and then self-edited.

"We've come from Brisbane," Ed informed me. "We slept in the van. It's not totally full, there was space for a sleeping bag in the back. For Emily," he quickly added. "I just slept in the front, in the seat. But I woke up when I was driving."

I thought, well, that was a good plan.

Emily finally detached herself from her mother with some difficulty, and came over to greet me. At least that's what I assumed she would do, but instead she planted herself in front of me, hands on hips, and looked me up and down with what appeared to be the deepest of suspicion.

"Petrus, yes?" she finally asked.

"That's me. Emily Moone, I assume?"

"Correct." Emily continued to appraise me as if I were a suspect in an identity parade.

"You used to know my mother in London." She made it sound like an accusation. I looked over her shoulder at Lila who had been looking into the back of the van, and was now sauntering across to us. I had no clear idea, or indeed no idea at all, what Emily knew about my relationship to her mother, now or in the past. I was more than somewhat worried about saying the wrong thing. I have a particular knack for saying the wrong thing at the wrong time, usually to the wrong person.

I decided to tread carefully, and merely plead guilty by saying "Yes," and nothing more.

"And you've been giving her somewhere to sleep and looking after her here since she left my father."

This struck me as a loaded question concerning our sleeping arrangements, or a loaded statement, or both. Whichever, the loading was pretty clear. I decided to avoid the elephant in the sentence, and focus on something more peripheral.

"I think 'looking after' is a bit of an overstatement. Your mother is very capable of looking after herself even under the most difficult of circumstances. However, as any friend would, I have assisted her a little by providing her accommodation here."

Emily gave me a final searching look, then held out her hand. As I took it, she took me completely by surprise by drawing me towards her, and kissing my cheek with more warmth than formality.

"Thanks, Petrus. You're a hero. Thanks for looking after my mum."

Clearly she had judged me not guilty of whatever crime she

might have believed me capable of. But I thought on for a moment. From her father's actions she has suddenly realised that not all men can be trusted, not all men are honest, and the motives of any man claiming to assist any woman need to be closely examined. Perhaps altruism doesn't really exist. I rather hoped that it did, but it was something that Emily would have to make her own mind up about, over the next fifty years or so.

Lila was now at my side, and Emily introduced Ed to her. "This is Ed, who helped me drive the van. He works at the removal company. When I explained what I needed, he said I'd save a bomb by just hiring a van. Then he said, if I liked, he'd help with the driving. Actually he did most of it."

Lila took it calmly. "Oh, you've just met. Well, that's nice. Ed, you must tell me all about yourself over lunch. Petrus, you lead the way upstairs and we'll see what we can rustle up."

"Not to worry, mum, we stopped off at the supermarket in Swansea and got some stuff. We didn't want to turn up uninvited and eat you out of house and home. Ed, bring up the stuff."

"All of it?"

"No, Ed, just the food we bought."

"Right, right," said Ed who wandered over to the van while we three trooped up the steps.

Emily was clearly impressed when she saw the view from the deck, and then the view from inside the house. "This is excellent. But mum, didn't you say your room is downstairs? So you don't get the view?"

"I get the peace and quiet of my own space," she replied, "but Petrus lets me come and go up here whenever I want."

"Ok, well that's good." I actually liked Emily's concern that her mum should get the best of everything. I guess we had that in common.

I became aware of noises from the kitchen. Ed thoroughly washed his hands, dried them on a clean towel that he somehow found first time in a drawer, and then he set about preparing lunch from the groceries they had bought. It was as if he had been trained as a chef and had known every aspect of the kitchen layout and contents for years. Emily followed my gaze, noted my raised eyebrows, and said "Ed was trained as a chef, and he's very good in other people's kitchens." Who would have guessed, I thought. I'm not going to deter him for one moment.

In a very little time, the table was spread with everything required for a cold lunch, to which Ed soon added a large spinach and mushroom quiche, warmed in the oven. "I'm sorry that it's just a supermarket one," he said, looking at it with some disdain. "I just didn't have the chance to make one myself. You know, we were driving and stuff." Emily beamed at him happily and we all made appreciative comments about the lunch.

"The best way to a man's heart is through his stomach," quoted Emily.

"So shouldn't you be doing the cooking for him?" I asked.

"Nope," said Emily firmly. "I let him cook 'cos he loves his own cooking and he hates mine, at least on the one occasion I've tried to entertain him just before we left. So that way, I'm finding my way to his heart through his own cooking. Not that I'm..." She trailed off as one who has accidentally made a confession.

I tried to make sense of this topsy turvy logic, and failed dismally. But whatever, if it worked for them, fine.

Once we had eaten the meal, another round of appreciation was declared. Comments were also made to the effect that a large and delicious lunch wasn't the best idea before convening a working party to empty the van, but at least with the four of us doing it, it didn't take too long when we set to. The contents were piled up in the lower room, and then Emily suggested that she and Lila should set to work right away to unpack and tidy away. I thought that it would be a very good opportunity for them to have a bit of one-to-one time, so I suggested to Ed that he and I should have an amble along the shore for a while, then we'd come back and make tea for everyone. To be honest, I was rather hoping that it would be him making the tea in some exotic fashion, and that I'd have little or nothing to do with it.

We set out. I'm really a lousy conversationalist, hopeless at parties and so forth, but I thought it incumbent on me to make conversation with the young man, so I started with what I already knew – which was close to nothing.

"So you work at the removal company?"

"Yup. Been there a couple of years."

"Driving? Heaving stuff around? Office work?"

"Bit of everything really."

Silence, while we trudged a little further along the shore.

"But you really wanted to be a chef?"

"Not really. Cooking classes at school was the best way to spend time with the girls. I did ok, I mean, with the cooking, and then that was the only thing I could really apply to college for."

"But you haven't managed to get a job in catering?"

"Got a sous chef job in a Michelin three star restaurant. Gave it up after six months. All blokes. No good to me."

"So you're a bit of a one for the ladies then? Emily certainly seems like a good catch, and she seems to like you."

"Emily? Nah. We're just good friends. She seemed to need a bit of help so I'm just along for this trip." He was silent for a minute, then said, "You think she likes me? I hadn't noticed. Does she seem ok to you? I hadn't really noticed that either."

"Well, I've only just met her, but I've known her mother for a long time. Emily seems to be a charming young woman."

"Oh. Hadn't noticed," he repeated.

"Ed – have you had many girlfriends, or dated much?"

"Me?" I thought for a moment that he was actually going to look round for someone else who I might be talking about.

"Yes. I mean, you seem to like working with women, having them around, so I thought maybe you'd been dating a few."

"Nope. None of them asked me so far." His eyes seemed calmly set on the distant horizon. "No rush," he said.

Bingo, I thought. Here is the first altruistic man on the planet. He really had driven several thousand kilometres just to be helpful to someone who happened to be an attractive young woman.

We walked a little further, then I suggested it was time to turn round and walk back.

"Shame we can't walk round in a circle so we don't pass the same stuff again," Ed replied.

"Then we'd get our feet wet, Ed."

"True. If we turned out to sea. But I meant inland."

He wasn't so daft as I thought. "We could, but you have to go a long way till there's a path inland to the road."

"Maybe next time."

When we neared the path up to the yellow house, I could hear Emily calling us from nearby. "Ed, Petrus, where are you?"

"We're in Tasmania," Ed shouted back. I thought, either he got that line from a TV show, or he really meant it.

"We're nearly there," I called back more informatively. "Is everything ok?"

"No! We need tea!"

Well, it's always nice to know that you are needed. And hopefully, one day Ed would come to realise that.

Chapter 16

It took a while to unpack the jumble of boxes and cases in which Emily had brought my belongings, and to somehow put them away in the limited space available. There were some items I wouldn't have bothered with, and I mentally noted them so that I could throw them out when Emily had gone. But there were other things, ranging from my precious laptop through to my essential clothes, that would make my day-to-day life in the yellow house much more viable. She had even gone through the box of family photographs and removed all she unilaterally deemed to be mine rather than Brian's. I suspect Brian hadn't been left with many. But the sight of Ed, who must have been at least six foot six, had persuaded him that no argument would be tolerated at any point. He had meekly allowed Emily to bring everything she chose, unaware that Ed would probably have simply wandered off in the event of a confrontation.

"So what's the deal with you and Ed?" I asked her as we stood back to survey the pile of empty boxes which bore testament to our efforts.

"Oh, he's just a friend. I mean, really I've only known him for a few days before we raided the house and drove down here."

"So..."

"No mum, I've not bedded him, and as far as I am aware, he's simply not interested. I don't mean as in gay, I mean as in, maybe I'm not his type. But that's fine. Perhaps there's a life lesson happening. Perhaps it's possible to have a close relationship with a guy, intimate even, but not sexual. Or even physical. Like with a woman. But he happens to be a man."

"Well that's going to make the sleeping arrangements interesting, as there's only one spare bedroom."

"Frankly, the way Ed is, we could share a bed and he wouldn't so much as touch me. However, it's me we're talking about. I know I'm totally irresistible, and I don't want to risk the experiment, so I've got my eye on that sofa in Petrus' study. For him, not me, needless to say."

"Well, that all sounds very sensible," I told her, trying to think back to the last time she had been sensible about a man.

"Anyway, I seriously need afternoon tea in some shape or form. Where have those two got to?" Mercurial as ever, Emily was striding down the yard towards the beach before she had finished her sentence. As I got to the top of the steps, I could see her at the end of the path, calling "Ed, Petrus, where are you?"

It was hard to hear, but I could have sworn I heard Ed call back, "We're in Tasmania," but I'm sure I was wrong.

Emily and I and Petrus sat in the lounge while Ed made afternoon tea. God knows how he did it, but it would have done a five star hotel proud. He put on a repeat performance in the evening, producing a vegetarian dish based around stuffed peppers, but with other things happening that defied description. Fortunately, they didn't defy eating.

I took Petrus aside after dinner out on the deck. "I need to talk to you about sleeping arrangements," I said, and then realised I had his full attention. "Petrus, calm down. Not you, not I. Not even you and I. I'm talking about Em and Ed."

"The guest room awaits them. Is there a problem?"

"Not a problem as such, just that they are not an item. They don't sleep together. Just good friends. You know, like you and me."

"Ah. Maybe it's to do with the colour of the walls of the house."

"I beg your pardon?"

"That yellow colour. A passion killer. How many weeks is it that I've lived under this roof, and nobody has had sex with anybody?"

I turned and gave him a shove. He rocked back towards me on his feet, and with a deft manoeuvre tucked his hand through my arm, so we stood there looking out to the darkened sea view arm in arm like old lovers. "Hoi," I said. But he didn't relinquish me, and I didn't pull away. Let's face it, we *were* old lovers, so it wasn't that inappropriate.

He said, "Well, the good news is that it's perfectly possible to sleep on that sofa full length, or in Ed's case, almost full length, him being the height that he is. And they brought up a sleeping bag from the car. He's young enough to cope with that, and let's face it, it's better than sleeping in the front of the van."

"Come on then, let's go inside and get them and ourselves settled down. They must be exhausted." As we went in, I realised that Emily had been sitting at the dining table facing the windows, watching our every move. She caught my eye, and then theatrically looked away as if to say, "I didn't see anything, and I'm saying nothing."

Later, almost asleep in the loft bed, I heard the phone ping. I hoped this bedtime messaging wasn't going to become a habit. But I knew it already had.

Hi Lila, are you all tucked in and ready for lights out?

Yes. Go to sleep. All quiet up there?

Can't hear anyone creeping about. They'd have to pass my door if they did. I've left it ajar so I can catch them.

Petrus, don't be an idiot. Close the door.

I was joking. I only left it open in case you decided to come upstairs.

Petrus, close the door. I'm not coming anywhere.

Me neither. Sad, isn't it.

Goodnight Petrus.

Goodnight. Sweet dreams. Xx

Chapter 17

When I staggered out of my bedroom in the morning, everyone else had already breakfasted. Emily was downstairs with her mum, doing mother-and-daughter things. Ed was sitting in an armchair in the lounge, reading a book.

"What's the book, Ed?" I enquired, chiefly to determine whether I was awake enough to have the power of speech or not.

"It's called 'The Rain of War – Collected Poems from the First World War' and I found it on your bookshelf."

"Ah yes, I'd forgotten I had it. What made you pick that one out?" It seemed to be rather serious reading for a removal company operative and former chef. But I'm an intellectual snob. I don't deny it.

"I've always particularly liked Wilfred Owen's poems, but I was trying a few of Siegfried Sassoon's. 'I knew a simple soldier boy...' - so powerful."

"I'm the other way round," I replied, trying to stuff my snobbery back where it came from. "Owen seemed to write a few that are of course justly famous, but Sassoon's are more consistent, more globally applicable perhaps."

"I do wonder whether their perspective in either case was simply for their own time, or were they leaving a dreadful warning for the generations to come?" Ed replied, looking pensively out of the window.

"Well – we shall never know," I said, trying to duck out of a conversation which was about to go way over my head. Of course, later in the day I would have been able to hold my own. Of course.

"Why's that?"

"Well – they are both long dead."

"Ah, I hadn't heard," Ed replied.

I thought, this guy is beyond strange. Of course they are long dead, but he doesn't know. But he's still able to conduct a conversation comparing and contrasting their works. Perhaps he's winding me up. Perhaps I should get us onto firm ground.

"I'd better get myself breakfast," I said. Ed got the hint. In fact I think he was out of his chair and stepping into the kitchen before I had finished speaking.

"What do you fancy?" he asked.

"Well, there used to be a place on the coast near Melbourne where they did something called 'The Big Breakfast' which basically included everything you could imagine. Eggs, bacon, sausage, beans, fried bread, mushrooms, tomatoes, hash browns, the lot. But I'll settle for any one thing from that list."

"Hmm. I think we've got all that. Give me a couple of minutes. Tea or coffee?"

Ten minutes later, I sat down to the breakfast of a lifetime.

"So how long were you thinking of staying?" I enquired. I couldn't decide between my privacy and Ed's cooking. This was going to be a good news and bad news thing.

"I've got to get the van back to the depot by Tuesday. I guess one more night here, then we start driving."

As I finished my breakfast, Emily and Lila came up the steps and through the door.

"So what's the plan, Petrus?" asked Emily brightly, unaware that I am not a person who makes plans.

I thought on my feet, despite being unable to stand up due to the size of the breakfast I had just utterly consumed.

"It's not a bad day for a walk," I said, still thinking. "Or maybe we could go out for a meal somewhere."

"Or both," said Emily.

"Tell you what. Why don't you and Ed explore along the beach a bit, then we'll have lunch here, then we'll head out in my SUV, and we'll find somewhere really good for dinner, to thank you two for all your help."

"Ok, Petrus, that sounds good. Come on Ed, let's go."

"I'd like to try to walk in a circle", said Ed, to the complete puzzlement of Emily, but she let it go.

"I'll go downstairs and do some dinner research," said Lila. "I'll try not to make it too expensive." She threw me a wicked glance, and followed Emily and Ed down the steps.

I finally managed to move from the dining table, and pottered around tidying up, not that there was much to tidy. Ed had rolled up the sleeping bag neatly in my study. He's a good catch, I thought. A bit, well, different, but aren't we all. I sat down at my laptop and tried to think of something to write. Then I dozed off.

I woke when Lila squeezed my shoulder. "Petrus! It's lunchtime and Em and Ed are still out there somewhere."

"He always will be," I said, trying to remember who I was and where I lived.

"Very witty. Can you go and find them while I finish making sandwiches for lunch?"

"Sure, sure. Give me a moment to remember where the beach is."

A few minutes later I stepped gingerly down the steps to the yard, not too sure whether I was fully awake. As I was about to turn towards the beach, I saw the missing couple coming down the drive from the road, either side of a man I didn't recognise. He was quite tall, not in Ed's class, but his lean build emphasised his height. He must have been in his late forties. He was informally dressed, like everyone in Tasmania seemed to be, but very smartly. A man of means on his day off. I walked towards the group.

"Good afternoon!" the stranger greeted me. "Do you know these two?"

"Yes, but I don't know you."

"Sorry, of course, I'm Jeff, from the house next door. These two were wandering up my path from the beach and they looked a bit suss, so when they said they had got lost trying to walk in a circle to the yellow house, I thought I would check the story. Sorry to have bothered you."

"Not at all, I'm sorry they got onto your property. Young Emily here is my... friend's daughter, and Ed is her... friend. Everybody's somebody's friend I guess."

"Well, all's well then. And anyway, I'm glad to have met you at last. You are...?"

"Petrus. Yes, it's an odd name. Petrus. You must come over one evening for a drink or something."

"I'd love to. Perhaps I could bring my wife? She is utterly consumed with curiosity about the house. She's been telling me to find an excuse to call for weeks."

"We're tied up tonight – I've promised these two a slap-up dinner somewhere or other – but maybe Sunday night, about 8pm? Just an after-dinner glass or two and nibblies, if that suits you."

"Great. See you then. Enjoy tonight! Where are you eating?"

"I have no idea. I'm open to suggestions."

"Richardsons Lodge. Only place to go. About 50 minutes' drive, but round here that's no big deal. Be sure to mention my name – Jeff Leigh – that should get you a good table. But do make a reservation."

"Cheers!"

Em and Ed bade Jeff as fond a farewell as they could, given his deep suspicion recently expressed, and we climbed the steps to the house.

I recounted my meeting with Jeff over lunch. Lila had prepared some of her excellent sandwiches. Ed had taken one from the dish with a degree of suspicion, and had been rude enough to open it up to examine its contents and construction, which drew a reproof from Emily, but he seemed not only happy with what he saw, but impressed with what he ate. He had several more before Emily cleared her throat loudly and moved the dish away from him.

Lila seemed slightly unenthusiastic about entertaining the next night, but agreed it was time we met our other neighbours. Then she asked Emily how they had managed to end up on the wrong property.

"Ed was so keen not to retrace our steps, so we walked up from the beach through a property a long way down, and came back along the road, but then we got confused, and went first down the wrong drive back to the beach, and then up the wrong path to the house next door. And then we were apprehended by that Jeff guy. He wasn't aggressive but a bit rude really. I mean, look at me. I paid a fortune for this outfit. Do I look like someone up to no good?"

"No, you certainly don't," Lila assured her. She probably didn't dare say otherwise. "But perhaps Ed gave him cause for concern. He's very tall, and…."

"Anyway," I said, trying to rescue Lila from the hole she seemed to be digging for herself, "Jeff said we should go to the Richardsons Lodge for dinner, so that's what we'll do. If we leave here in about half an hour or so, and maybe make a few stops along the way, we'll be in good time for a 7pm meal. I'll ring and book."

Emily disappeared into her room to renew her makeup or whatever young people do for half an hour before going out. Ed went to see what else he could find on the bookshelves. Lila and I cleared the table and dealt with the kitchen. Lila was frowning a bit, I noticed.

"What's up?" I asked. "I can see something's on your mind."

"Well, I don't want to seem tight, but from my researches, the Richardsons Lodge is seriously expensive."

"That's ok, I'm paying. It'll be good to give those two a treat, and heck, we deserve a treat too. And I'm very grateful to them for bringing all your stuff here so you are that much less likely to run off and leave me in the next few days."

"Petrus, don't get serious on me, ok? I don't know... back in London you used to get pretty intense, and that was kind of flattering, but scary too. It can teeter into emotional blackmail territory, controlling even. I know it's just you being a romantic idiot, but even so, well, I just don't want to feel too wanted right now. Just a bit wanted. Ok? Feelings not hurt?"

"It's fine. You're right. I'll get a grip. Me paying for an expensive meal tonight will be nothing whatever to do with you. It's just me fancying a decent meal for once. I mean, you cook quite well sometimes, but..."

Lila slapped me with the tea towel she was holding. Then, to my considerable surprise, she took my arm, kissed me, briefly, on the lips, said "I've got to get ready," and went downstairs.

Trying to speak with a steady voice, I rang the Lodge, booked a 7pm table for four, and said that we'd been recommended to dine there by Jeff Leigh. The reception guy's slightly bored tone instantly changed to something more motivated. "We'll make sure you have a table with a view. Looking forward to seeing you at 7pm."

When Lila and Emily appeared from their separate rooms, I could not decide which of them looked more stunning. At least, not for a moment or two, and then Lila got the loyal vote.

We drove a slightly scenic route to the restaurant. The journey took us through the small town of Coles Bay, which although not far from the yellow house as the crow flies, can only be reached by driving all the way round the large lagoon behind the beach. It was tempting to take a detour to the interestingly named 'Friendly Beaches' area, but time did not allow it on this occasion. We drove along the esplanade at Coles Bay, and stopped for ten minutes or so at the boat ramp to look at the view and stretch our legs. Ed's legs needed serious stretching, as even though he'd been in the front seat, his knees ended up somewhere near his chin.

Lila took his arm and steered him off along the waterfront a little. I suspected she was doing a bit of motherly checking-out. I sat down with Emily on a bench facing the bay, where the boats tied there bobbed peacefully in the late afternoon swell.

"One day I'll bring my ocean-going cruiser down here," Emily said wistfully.

"You have one? Ah, I get it, your imaginary one. Well, keep working hard and one day you might get yourself one. Shit, that sounds patronising."

"You're right. I could work hard for years and save up. Or I could marry an elderly billionaire."

"First you've got to find one."

"I've been looking, believe me."

"And here you are with Ed."

"I'm not *with* him, I'm with him. Having said that, I like him a lot. And if he would quit the removal business and go back to being a chef, he'd make a fortune. I've had a rummage online, and he made a real reputation for himself in a very short time. He only quit because he was concerned about inclusiveness in the business. Not enough women."

"That's not quite the way he described it to me."

"Oh, I know what he says, but having got to know him rather better on that long drive, a lot of what he says is a cover for his real feelings."

"He's something completely different, isn't he. I just hope you have the patience to take things really easy and slow with him, and you could build a very special bond."

"I could say the same thing to you."

"What, about me and Ed? I wasn't planning on going beyond good friends, actually."

"No, Petrus, I mean you and my mum. You've just been giving

me relationship advice, now let me return the favour."

"You're young enough to be my daughter. I'm not sure that you are old enough to be my counsellor."

"Rubbish. I'm an adult. And I know my mum."

"I've known her longer than you have."

"No. You knew her for about nine months in London before I was born, and you've had a few weeks here with her. Ok, plus some messaging. I've known her for over twenty years, if you don't count the toddler bit."

"OK, point taken."

"And think about it. Technically you are old enough, legally, to be my mum's father, and I could be your granddaughter."

I thought about the maths, gave up, and conceded she could be right, even though I wasn't sure. But I pointed out she was being a bit unkind.

"I don't think I am, actually, Petrus," Emily responded. "Look, I like you a lot. I love my mum. I just don't want you or her getting hurt. I've got two things to say. First. Take it slowly, like I said before. She's had an appalling experience very recently, and she's either going to need time to recover before she so much as wants to be touched, or she's going to rebound bigtime, and that's not a recipe for lasting happiness. Second. No, Petrus don't interrupt. Second. What went wrong in London? Age difference. Plus other stuff, but much as she liked you, maybe even loved you, she couldn't get over the attitudinal differences that come with that kind of gap. Now, whatever else has changed, your age difference remains the same. You can never get past that. Except now, it's even worse. What's your life expectancy? Got any health problems? Yup, she told me. She's terrified of you having another heart attack. Do you really want her to have to live with that for years? Until you die with it?"

Christ, I thought, that was brutal. Just brutal. And probably right.

"Can I get a word in?"

"No. You'll have to wait a moment."

And Emily leaned across and kissed me warmly on my cheek.

"Remember, this is coming from a place of love, ok? I really, really care about you both."

We sat in silence for some moments. Lila and Ed were still talking out on the boat ramp. I hoped his interview was going smoother than mine.

"Let me explain one thing," I said eventually. "Yes, you've known your mum much longer than me. But you talk of loving her. Well, I've loved her longer than you, of that I'm certain. You didn't start until you were born, and I bet when you were a teenager there were times you didn't love her at all."

"True," smiled Emily. "But so what?"

"The thing is, as you get older, you don't lose those feelings at all. The emotions I felt twenty-seven or whatever years ago are exactly the same now. The physical responses. Ok, I admit, the sexual responses too. There is no time gap between then and now. In the falling in love department, I'm still a teenager."

"But you both married other people," interrupted Emily.

"Your mother would have to speak for herself, but for me, that doesn't mean you stop loving the first person. Not unless you parted the way your mum and dad have parted, with betrayal and a complete breakdown of trust. You mum didn't do anything that stopped me loving her. Yes, maybe she hit the age difference wall, but that wasn't an 'I don't love you any more' thing. So what do you expect me to do now? I guess you'll say, 'if you really love her you won't risk running headlong into that wall again'. That's fine, but that's a head thing, not a heart thing. How many fucking times in my life do I have to do the noble thing, excuse my language, and love someone to the point of losing them? Look, this whole thing would be totally different if she was still with your father. It was different, in fact. We were messaging like old friends, Brian knew about it, I had nothing against him, I wasn't even jealous. But now, it's a whole other thing. This is a rest of my life thing now."

"You keep saying 'me', Petrus. I can't see it that way. I need to be convinced that anything happening with my mum is going to be good for her, and good for you for that matter. And right now, I'm far from convinced. So, like I said, please take it slowly."

"Fair enough, Emily. I respect your concerns. But let me add one thing. You say I keep saying 'me'. That's because I've only been talking about me so far. The other side of the equation is, what if your mum actually had the same feelings as me? What if she thinks, stuff the age gap thing, we can work that out? Let's face it, if you thought she was hostile to the very idea of having a relationship, an intimate relationship, with me, we wouldn't be having this conversation."

Emily looked down at the ground for a moment and said nothing.

I continued, "It seems to me that relationships usually founder on problems that were not perceived at the outset. I had a friend who married a woman with a severe disability. They knew they were going to have to take that into account and make things work nonetheless. But what of a couple who marry when they are both young and fit, and then one has an awful accident, a life-changing accident, and then the whole deal has changed, the whole premise? I'd say it's the unforeseen stuff which wrecks relationships, not the stuff that's obvious at the outset." We were silent for a moment. Then I added, "But Emily, I will continue to take it slowly. And if you have concerns down the track, I will listen to them."

I checked the time on my phone.

"Shit, we're going to be late. Lila, Ed – come on!"

We reached the Richardsons Lodge via the narrow roads of the Freycinet National Park just in time for 7pm. It stands on a very small promontory on the side of the bay, and the stunning location is reflected in the prices.

"Wow, they've even got a Tesla charging station over there," said Emily as I parked.

"I could tell you something about that later," I said, glancing in the direction she was looking. And I looked again. There with its personalised number plate facing me was Colette's Tesla. I put my hand on Lila's arm and pointed with my other hand at the car. "Look who is here," I said.

Lila was equally surprised. "Well, well. I guess this is the kind of place she can afford to visit when she fancies a bite for supper. And in that car it probably only takes her ten minutes to get here."

I flung open the door of the Lodge with suitable flamboyance, and my three guests trooped in. Near the door was a small reception desk for the restaurant, and there at the desk stood Colette. I should have known. Ezra's latest little earner.

There was mutual recovery of dropped jaws. "Hi Colette. We're here to dine," I explained. "Not following you around, honest."

"Wow, great to see you!" she replied, looking with interest at Emily and Ed. Lila performed the introductions.

Colette lowered her voice. "Did you book? If not I'll sneak you in anyway."

"You'd get fired again. But we booked. Our neighbour Jeff Leigh recommended we should come."

"Ah, that's why they've given you the best window table facing the bay," she said, checking her list.

"So who is Jeff Leigh and why do people jump around him?"

"Well, for a start, he owns the Lodge. And a whole lot of other businesses around here. Pots of money. But for all that, a really nice guy, likewise his wife. He basically tries to kickstart businesses around here because he loves the area and wants it to do well. So you should get to know him. If he invites you to his house inland, say yes. Ezra and I have been up there a couple of times and the hospitality is amazing. And he even said, 'bring the kids'. Almost the nicest guy on the planet." And she looked at me with a certain smile.

"Well that's an eye opener," I said. "I'd been meaning to ask you if you happened to know about them, and I kept forgetting."

Colette took us to the table, which was indeed the best in the room. We studied the menu folders which awaited us. Ed looked at his with the air of an Egyptologist who had just opened up a freshly excavated mummy. Believe me, I've seen them. Well, on the TV. Then he stood up, and wandered towards the open kitchen at the side of the room. Perplexed, I wandered after him to make sure he didn't get lost.

When I caught up with him he was watching the busy team within with great interest. The head chef turned in his direction. "Hey, Trent, over here!" called Ed.

The chef's jaw dropped. There was a lot of jaw dropping that evening. "Ed Delany! What are you doing here, mate?"

"Just having dinner, or we will be when you guys get round to cooking it."

"I don't believe it. Come around, come in, let me introduce

you to the team. I've often told them about you, you legend. But it's got to be quick, there's some friends of the owner in tonight, so we're on our toes."

"That's me," I interjected. "Ed is with us. It's not a problem if Ed wants to catch up for a moment. There will be no complaints, don't worry."

Ed said, "Thanks Petrus. Trent and I worked in Brisbane together. I didn't realise he was here. I'll be back in a moment."

I made my way back to the table and reported the developments to Lila and Em. Em buried her face in her hands. "We won't see him again this evening. Still, if it reawakens his interest in being a chef, that's ok."

But Ed did rejoin us in a few minutes, and made some suggestions about menu choices and wines to match. We were all very happy to place ourselves in his hands. He dealt with the ordering with the pleasant if slightly obsequious waiter, and then looked again at the description of the main dish he'd ordered for Emily, 'Cape Grim Eye Fillet Steak'. He thought for a moment, then said, "I'll be back in a moment," and returned to the kitchen. We watched him as he pointed and explained and gesticulated, and finally he returned to the table. Well, to be honest, he almost returned to the wrong one but I rescued him.

"I just suggested some tweaks to the steak dish," he explained. "It'll be really good now."

It was a spectacular meal. After some excellent starters, Lila had the 'Seafood Laksa' with Atlantic Salmon, Ed had the 'Scottsdale Pork Belly', and something made me settle for the 'Nichols Chicken Maryland', which was pretty special. Ed's choices of wine went very well with our meals, and the service was excellent, with the staff being fully aware that their jobs were on the line. Ed stole a tiny piece of Emily's steak, which given her love of meat was perhaps a risky thing to do despite the substantial size of her portion, and professed himself satisfied with the outcome of his suggestion, which as a secret of the trade he refused to explain to us.

Coffee and petits fours completed the meal, and finally it was time to ask for the bill. "There's no charge," the waiter informed us, slightly shocked at the suggestion that we might pay. "The meal is with the compliments of Mr Leigh."

"Wow," I said to Lila as the waiter drifted off. "I'd better get some pretty fine wines in for tomorrow night's get-together."

Chapter 18

I felt like having a little cry after we had said goodbye to Ed and my dear Emily that morning. Petrus and I waved until the van lumbered through the gate out to the road. Ed tooted the horn, and they disappeared from view.

I walked heavy-footed to the entertainment area in the yard and sat down on the bench. Petrus stood a little distance away, and said "Shall I join you, or would you prefer to be on your own?"

"No, come and sit with me if you want." Petrus ambled over and sat down next to me, quite close. "So what do you think of my dear daughter? And what do you make of Ed?"

"Ed is, well, something completely different", he said. "It's hard to guess where he, or they, might go next."

"Yes. I had a long talk with him and came away knowing nothing more about him than at the start of the conversation. I can't picture him being right for Emily. He's just too different from her usual friends. But she seems fascinated by him."

"As for Emily, she's lovely," Petrus assured me. "We had a bit of talk on the way to the restaurant."

"I noticed. She's worried about you and me getting involved."

"I'm worried too. Let me guess – you're worried as well, just to complete the set."

"I don't know what to think, Petrus. Sometimes I think that at one level we never stopped being involved. At other times, I think, maybe it was just sexual attraction back then, and neither of us can face the fact that those days are over."

"Over for us, or we're past it for all purposes?"

"Over as a thing in itself – if it was a thing in itself."

Petrus thought for a moment, as if for once thinking through what he would say before he said it. "Firstly, I don't think for a minute it was just a sex thing in itself. For me it was an expression of what I felt about you, not just sex for sex's sake. I mean, it was great sex, the best, but there was something on top."

"Me?"

"Lila, I'm trying to be serious! And now - well, let's be glad of where we are at this moment, wherever that is. And if anything develops, for one or other or even both, let's try to be open and honest about our feelings. We haven't got time for guesswork." After Petrus said that, I thought, you've got less time than me, statistically, and sadly that must influence your thinking.

"Fair enough," I agreed. We sat in silence for a moment, and then I said, "Anyway, let's get sorted out ready for these good people tonight. We need two good bottles of red, two of white, and some nibblies. I reckon we could get the wine at the Bark Mill and the rest at Morris's Store. Shall we go together?"

At the shops, Petrus followed me round with the trolley as I picked up the things I thought we would need. After not having to pay for last night's meal, I didn't feel the need to cut corners with our purchases. The flicker of Petrus' eyebrows at the cash desks made it necessary to remind him of the circumstances.

As we drove back, Petrus said, "This sort of occasion always raises the interesting issue of whether I should be frank about my occupation. You know, author of erotic stories. If I just say 'I'm a writer' then inevitably people want to know more. And if I do give them the full job description, I can feel them looking at whatever white hair I have left, and wondering how someone who probably hasn't seen a naked woman in years manages to write in that genre."

"I have to say I wonder about that myself."

"I just think back to London."

"Petrus, keep your mind on the road."

"You can't blame a chap for remembering his youthful conquests."

"Petrus, you weren't youthful even then, and no conquest was involved. I was just being kind to an older man."

"I wish I was confident that you are joking."

"I wish I was confident that you are watching the road."

Petrus took the purchases upstairs. I called after him to remind him to put the cheeses in the fridge. And the white wine. I thought that I'd better pop up there later and check. And make sure the place was tidy. Then I thought, am I making excuses to go upstairs and see Petrus?

We had lunch independently. At least, I hoped Petrus had lunch. He was perfectly capable, if unimaginative, in the kitchen, but recently he'd not had to exert himself too much on the catering front. And for the last couple of days, with Ed around, not at all.

One way and another, I had got seriously behind with my writing. I had deadlines for two magazines coming up. If I got the pieces in promptly, I could relax for some days. I settled down at my desk under the loft bed, and found that the room was actually quite conducive to concentration. The temptation to go upstairs for afternoon tea only occurred to me when it was much too late. I finished one article and completed a draft of about half of the second one. Good going really. I shut the lid of the laptop and spun round in my chair to face the room.

I found myself trying to decide what kind of room it was. A bolt hole in which to hide? A private area in an otherwise shared house? A space from which to launch my new business, whatever that was going to be? I had no idea where I was going with anything. Well, whatever my destination, the journey would be an interesting experience at the very least.

My eye lighted on my camera which Emily had left on top of one of the chests of drawers. "You should do some photography again, mum," she had said. "You used to be good with a camera." I picked it up and switched it on. Nothing. Flat battery. I tried to think where we had put the charger. 'Come back Emily, all is forgiven,' I thought. Then I remembered the box of such things in the bottom drawer, fished out the charger, and inserted the battery. 'That's something for when I've finished the second article,' I promised myself. 'Maybe I can treat myself to a photography trip later in the week.'

I finally went upstairs to see what was left in the fridge for supper from Emily and Ed's visit. Petrus came out of his study when he heard me in the kitchen.

"Hi Lila, how have you been doing?" he asked.

"Finished one article and uploaded it, made a good start on the next one. I'm thinking that if I can get that one done tomorrow, maybe later in the week we could go somewhere photogenic, I mean apart from round here. Emily reminded me that I haven't taken any photos for ages."

"Sounds like a plan. Perhaps Jeff would have some ideas about a destination tonight. He clearly knows the district very well."

I rustled up some kind of meal for us from the various good things that Em and Ed had left behind, and we sat opposite each other at the dining table, trying to think up lively topics of conversation for the evening ahead. But knowing very little about the Leigh's, we were left with winging it as the only real option. I cleared away the meal, did a rapid spruce up of the kitchen, and laid out on the dining table the cheeses and biscuits and dips and things we had bought. I opened the red wines to breath a little, made sure the whites were good and cold, and turned on the outside lights to greet our guests.

The weather being now a bit on the cool and windy side, with rain clouds mostly obscuring the moon, we were not surprised when Ann and Jeff arrived in their car rather than on foot. Warm greetings were exchanged at the door, and we ushered them in. Petrus had already described Jeff to me, but neither of us had met Ann. She was a pleasant looking woman of about Jeff's age, and there was something about them as a couple which was apparent very quickly – the word 'integrated' sprang to mind. They also proved to be very easy guests, unpretentious, amusing, polite but not stuffy, clearly well educated but without any tendency to wave their uni degrees in the air.

Obviously our first duty was to thank them profusely for hosting our dinner at the Lodge the night before.

"Perhaps it was a bit naughty of me not to have declared a financial interest in the Lodge," said Jeff, smiling happily at our compliments about the meal. "I gather one of your party is himself a talented chef? Perhaps he would like to join the team in the Lodge kitchen? Though Trent said he would be more suitable to lead the team than to be any kind of junior member."

"He's based in Brisbane at the moment," I explained, "and I don't think he has any thought of coming down here again, but thank you anyway."

"You neighbour the other side, young Colette, is already on our staff," observed Jeff, "so you might get the impression we are trying to employ the entire population of Dolphin Sands one way and another."

Petrus took a slight risk, but the Leigh's gave the impression of being hard to offend. "We saw her there. She seems to pop up in a variety of roles all around here. She mentioned that you are involved in other enterprises in the area."

"Well," said Jeff, "to be honest we don't mention it to many people, but the fact that we are able to invest locally is entirely due to some good fortune we encountered here a few years ago when we were staying in a rented house for a holiday. We weren't particularly well off at the time -"

Here Ann interjected, "Bloody poor actually!"

Jeff smiled fondly at her, and continued, "and I was in the habit of buying one lottery ticket each week from whatever outlet was convenient. I suspect you can guess the rest of the story."

"You bought a ticket at the local store, won the jackpot anonymously, and have been spending the proceeds in the area ever since?" I suggested.

"Exactly, though we don't simply spend it. We invest it on a perfectly commercial basis, but taking much bigger risks than banks would. We look for people who have good ideas but are short on opportunities to bring them to life. Then if the idea seems reasonably likely to succeed, or deserves to succeed, which is slightly different, then we invest."

"And the Lodge?" I asked. "That seems to be a normal kind of business not needing help from an angel."

"It was – until the previous owner was suddenly arrested for running a money-laundering operation via the Lodge accounts, and a lot of local people would have lost their jobs if we hadn't stepped in and taken it over," explained Jeff.

"And Jeff likes a good meal and a fine wine!" added Ann with a laugh.

I took the hint and topped up their glasses liberally. On the way home they would only be driving for about a hundred metres on a deserted public road, so I wasn't too fussed about how much I was pouring.

"So now you know all about us, tell us about yourselves, and this gorgeous house," prompted Ann.

This was the question I had both anticipated and dreaded, and having thought carefully about it for much of the day, I really hadn't got an answer ready. But Petrus jumped in before I could respond. Given his ability to say the wrong thing at the wrong time, I immediately prepared to cringe. But actually he spoke well.

"We're really here by accident, you could almost say. First I had some domestic difficulties which I won't go into, but I needed to find somewhere quiet where a fair bit of restorative contemplation would be possible. And then Lila had to leave home suddenly as well, and rang me and said, 'help!' and I did. So now she lives downstairs, and I live upstairs, and we both lead our separate lives but overlap in the kitchen and laundry. Probably a strange arrangement, but it works."

"That's the main thing, whatever works," said Ann. "But you must have known each other before, unless Lila chose your number at random, which would have been very romantic, but not very likely."

"Oh, there's nothing romantic about it at all," said Petrus. I entirely endorsed that as a reply, but felt strangely sad that he had said it nonetheless. "We worked in the same office in London decades ago, and kept in touch on and off. Nothing more romantic than that."

I could have sworn that I saw a little glance exchanged between Ann and Jeff, but perhaps I was wrong.

"And what do you both do?" asked Jeff. "Everyone has to do something. Like most people on the planet, I'm afraid I pigeon-hole everyone by their occupation. Including the retired category."

Once again, Petrus led. "By coincidence, we're both writers," he explained. "I write short stories mainly. Lila is more of a journalist in the field of design and interior decoration and suchlike."

Ann frowned. "Lila – you're not Lila Moone are you? Not *the* Lila Moone?"

I thought, what is it about my reputation that it has preceded me nowhere but to Dolphin Sands? Still, it will distract them from asking for more details of Petrus' writing.

"Well, yes, I guess I am that particular Lila Moone."

"Good grief," said Jeff. "Ann wanted to completely overhaul our décor, and adopt your principles of colour and pattern that you've been expounding in 'The Decorator' magazine, but I said, over my dead body."

Ann said "Jeff! That's not true, you said nothing of the sort!"

and there was a sudden awkward silence.

Then Jeff burst out laughing, and said, "I'm sorry, I'm a terrible tease, and when I get home I will be made to suffer for my misplaced humour. Lila, I love your eye, and indeed we have followed a great many of your suggestions. And I look forward to showing you our house in due course, so that you can both admire your influence at work, and also advise us on where to go with the process next."

Jeff was such an affable character that I took no offence at his humour, but I decided I'd take the chance to ask for advice myself.

"We would really love to come over in due course. But before you pick my brains, for what they are worth, could I have a pick of yours? I'd love to get away for a couple of days to somewhere photogenic, to brush up my photography skills. I've really hardly taken a single photo for the last couple of years, and while there are some spectacular beach scenes around here, I'm looking for something more varied, more wildlife, you know the sort of thing."

"Maria Island", he replied at once, and Ann nodded her agreement. "Loads of wildlife, fantastic scenery, and nobody actually lives there apart from rangers. You have to drive down to Triabunna, get the ferry from there, and you can stay in the old Penitentiary buildings quite cheaply. Great unless you like five star hotels. Or, you can camp."

"Sounds great. Do you own it?" I immediately wished I hadn't been so flippant, but Jeff's sense of humour worked both ways, and he roared with laughter.

"Well, I'm on the board of the National Parks Service, but that's hardly owning the island. It does mean I get free ferry travel but sorry, it's not transferable. You'll have to pay your own fares."

"Thanks, Jeff, that's a really helpful suggestion."

"Oh – Petrus – I didn't ask what genre of stories you write. Do you publish under your own name?" Jeff clearly had an eye for detail and hadn't been distracted at all.

"I use a variety of pen names," said Petrus, "but I doubt whether you would have come across any of them. The genre is not everybody's cup of tea."

"Aha. I get you. Say no more, mum's the word, and all that stuff." And the way Jeff winked at Petrus made it abundantly clear he was fully aware of the genre.

"But we must be going," said Jeff. "Must let you two get to your bed. Or beds, sorry."

That wasn't a slip of the tongue, I thought. He's a rogue, but a loveable one.

Ann bade us a very warm goodnight, cheeks were kissed all round, and we saw the Leighs to their car. It was actually more of a limousine. And we hadn't needed to worry about how much they were drinking, as their driver had been sitting at the wheel waiting for them the whole time. How the rich live, or how the philanthropists live. I guess they were somewhere between those two states. The car glided back towards the gate to the road.

At the foot of the steps, I asked Petrus whether he would be ok with clearing up in the house. He said he thought that would be within his capabilities, and he gave me a little bow and said goodnight. He turned to go back upstairs, but I said, "Petrus, wait. Come here."

He turned back to me, and for a fleeting moment seemed to hesitate, and then with a simultaneous movement, we drew together, and wrapped our arms around each other, and just hugged, rocking very slightly, with no sound other than the lapping of the waves beyond the end of the yard.

Eventually I drew back a little, Petrus releasing me with a little reluctance. "Thank you for all your support, Petrus. I feel a little healed. Happier. Thank you."

We kissed goodnight, not lingering, but it was the kiss of former lovers perhaps remembering a little of their past.

There was no messaging that night. Maybe our communication was on another level.

Chapter 19

On our first night in the Maria Island Penitentiary building, I lay in the almost pitch black darkness, in a sleeping bag on a narrow bunk bed with a near-solid mattress. Just a faint outline of a window could be seen at the end of the room. Another bunk bed was against the opposite wall of the narrow room. Lila lay there wrapped in her sleeping bag. I heard her sigh.

"Petrus, what have you done to me?"

"What is it? Are you ok?"

"This wasn't supposed to happen."

"What has happened, Lila?"

"You know. I think it has happened to you too."

"Love? Desire?"

"One or both. Which one? I don't know any more. I don't know anything. I just want to take those last two steps to you."

"Me too. We should have known this would happen."

"Maybe we did know."

"Maybe."

There was silence for several minutes. The moon had been partly obscured by broken cloud. Now it emerged, only a half moon, but enough to illuminate the space between our beds.

"So shall I come to you, or will you come to me?" I finally said. "Or we can stay put. And probably not sleep all night."

"Unzip your sleeping bag, Petrus. I think perhaps we could manage to just cuddle for a while."

I sat up and wrestled with the zip for a few moments. Lila, wearing only pants and a t-shirt, wriggled out of her sleeping bag, unzipped it all round, brought it with her across the boundary of the floor, and squeezed onto my bed. My bag lay below us and she arranged hers over us as a blanket.

"Hi," I said.

"Hi," said Lila in almost a whisper.

We clung to each other, scared that the very thought of separation would end us, or that this very act might undo us.

* * *

The first day of the Maria Island trip had proved to be a bit more of a challenge than we had expected. The island can only be reached by a small ferry which crosses from Triabunna, somewhat south from Dolphin Sands. There are no shops on the island. Everything you need for your stay has to be taken with you, including food and water. We had to make lists, we had to plan, we had to buy all sorts of things at Morris' Store. Fortunately they sell everything, including cheap sleeping bags and backpacks. Accommodation on the island consists only of rooms in the old Penitentiary, or you can bring your own tent. I drew the line at that. Camping is not my thing. The Penitentiary on the other hand seemed very like the dormitories of my English boarding school, where the beds had consisted of an iron frame, wooden slats, and a thin horsehair mattress. I thought I would be at home in that environment. We booked two nights.

The drive from Dolphin Sands to Triabunna took about 45 minutes. We had booked tickets for the 10am ferry, and we were just in time. It was a windy day with occasional glimpses of the sun. The sea was choppy and the small ferry bounced across to the island in about 20 minutes. I was glad that breakfast had been minimal. Lila seemed unfazed, a better sailor than I. Signs above the windows decreed that passengers were not to eat or drink. Nobody in their right mind would have wanted to. Even at the island jetty, the boat still bobbed up and down, so that some agility was required to disembark at the right moment.

The scene as we walked from the jetty onto the island was somewhat bizarre. At one time, the island had been used for the production of cement, with a substantial industrial plant ranged along this part of the shore. Three great concrete silos remained, towering over the jetty terminal. From there, an unmade road led to the 'township' of Darlington, now just a small mixed group of both functional and abandoned buildings, a short walk from the ferry. The buildings reflected the history of the settlement, firstly as a prison camp for convicts, and secondly as an industrial and agricultural centre. There had been enterprises related to the growing of vines and mulberries, cement manufacture, timber, and fishery, but these gradually failed, and the buildings fell into disrepair. Finally the island became a wildlife sanctuary and historical site.

Having found our allotted accommodation and shed our load of supplies and bedding, we first set out to look around the historic buildings of the settlement. Here I was sure Lila would find any number of photographic opportunities. It was to find her some Kodak moments that we had made this trip. On my side, we were also making it because at the house, our mutual respect for each other's privacy seemed to be inhibiting what I hoped would be the development of our relationship. Since we had embraced after the visit by Ann and Jeff Leigh, we had kept much more to our respective territories, and there were no more kisses. In fact, ever since Lila had moved downstairs, I had always avoided visiting her there, because it seemed to me to be her territory, her sanctuary, and therefore not a place for me to intrude.

But here on the island, there were no such considerations. We were thrown together, in fact closer together than I had anticipated. I had been almost taken aback by the proximity of the beds we were to occupy.

Lila looked carefully around the various disused or even ruined old buildings. She was of course using a high quality digital camera, but she was using it more like a film camera, as in the days when every shot was carefully considered, due to the cost of the film and of processing and printing. On the island, as there was no electricity, there was therefore no way of recharging the camera batteries, and therefore Lila kept it by her side and not switched on until she was sure that there was a photo to be taken.

In the ruins of the house of the lessee of the island who was responsible for the attempts to develop the commercial enterprises in the late 1800's, Lila took a series of photos which contrasted the crumbling brickwork with the great expanse of land, sea and sky visible through the gaping holes where once there had been windows. Behind those windows, the entrepreneur and his family had battled against inevitable business failure. The bricks themselves were a testament to the labours of the convicts who had manufactured them on the island.

Close by were the ruins of the 'Grand Hotel' of which nothing remains but the brick fireplaces and chimneys. Where the grass now grows there were once lavishly furnished rooms for over thirty guests, who were drawn to the island by the promise of a 'happy hunting ground of the Geologist, Naturalist, Conchologist, Artist, and Alpine Climber'. Now the photographer such as Lila and the romantic such as myself could be added to that list. Lila found only one subject for a photograph here, when a wandering wombat helpfully positioned himself in front of one of the ruined fireplaces. Or the wombat positioned herself; determination of the sex of wombats is a skill I do not possess. They can bite, so it would be a foolhardy person who chose to examine the animal so as to know whether to call it him or her for the purpose of a diary.

The great brick-built barn proved a more fertile photographic subject. Historic farm and mining machinery have been stored there but not under museum conditions. The machines were mottled with the droppings of birds which could freely enter via the open doorway, perching on the massive timber frame supporting the roof. I could see that Lila was finding visual treats in the details of the machines as much as in their overall appearance. Massive bolts, spokes of ancient wheels, haphazard piles of timbers.

From building to building Lila hunted for elusive original images, saying little, concentrating on the promptings of her artistic eye. I kept out of the way, knowing that to some degree she would have preferred to be alone. I simply observed the observer.

The late morning slipped past as we wandered from one ruin to another, and we visited the museum, in a building where time seemed to be frozen in the late 1800s. Here Lila took a particular interest in the décor, and took close-up photos of parts of the peeling wallpaper, the patterning around the fireplaces, the details of old furniture.

Eventually Lila surfaced from photo mode and gave me a beautiful smile, followed by an unexpectedly affectionate kiss. "Thanks for being so patient. I know I'm no different from any other amateur photographer but I can't help getting immersed in trying to capture that elusive perfect image."

"You have your artist's eye, and that kind of drives you. And I think it's that eye that makes you not quite the same with a camera as many others. And the discipline of having to ration your shots to make your batteries last perhaps adds to the need to make every one a good one."

"You flatter me, but thank you. Anyway, let's get back to the real world – time for some lunch."

We returned to the Penitentiary and unpacked our first meal. Lila had made up exactly what was required for each meal of our stay, in order to minimise having to fuss with food in a kitchen-free environment. My function in this matter had been to push the shopping trolley and to admire the assembly of the items back at home. "It's a bit like putting together Emily's school lunch packs," Lila had said as she stood back to admire the neat series of bagged meals.

For the afternoon we had planned a walk to the 'Painted Cliffs', sandstone cliffs of patterned sandstone, which had been eroded by the seas of centuries into remarkable shapes. Nearby are rock pools teeming with marine life. The guide book had emphasised that they should be visited at low tide, and we had done our homework and calculated that arriving at about 3pm would be ideal.

We made our way along a gravel path, and after a little while I made sure the crunch of my walking boots matched Lila's stride. When she noticed, she grinned at me, said "Idiot!" and took my hand. Thus we walked like a couple of teenagers, exchanging a few shy glances at each other, companionable smiles, saying little. Soon we left the path to cross a paddock towards a cottage on the hill.

"Mrs Hunt's Cottage," I told Lila.

"I know, I read the same guide."

"Don't get smart with me, young lady," I teased, and withdrew my hand from hers, which actually coincided with Lila doing much the same movement in order to turn on her camera.

"There should be a couple of trees here. Yup, there they are."

Part way across the meadow, two spindly trees grew close together but otherwise in splendid isolation. Years of being buffeted by the prevailing winds had bent them over, and thus they framed the view of the old cottage beyond.

"Wow, that's going to be a great photo," I enthused.

"It's as common as mud," Lila disenthused, if there is such a word. "Everyone who comes up here takes that shot. I'm hoping for a small variation in mine which will really nail it, though."

"It said in the guide that Mrs Hunt used to hang a lantern in her window to guide the incoming mail boat, but I wonder whether it was for a different purpose."

"Petrus, get your mind out of the gutter."

We made our way back across the meadow on the other side of the house and rejoined the main path. As the path neared the coast, Lila pointed out a small group of kangaroos grazing about 50 metres away, and she photographed them against the backdrop of the coastline of mainland Tasmania, far across the water.

Soon we came to the beach. "We should be able to see some interesting birds here," said Lila, pulling a face because of the stench of rotting seaweed. Almost at once we saw hooded plovers running along the beach in front of us, and the cry of Pacific gulls came from above us as they wheeled in the wind with graceful ease.

We made our way along the sand to the end of the beach where the Painted Cliffs began at a sandstone outcrop. It was indeed a remarkable sight, and we stood and gazed at the dramatic formations wrought by the coming together of groundwater, spray and wave actions. Lila spent a long time almost cataloguing the cliffs in detail, commenting that there was considerable scope for harvesting some of the natural patterns for fabric or wallpaper designs. After a while I wandered back along the cliff to the rock pools filled with seaweeds, shell fish and anemones. Here Lila eventually joined me and with her camera gathered more material for future use.

The tide had clearly turned and the late afternoon sun was providing less warmth. We made our way back to the Penitentiary, with Lila stopping from time to time to photograph the wombats and kangaroos emerging for their evening feed. Finally she put away the camera into its case.

"Petrus, maybe tomorrow I should go out without the camera. I've really ignored you for most of the day."

"Hey, don't worry. I've got this thing about being with someone, but alone at the same time. I don't mind you being on your own with me if that's what you want."

"Yes, it is. I like it. I like you." Lila slipped her arm through mine and we strolled towards the Penitentiary closely linked.

Our room was equipped with a wood burning stove, and despite never having been a member of the Scouts, I managed to get it going, and its warmth soon permeated the chilly space. Well, some of it. Lila rummaged in the backpack of food and surfaced with the container for our evening meal, a simple barbecue meal, with meaty sausages for me and vegetarian ones for her.

"I shall put on an extra layer of clothing I think for when we go down to the barbecue area," Lila said, pulling out a fluffy pullover from her backpack. Unselfconsciously she peeled off the lighter sweater she had been wearing, and in doing so revealed her abdomen and briefly her bra before she rearranged the tee-shirt that she had pulled up. She caught me looking.

"Calm down, you've seen it all before," she said in mock reproval.

"Not for a couple of decades," I said, aware that my face might be reddening.

She slipped the warmer pullover over her head and arranged it over the tee-shirt. She looked at me with an appraising manner. Then she pulled up both garments above her bra and grinned one of her most wicked grins.

"So what do you think?" she asked. "Not bad for a woman in her mid fifties, huh?"

"Bloody hell, Lila. First, you look amazing. Second, you are turning me on and there's no cold shower to turn me off again."

She rearranged her clothing, and turned away for a moment. Then she turned back and said, "Sorry, I was just being a bit naughty. Sorry."

I held out both arms towards her. "That will cost you a hug."

"If I have to," she said, pretending reluctance. But the hug was warm, long, and close.

Chapter 20

Petrus and I huddled together arm in arm on a bench in front of the fire after we returned from the barbecue on our first night. It was the only ongoing source of illumination in the room. We used our torches when necessary but there is a particular magic about a room lit only by a fire.

"I'd love to look through the photos, but that won't help the battery last," I told Petrus.

"Maybe we could watch a movie or something. Oops, no TV."

"Perhaps I should sing for you?"

Petrus looked at me as if I was crazy, but then looked puzzled, and said, "You know, I don't think I've ever heard you sing, not even quietly to yourself."

"I guess I don't. Not when anyone might possibly be listening."

"We could have brought a pack of cards with us. We could have cheated each other rotten in the dark."

"I'm sure you wouldn't dream of such a thing, Petrus."

"I dream of many things."

We both stared at the fire. I could feel he was squeezing a little tighter with his arm. For a moment or two we sat silently. Eventually I spoke.

"Petrus, not all dreams can come true. Most don't. Some dreams turn into nightmares in the real world."

"I know," he replied in a low voice. "But I can't associate you with anything nightmarish."

"Not even when we split up in England?"

I could tell Petrus was pondering how to answer that.

"Well, perhaps a bit. You know those horror movies where the hero is trapped in a small room, and then the ceiling slowly starts to descend, and he is desperately trying to find a way out before he gets horribly crushed? Except in this movie, the hero had been told before he went in the room what would happen. He had only himself to blame for anything nightmarish to follow. But he was told, before the ceiling crushes you, you will enjoy pleasures that will exceed your wildest dreams, joys beyond telling, happiness like no other. And at the last moment, the heroine rescued him, before she disappeared for years and years. For a while he was out of his mind from the horror of it, and he did all sorts of crazy things. Then he gradually got himself back together, and he held onto the belief that one day he would see the heroine again, and finally he found her, and then... then I don't know how the movie ends."

I tried to relate what he had said to how I had experienced those same events, but with our different perspectives I could not entirely agree on the accuracy of his allegory. Perhaps that was inevitable.

"I don't know either," I said as gently as I could. "Maybe the next time they enter the room of delights, it is upon her that the ceiling would descend, when the hero gets written out of the movie altogether. Knowing that, should she step into the room?"

A look of infinite sadness clouded Petrus' face. "You mean, when I die? And you are left?"

I wished we hadn't started the conversation. I tried to unsay everything. "Petrus, we don't know the future. Statistically you might be the first to go, but there's no certainty. I promise you this, I'll come back and haunt you if I go first, ok?" I did my best to make a joke of it all. And Petrus, being the person he was, grabbed the lifeline and laughed a little.

"All promises have to be sealed with a kiss, else they don't count."

I gave in with no difficulty, and we kissed with more warmth than we had for decades. It was a kiss for the future rather than in remembrance of times past.

We went to bed early, as the fire burned itself out. Its light in the room was gradually supplanted by the varying light of the moon as it slipped gracefully among the broken clouds. I stripped to my tee-shirt and pants, turning my back to him as I removed my bra. I told him to look the other way, but I wasn't sure whether he did. But he took the opportunity to likewise undress to a similar level. It was strange to be in the same room, undressing if only partially, and then to get into separate beds.

I wished Petrus goodnight, and he said something like sweet dreams, and we both lay wrapped in our sleeping bags, wide awake. At least, I was wide awake, and I couldn't believe he was any less awake than me.

Maybe an hour passed, I'm not sure. There were sparks crackling across the narrow space between his bed and mine, sparks of desire, sparks of craziness, sparks of youthful fire rediscovered.

Finally I could bear it no more.

"Petrus, what have you done to me?"

"What is it? Are you ok?"

"This wasn't supposed to happen."

"What has happened, Lila?"

"You know. I think it has happened to you too."

"Love? Desire?"

"One or both. Which one? I don't know any more. I don't know anything. I just want to take those last two steps to you."

"Me too. We should have known this would happen."

"Maybe we did know."

"Maybe."

There was silence for several minutes.

"So shall I come to you, or will you come to me?" he finally said. "Or we can stay put. And probably not sleep all night."

"Unzip your sleeping bag, Petrus. I think perhaps we could manage to just cuddle for a while."

He sat up and wrestled with the zip for a few moments. I wriggled out of my sleeping bag, unzipped it all round, brought it with me across the boundary of the floor, and squeezed onto Petrus' bed. His bag lay below us and I arranged mine over us as a blanket.

"Hi," he said.

"Hi," I replied in almost a whisper.

We clung to each other like babes in the wood.

Time passed. We simply held each other, not speaking nor daring to move. He had his underpants on but his desire was unmistakable. I thought, this is crazy, in this bed there is nothing we can do, at least nothing that would reflect the significance of the occasion.

At last I felt Petrus move. He brought his hand to my face, and gently stroked it with the back of his fingers, down my cheek, across my brow, then with one finger tracing down my nose and brushing across my lips. He moved his finger across my lips again, and then gently parted them, and stroked his fingertip barely inside, just caressing the inner edge. It was an incredibly erotic movement, as if he were parting between my legs, which I had no doubt was what he meant me to think. I could not stop myself, and took the finger into my mouth, and played my tongue over it, while Petrus gently moved it a little further in, then withdrawing it, unbelievably suggestively.

But I was suddenly aware of something in my mind and my body rebelling at this seduction. I was not ready, it was too soon.

"Petrus, we can't make love."

He gently took his finger out of my mouth – I could not help but kiss it as he withdrew.

"Wrong time of the month?"

Despite everything, I could not help rewarding him with a giggle at that one. "Idiot. Petrus, I am just about exploding with lust and desire, but something is screaming in my ear, don't, don't. I want it to be consensual, I mean, consensual within me when it happens. I don't want there to be a shred of doubt. Am I being a total shit? I am so sorry, I want you but I don't all at the same time."

"I don't want anything that isn't right for you, Lila. You know that. What do you want to do? Do you want to go back to your bed? Shall we try to just sleep now? Is that going to work?"

"If I turn with my back to you, maybe you can just cuddle me, and perhaps sleep will come. Can we try?"

So Petrus fitted himself to the contours of my body as I lay on my side, with his arm around me but being careful not to touch my breasts. It was as it had been when I was taking the photographs earlier on. We were alone, together.

After a long time, I felt his body relax and his breathing slowed, and I knew he had drifted off to sleep. The fire went out and the moon was overcome by the clouds. A little while later, in the deep darkness, I followed him into sleep, weary from the day's activities and from the night's struggle within myself.

Chapter 21

The dawn, the birdsong, the discomfort, and the need to pee woke us early. Lila went along the corridor to the communal bathroom first, having pulled on her jeans in case she wasn't the only early riser. I made the journey when she returned. She had gone back to her own bed.

I couldn't help noticing that it was not much of a day outside. The rain while not heavy certainly appeared to be the wet sort, and the wind was flicking the trees around on the far side of the Penitentiary courtyard. My enthusiasm for the walk we had planned was waning somewhat as I climbed back into my sleeping bag.

We slept for a further couple of hours. There really hadn't been room for two on the narrow bunk bed, and although we had both managed to sleep, it was not the most refreshing sort.

In fact I would probably have slept longer, had it not been for Lila waking me for breakfast. This turned out to consist of a couple of nut bars. Come back Ed, I thought, all is forgiven. I still have occasional dreams about that breakfast he prepared.

"So how are you this morning, passion flower?" I asked Lila when we had finished chomping on the bars.

"Grumpy. Tired. Confused. Don't try to start anything." Lila gave me one of her warning looks, which would probably have stopped a German shepherd police dog in its tracks at a hundred metres.

"Nothing was further from my mind, I can assure you," I assured her. "There is only so much sex I can handle in any twenty-four hour period."

"Don't push your luck."

"Ok, ok. I knew it was the wrong time of the month."

Lila threw her nut bar wrapper at me. Sadly it was empty, as I was still hungry.

"So what's the plan on this dull and miserable morning?" I asked. "I think the forecast was for sunny intervals this afternoon. In England that's what they would say, anyway. I notice here they call it 'partly cloudy,' which is a bit of a glass-half-empty way of saying the same thing."

"'Bishop and Clerk' walk, as planned. We're not going to let a bit of drizzle put us off."

"I'd happily let it put me off, but if you insist..." I decided that if I wanted to depict myself as a fit and passionate potential lover, I'd need to depict myself as a fit and passionate walker. Would it be worth it? I very much hoped so.

We donned warm clothing and waterproofs on top. I kept my back to Lila as she dressed, in the interests of living till the end of the day. And not getting over-excited.

'Bishop and Clerk' is an outcrop of rock some 630m high, on the north side of the island. We set off along a gravel road, Lila with enthusiasm, me with a disconsolate air, and that air was full of the still-falling fine rain. At least the wind had dropped somewhat. Lila kept her camera dry in its case, so I did not get the excuse of waiting for her to take photos in order to take a rest. And perhaps a rest after the first hundred metres would have been inappropriate. The local wildlife, aware that cameras don't come out in the rain, was out in force. Cape Barren geese, bush-hens, scarlet robins and black cockatoos all made appearances among the big blue gum trees, together with the occasional kangaroo and a few wombats. These last are generally nocturnal, but the day being so gloomy they probably thought they were out at the right time.

We crossed a creek and soon found ourselves on open grassland, sloping upwards. The guide sheet we were following suggested that when the grassland reached the cliff edge, we should turn to the right. This struck me as being the best piece of advice I'd seen in a long time, as otherwise we might have just kept going straight ahead and over the precipice.

As we walked near to the cliff edge, but not too near, for a while we could see our destination intimidatingly above and ahead of us. Then the view was obscured as the path weaved through a stand of she-oaks, where currawongs searched for good things to eat among the debris beneath the trees. This gave me an idea, namely food, and I sat myself down on a damp log and waited for Lila to come back to find me. She had disappeared ahead round a bend in the track. She had the supplies in her backpack. For some reason she did not trust me with the food.

After about ten minutes, I gave up waiting and trudged on. Just round the bend, Lila was sitting on her own log, which appeared to be significantly drier than the one I had chosen, just finishing a snack bar.

Words were said.

I had to eat my bar on the move, but at least on the move I wasn't getting a damp bottom. However, around the point when I had finished it, Lila stopped again, and found another reasonably dry spot to sit. She beckoned me to do likewise, and brought out her camera, the rain having more or less stopped.

"Apparently if we sit quietly we might see a forty-spotted pardalote here among the stringybarks. They are quite rare now. Sit still and don't fidget."

I did as I was told, the habit of a lifetime. I had no idea what this creature might be, until Lila, reading my mind as usual, or anticipating my ignorance as usual, quietly explained that it is a tiny bird that feeds on a secretion from a particular gum tree growing in those woods.

"We might also see some other Tasmanian birds – look out for green rosellas and dusky robins." I tried my best but saw nothing, neither green nor dusky. But after a few minutes I saw Lila bring the camera slowly to her eye, pointing into the trees, and I was about to turn to see what she had spotted when the thought occurred to me, just in time, that doing so might frighten her target away, in which case the rest of our walk would be conducted in a frigid silence. So I froze. I heard the click of the camera, and Lila said "Got it!".

"Nice one!" I responded. "Can I see?"

"Here." Lila passed the camera to me, with the display showing a first class image of the tiny bird brought close by the long zoom. Lila certainly knew her stuff. I would probably have produced an out of focus image of a pigeon of no interest.

"That's fantastic. You should be doing more of this."

"Thank you," responded Lila. I passed the camera back to her, she restored it to its case, and then she leaned to me and kissed me with a combination of tenderness and passion that took me totally by surprise.

I was even more surprised by what came next.

"Do you think anyone else is coming up the path?" Lila asked me. "I have this urge to lie down in these fallen leaves and...."

Right on cue, there was a sound of youthful voices from not far away. Looking ahead along the path, I could see a group of four, perhaps parents with two teenage children, coming down the track.

"I don't know what you had in mind, my sweet, but I suspect now is not the time, without any consideration of whether this is the place."

"Damn," said Lila. "It's something to do with the great outdoors. Always makes me, well, needy shall we say."

"Ah. I thought perhaps it was an effect I was having on you. Well, maybe there will be somewhere more suitable before we get back. Or even when we get back."

"That's not the point, Petrus. It has to be somewhere unsuitable, somewhere a bit risky. That's the turn-on."

"Ok... like where we get to the top of the climb and the whole of Maria Island could see us."

"Now you're talking," replied Lila. I wasn't altogether sure whether she was joking or not. She certainly seemed to be less in two minds than she had been last night.

We continued on along the track, as it gradually become more rocky, until we came to a scree slope where the track was marked out with yellow arrows and cairns of rocks piled up as markers. The scree shifted and slid beneath our feet. I was tempted to offer Lila a hand, but then reminded myself that I was probably significantly less sure of my feet than she was. Finally we were across, and confronted with the final section of boulders, steeply piled to the top of the peak.

"Rest a moment?" Lila suggested.

We sat on the flattest rock we could find and gazed out at the view, which was misted but not totally obscured by low cloud. The mainland was a broad dark line to the west, and Freycinet to the north.

"Feeling ok?" Lila asked.

"You mean heart-wise? Well, thank you for asking, I'm fine, and yes, I do have that spray with me and I did take my pills last night."

"I think you are cranky with me for asking."

"No, Lila, I'm glad you care. But actually, I almost never think twice about it, unless I'm taking advantage of it to get some feminine sympathy."

"Well, in that case, back on your feet and let's clamber to the top."

"Last one up's a cissy. Or someone who likes looking at your bottom as you go up."

"Randy little bugger. I should make you go first."

"Gentlemen always come last. After you."

The last climb up the rocks was only about 50 metres, but almost like a 50 metre ladder. Once at the top, there was a sheer drop down the other side. I kept well back from that, but Lila went close to the edge and took photographs, looking remarkably vulnerable to any little puff of wind that cared to send her over the edge. Suddenly, she called out to me, very excited.

"Petrus! Petrus! Come here! I can see a whale!" And she brought the camera to her eye again. Curiosity and the need not to appear a total wimp overcame my natural desire not to perish in a fall, and I joined her at her vantage point. There was indeed something whale-like out in the sea, although I wasn't entirely sure of the identification. But it made Lila's day, and I wasn't about to cast any doubt. Doubt was the last thing Lila needed at this time.

Chapter 22

Petrus was pretty tired by the time we returned to our accommodation. But he managed to finish all the barbecue meal I prepared for him, despite muttering that the once-frozen beef burger patty in his bun was probably going to kill him with salmonella. After that, an early night seemed to be a good idea. Petrus seemed very happy at the thought, even though I hadn't indicated any desire to join him on his narrow bunk. I hadn't indicated any desire, even though I felt it almost overwhelmingly. There was a complete disconnect between my sexual impulses and my intellectual restraints.

I knew what the problem was. As soon as the thought of a naked man came into my mind, even if it was dear Petrus, the man turned into Brian, and I turned into someone who couldn't be less like a nubile schoolgirl. I felt inadequate and somehow defiled all at the same time. And yet I knew that Petrus was coming from a completely different situation, one of direct rejection by his wife, a loveless marriage, a celibate marriage for an unbelievable number of years. I could not bear to be the instrument of a further rejection, the cause of yet another night of celibacy.

I hesitated beside my bunk bed. I could not totally deny him. I said, "Petrus, can we spend a little more time together without actual sex? Can I lie with you again? Perhaps we could just... explore."

He said nothing, but opened out his sleeping bag. I realised he hadn't zipped it up in the first place. I brought mine over, and once again used it as a makeshift top blanket. We lay facing each other for a moment, and then I brought my lips to his, and stroked his with mine, and then kissed him open mouthed, and allowed his tongue to briefly play with mine.

His upper hand was on my shoulder. There was so little room on the narrow bunk, but just enough space for me to pull up my tee-shirt, and to take his hand and guide it to my breast. In the darkness I could barely see his face but I sensed his eyes gazing into mine.

"Do my breasts seem a bit different after a couple of decades?"

I asked him, trying to restrain a chuckle.

"A bit fuller," he replied judiciously, after a little more exploration. I thought, last time he caressed my breasts they were almost like those of a schoolgirl. And then that word wrenched me. But I rammed the thought to the back of my mind. I thought, I will not have this moment derailed. I deserve this. I deserve so much.

"Motherhood must have had quite an effect on your body," Petrus almost whispered. "God, I have so much respect for what mothers put themselves through to bring kids into the world. Or perhaps they don't put themselves through it, it's their men who do that to them. Or somewhere in between."

He continued to gently caress and explore each breast in turn, initially avoiding my nipples, unsure of whether he would cross a boundary by touching them. I just said, "It's ok to touch them," and he knew what I meant, and very gently took my nipples alternately between his fingertips, until they grew firm under his touch.

"You are fuller," he said, "but you have such shapeliness, such proud, firm breasts. I rather suspect you are quite pleased with how they have become."

"You're probably right," I acknowledged. I felt dreamy under his touch and I was in no hurry to speak, in no hurry for anything. He was making me float in a warm sea of desire, soft desire, desire without urgency.

His caresses ceased at my breasts and I felt his hand travelling down my abdomen, not all at once, but by degrees, circling, stroking across, stroking down. Somewhere deep inside my body I felt a melting sensation. But somewhere deep inside my mind, I felt unready. It was with so much effort that I held my nightmare thoughts in check.

"I'm going to keep my legs together, Petrus. The simplest contraceptive. Just for tonight. Soon I will be ready, I promise you."

His fingers slipped inside the front of my pants and played in the borders of my pubic hair. I almost wished he would gently coax my legs apart, but I knew that his respect for my wishes would be absolute, no matter how frustrating for him. I said,

"Perhaps I can do the same." And I took my hand from his back, and slid it down him to his boxer shorts, until I could gently stroke the hair there, like he was doing to me. The backs of my fingers were against his erection.

"And does my erection feel much different after a couple of decades?" whispered Petrus, mimicking my question.

"I can't tell."

"You could if you just held it for a moment."

I did.

"Perhaps a little softer."

"You could work on that."

"I could, but I won't. I've heard that older men take quite a lot of work."

Petrus chuckled softly. "True, but think what it's going to do to you to have a man inside you for half an hour or more."

"Christ, it would probably make me very uncomfortable for a week."

"We'll have to see, won't we."

"But not tonight, Petrus. I rather suspect that when we get home, one thing will quickly lead to another, and I'd rather you saved your ammunition till then. I'd rather you came inside me then, then come in a tissue now. And they're somewhere at the bottom of the backpack, anyway."

I gave his erection a final valedictory squeeze, and brought my hand to his face. He withdrew his hand from my underwear and gently stroked my back.

"Soon, Petrus, it will be soon. I think we have started something that can't now be stopped, and which was inevitable in any event. It's a force of nature thing."

We kissed long, slow and deep.

When I slept, I dreamed of whales and dolphins and mermaids.

When Petrus slept, I suspect he dreamed of my breasts.

Chapter 23

Lila and I watched Maria Island recede into the rainy distance as the ferry took us back to the mainland. Our morning activities on the third day there had been curtailed by heavy rain, and we had simply spent the time repacking our backpacks, and making sure we had left the accommodation clean and tidy. The noon ferry crossing was uneventful but rough, and we decided we would head straight home rather than have lunch in Triabunna. Speaking for myself, my digestive system wasn't up for it there.

The yellow house was cold on our arrival, and my first task was to get the wood burning heater in the lounge fired up. Downstairs was heated by a rather more soulless electric panel heater. Lila was desperate for a shower, even before the room heated up, but I was still splashing about in mine when she called out to me that she had made her way upstairs and was putting together some lunch in the kitchen.

I dried myself in front of the fire, which was starting to heat the house through, but my bedroom still felt too chilly for dressing. We were back into privacy-respecting mode, and Lila did not comment on my state of dress as I wielded the bath towel with as much modesty as I could. I finally wrapped myself in it fully and went through to my bedroom to dress.

We ate our lunch side by side at the table, both gazing out at the rainswept sea. On a clear day, Maria Island was just visible on the horizon, but today there was little to be seen apart from the sea itself.

"Perhaps we picked the wrong time of year, but I'm still glad we made the trip," said Lila. "Perhaps we could go through the photos on your TV screen in a little while?"

"Sure. Maybe I'll clear up the kitchen a bit and get the laundry going, while you make a backup of them right away on your laptop. Then we can sit with some tea and cake and re-live our trip."

The TV occupied a corner of my study, opposite the sofa. In a little while we were sitting side by side with our afternoon tea on the coffee table in front of us, while Lila paged through the photos with the remote. She scrutinised each photo with a dispassionate eye. "Crap". "Oh God." "Not bad." "Could use that."

As far as I was concerned, they were almost all very good, but she was the artist, not me. She seemed particularly pleased with some of those taken at the Painted Cliffs.

"You know, those give me an idea. Just look at those colours and sensuous abstract shapes. It would be perfectly possible to derive fabric designs from some of those. Then get them printed, and sell them locally, or online. Both perhaps. Something like that."

"Sounds like the sort of project that Jeff Leigh would be interested in."

"Funding from our next door neighbour? Wouldn't that be a bit tacky to ask?"

"He's a businessman. He's not a charity. If he thought it had a local flavour and deserved to succeed, he'd help. As long as you didn't cut him off socially if he turned you down, it would be fine."

"Of course I wouldn't do that." Lila was quite offended.

"Well, I know, I'm really just saying there would be no harm in asking when you've got it fully thought through."

"Hmmm." Lila started going slowly through the cliff images again. I watched for a couple of minutes, then found my attention wandering. I was so tired after all that outdoor activity. So tired.

When I woke, the room was in near darkness. Lila had gone. The house was silent. I sat for a few moments gathering my wits. That sofa always sends me to sleep as soon as my behind makes contact with it. In my married days it was the sofa I was sent to when my wife threw me out of the bedroom for some imagined transgression or other, so I associate it strongly with sleep. I hoped Lila hadn't gone off in a huff when I'd dozed off. I'd at least had the good manners to stay awake for the first time through the photos. Protocol allows the audience to fall asleep the second time around. It's in the rules of photo shows.

I was dressed a little too warmly now the house had heated up. I heaved myself onto my feet and went out of the study into my bedroom. As I opened the door, in the dim light of the clouded sunset I realised with a shock that Lila was on my bed. Her clothes were on the floor. Although she had pulled the blankets partly across herself, I could see she was wearing only her underwear. She turned her head to me as the door opened.

"Sorry, Petrus. I was tired too. I hate sleeping sitting up, it gives me a neck ache. And the spare bed isn't made up. So I came in here and helped myself to your bed."

"Any time. My bed is your bed, and so on." I turned on the small lamp on the bedside table.

We both hesitated. I felt my body reacting to the sight of her. Perhaps it showed in my face.

"I think I've teased you once too often," said Lila.

"You're not a tease. I want you so much anyway, teased or not."

"I want you too. Very much. Can it be now?"

By way of reply, I undid a few of my shirt buttons and pulled it over my head. I dropped it on the floor on the small pile of her clothes. My clothes on her clothes. Just that gesture seemed an erotic move. I sat down on the wooden chair beside the bed and removed my shoes and socks. I stood up, and took off my jeans and boxer shorts, turning away from Lila a little, feeling embarrassed about my nakedness and my erection. But there was no way of joining her on the bed without her seeing the degree of my desire.

"My Petrus. You look so ready."

"It's still optional," I replied. And actually, I meant it. I wasn't going to make love to her unless it really was right for her. I wanted what was about to happen to be the beginning of us, not the end.

Lila's response was to sit up, and reach round behind her back, deftly undoing the strap of her vivid red bra. As she brought her hands to the front, it slid from her, and her breasts broke free, firm, beautifully shaped, crying out to be touched, held, caressed, stroked, and kissed. I sat down beside her, facing her, and then did all of those things, as my erection grew even firmer.

"I hardly dare touch you, Petrus. You look like you might come just like that, and I want you inside me."

"I don't know how good I will be, Lila. It's been a long time. But I suspect I won't come very quickly. Or maybe I'll be over-excited. Perhaps you will just take what comes this time. In a manner of speaking."

We giggled. Laughter during lovemaking is always a good sign. It is in itself an absurd activity, which has been given a veneer of seriousness by movies and books, but nonetheless, it would probably make an alien fall about laughing to see.

We kissed, many kisses, with a complete intermingling of love and longing, lips and tongues. Finally I gently laid her down, her rich red hair spreading across the pillow, and she arched her hips a little so that I could help her to slip down her red pants. Then she brought her knees upwards and outwards so that I could kneel between her legs.

"Maybe just simple this time, Petrus," she whispered.

I was positioned so that I could readily kiss and tongue-caress her firming nipples, while stroking upwards along her inner thighs. She shivered. As the back of my hand brushed against her between her legs, I felt her readiness, and I gently caressed and played with her there, patiently waiting until she naturally parted beneath my fingers. I repositioned myself, and I felt her reach down and guide me into her, little by little.

"Petrus. Petrus, this time all of me wants all of you."

Then I was fully within her, buried deeply in a place that two decades of lost time had denied me. Yet as I slowly thrust inside her, I was transported back to our first night together, so long ago. I could hear the music, I could hear the growl of London buses rumbling past the window. I could feel her young body so firm beneath me, proud, confident, unashamed of her desire. And I could feel my climax coming too soon.

But this time, I knew to slow down, to stay still, and Lila gently rocked her hips against my erection, just holding us both at the very edge, so skilled, so knowing. Then I saw her smile at me as if to say, now come, come, release what you have in store for me, I am open to all you have within, I want you to come home to me. And with three final slow penetrations, I came, and my climax brought her over the edge too, gasping as she felt my pulsing and flooding inside her. Her hips arched up to take every last part of me into her, I felt the clasping and rippling of her body around me, and I knew that we had at last reached both our destination and our commencement at the same time.

Now there was no going back.
Our past was set to rights, and our future was set on end.

Chapter 24

In the months following that night at the yellow house Petrus and I slipped into a new way of sharing it. I still maintained a base in the downstairs room, and sometimes slept there. But most nights as the evening drew to a close, we would find ourselves with our arms around each other, and I would say, "Can I sleep upstairs tonight?" and Petrus would say "that would be very nice" or something equally English, or sometimes he would say "Do you have to?" - to which I would respond, "Yes, because you can't wait to have your evil way with me."

But he never asked me to join him, as he knew that I knew that he wanted to sleep with me every night, and he never asked to sleep with me downstairs, because he wanted me always to have that as my private space. Also, the height of the loft bed scared him.

We made love cautiously at first, both fearing to cross some line in the others' preferences or comfort zones, but gradually we developed an understanding of what was good and what didn't work. Petrus was inherently more conservative in bed than myself, and there was no getting around the fact that this reflected a generational difference. I suppose my generation had grown up with raunchier movies than his.

It took him a little while to become comfortable with oral sex. He found it hard to accept that I actually enjoyed taking him into my mouth, (enjoyment chiefly derived from knowing how intense an experience it gave him), and he simply lacked confidence and practice when returning the favour. It seemed strange that he was able to describe in his erotic writing some acts of which he had little experience himself.

Neither of us was interested in anything with a sadistic or masochistic tinge. His only quirk was sometimes enjoying ejaculating onto my body rather than in it, but to me that hardly ranked as a perversion. He seemed not to want to humiliate me in that way; rather it was perhaps a way of trying subconsciously to impress me, or himself, with his ejaculation, although in fact he inevitably now produced less than he had in our London lovemaking. He took longer to climax, and sometimes his mind was more interested in sex than his penis was. But his ability to keep going much longer than a younger man gave me no cause to complain. Once I had to beg him to stop when I had already climaxed twice and he was happy for more.

Always though he was gentle and he was concerned for my pleasure. Consent was vital to him. "No" meant "no" to such a degree that on the few occasions I asked him to stop, I could almost imagine the squeal of brakes and the odour of burning rubber. And invariably I only asked him to stop simply because of something stupid, like the need to sneeze in mid-coitus.

We tended to gravitate to the bed for our sexual encounters, but other parts of the house were brought into play if the mood took us. Being exploratory and adventurous in sex is not the sole preserve of teenagers. Older lovers such as ourselves can also give their imagination free rein. A few days after we first became lovers again, there was an embarrassing moment when Colette decided to drop in to see how we were, and Petrus had me sitting on the kitchen bench semi-clothed and gasping. Colette was less than taken aback, merely saying "Hi! I guess if you're busy I'll come back a bit later on." After that, Petrus fitted a bolt on the inside of the front door. The sound of that bolt being slid across began to be not the least pleasurable part of our foreplay.

We sometimes indulged my own little foible. I have always taken a particular delight in outdoor sex, as Petrus almost found out on our trip to Maria Island. I am naturally drawn to outdoor places, remote places, and sometimes I feel a need to express sexually the affinity I feel with the natural world in a beautiful place. But on other occasions it is the thrill of risking discovery. For instance, we would sometimes indulge in some form of sex among the shallow sand dunes at the end of our property, just above the beach, accompanied by the sound of the waves and the evocative cry of sea birds. At other times, we cavorted at the end of someone else's property, where the risk of discovery was somewhat higher and the excitement therefore that much greater.

Perhaps I sound like some kind of nymphomaniac with my account of the flowering of our sex life. That I believe is not the case. As I explained before, I had gradually become starved of sex as my marriage deteriorated. And Petrus had been entirely celibate for many years. We simply had a lot of lost time to make up. And we did our best.

My original inhibitions, relating to my experience in discovering my husband mating with one of his school pupils, gradually faded, although during one of my early lovemaking sessions with Petrus I was taken by surprise by a sudden throwback to that episode. We had been tired after we had each been busy for much of the day in our own working spaces, writing. But I was weary also of my own company, and at bedtime I had invited myself to share Petrus' bed.

He was really too tired for anything other than sleep, but as we settled on our sides, me with my back to him, and he playing languidly with my breasts (always a source of great interest to him), I felt his erection growing against me, and I reached down and tucked it between my legs, close to my entrance but not within.

Although I intended just a closer cuddle, almost automatically he began to move himself against me, not penetrating, but slipping to and fro across my labia, just as a teenage boy might do in an effort to reach his own climax without doing a great deal for his girlfriend, other than reducing the risk of pregnancy (and that not by much).

I had a sudden need to feel him fully inside me, to be taken almost roughly, and I said to him, "I want you like this." I lifted myself from the bed and onto my hands and knees, and even in his sleepy state, Petrus could not resist kneeling behind me, and plunging himself into me, full length, with accelerating strokes, holding me by my hips, pulling me onto himself. And I suddenly found myself calling out to him, "Do I feel like a schoolgirl? Do I? Am I almost like a virgin? Is that what you want?" Rather than shocking him, my words seemed to drive him on, and for once he came quickly without regard for my pleasure, and I knew that we were enacting a tableau just as I had seen. Then my tears suddenly came, and I brought myself brutally away from him.

Petrus' confusion was total. He was aghast at his own sexual response, horrified at my tears, and dismayed that perhaps all the progress we had made towards a stable sexual relationship had been lost. But he cuddled me and hugged me and told me how mortified he was at what had happened, and said that I was twice as desirable as any schoolgirl on the planet. (Not entirely an appropriate comment but he meant well). In the morning nothing more was said, though he brought me all my favourite things for breakfast in bed. But it was some days before I asked if I could sleep with him again, and we simply slept, and in the morning made the most gentle love that could possibly be made. And all was well.

For some years, Emily and I had exchanged messages on Facebook every few days, and depending on where in the world she found herself flying, we would talk on the phone more or less weekly. Since her visit with Ed to the house, she would usually ask how things were going with Petrus during these calls, and I would ask about Ed, and we would be politely evasive in both directions. She was evidently still seeing Ed, but I didn't ask on what basis. She seemed to assume that the situation with Petrus was still as it had been at the time of her visit. But one afternoon, after some initial small talk on the phone, she suddenly tackled the elephant in the room.

"So Mum – there's nothing more gross than the thought of parental sex, but has Petrus bedded you yet?"

Emily was never one to mince words and had no time for an elegant turn of phrase. But I was so unprepared for the question that I was lost for words for some moments. Before I could gather my wits, Emily stepped into the silence.

"Well, I'm happy for you both. Your silence was deafening."

At last I recovered the power of speech. "I'll spare you the details, but yes, guilty as charged, and we're both very happy. But we still maintain our separate spaces, though when we're in the mood -"

Emily cut sharply across me. "Please, no details! And you are about to not spare them!"

There was a further silence. I sensed that I was supposed to pop the question too.

"And you and Ed?"

"Funny you should ask that," Emily replied innocently.

"Congratulations. Any… plans?"

"Well, actually, yes, we're going to be working together."

"Don't tell me. He's going to be an airline pilot. But come to think of it, maybe not, though he'd be good at the circling stuff. Tell all."

"Catering, Mum, catering. Home delivered meals ordered online. We're starting from my apartment to keep things cheap, the kitchen is just big enough. He's going to do the cooking -"

"You surprise me. And you'll watch?"

"No Mum. I'll handle the business side and the promotions and website and so forth. But that will include photos of the two of us looking like we're cooking together. Him looking competent, me looking glamorous. And my flying days are over. My notice is in."

It was evident that Emily still took much pleasure in her power to surprise. She and Ed would make an odd team, but Emily was never one for the conventional. And Ed certainly wasn't that.

A feature of this phase of my relationship with Petrus was our growing friendship with Ann and Jeff Leigh next door. After a few weeks we went for drinks to their house as they had come to ours, and I admired, genuinely, the work they had done on its design and décor. We gave them a full account of our visit to Maria Island, and thanked them profusely for their recommendation.

I did not on that visit raise the subject of my idea of using locally inspired designs on printed fabrics, but on an occasion about a week later, when the four of us simply went for a walk along the beach together, I did mention the scheme to Jeff. He listened intently, asked some very pertinent questions, and then invited us to lunch on the following Sunday in order to discuss things further. But he did say he would expect to see a well put together business plan, or at least an outline.

Early on that Sunday morning, it was already warm. The top sheet of Petrus' bed had been swept aside. I lay back on the bed, naked, after Petrus had taken away the breakfast tray. While he was out of the room, I arranged my legs casually but provocatively apart, and stared at the ceiling with as much wide-eyed innocence as I could muster. Petrus hardly glanced at me as he came back to get dressed. "No," he said, trying to keep the non-glancing going, "I'm cleaning the car and then we're going to Ann and Jeff for lunch, remember? They always look at us with suspicion to see if they can see signs of sex happening. They can't believe that it can still happen beyond fifty, but for their own sakes, they're hoping."

"Speak for yourself, you're into your seventies," I replied perhaps unkindly. "And anyway, I didn't ask for anything."

"Not much you didn't. I can see the steam from here. And I'm only just seventy, by the way."

"Well - if you are offering..."

"I'm not. Well, not much." He paused. "Just a little." He paused again. "OK, five minutes sex therapy then. No orgasms. I need to clean that car."

"I've never heard it called that before. Clean the car. You can buff my bumpers any time."

"Ok, message received." Petrus pulled off the tracksuit pants he was wearing, climbed on the bed, and straddled my midriff. "I'll give your bumpers a very gentle polish, OK?"

"Go for it." I tucked my hands behind my head, closed my eyes, and relaxed with a half smile of anticipation on my lips.

"Your five minutes starts... now!" I said. I saw Petrus actually checking the time on the bedside clock, but I suspect he promptly forgot it as he reached forwards and took my breasts in his hands, drawing them together, cupping either side.

He stroked beneath first, gentle but firm, like a delicate massage, flexing his wrists so that he lifted, separated, brought together. He made my breasts so young, my nipples so pert, swelling in response to his touch. He passed his hands across them, separating his fingers so that the nipples slid between them and received a stroke above and beneath at the same time. Concentrating on my left side first, he brought his hand around and around, the motion becoming wider each time, my supple breast moving as if following his hand. His thumb and first finger softly squeezed and teased my nipple, and my breathing quickened a little.

He moved his attention to the other side, and with his thumb on the tip of that nipple he made a slow rotary movement that he knew I particularly liked. My breasts firmed under his touch. His cupped hands held them while he pinched delicately on both sides, then stroked down from above. Finally he leaned forward and took each nipple into his mouth in turn, flicking his tongue around and

143

across, suckling lightly, listening for my response.

I murmured "I think my time is up, if you don't want me to come." I was feeling the swirls of pleasure spreading from my breasts downwards, strongly aroused now, and I was wishing we weren't going out. "Let me do something for you," I said.

"I think you can see something needing attention" he said, kissing each nipple and then, still astride me, sitting back. "But I think I would survive about one minute before exploding, so take it easy."

His erection was complete. The head was held proudly aloft, the foreskin slipped back. I gathered the pillows behind my head so that I could see Petrus more easily. I thought, When we were first lovers, all those years ago, there was more substance to him. Something had been stolen from him by the years. He had not lived a sedentary life but lacked aerobic exercise. His physique was no more impressive than might be expected at his age. His diet needed significant improvement – in that department I had been doing my best. He had been cheated of most of his sex life, and consequently lacked experience and confidence, though I had wrought considerable improvements since we had been reunited - he had seemed more than happy to make up for lost time.

But he gave me love. He was in love with me. He made love to me, only rarely just having sex. On most days he wrote me an erotic story, and I knew these were his love letters to me. He did not ask for my love in declarations, but I showed him in so many ways of my own that his love was returned abundantly. In short, I judged him not by the size of his erection but by the size of his heart, and I had no complaints.

I licked my fingers generously and with a feather touch lubricated the head of his penis, repeating the gesture twice. Already his breath came in short soft gasps. From above I lowered my fingertips just below his foreskin and delicately drew it up onto the head, paused briefly, then moved my hand downwards until the head was again fully exposed and the tip touched the palm of my hand. Three times I repeated this movement; then once more, and kept my hand still, as I could feel that I had already brought him close to a climax. He gasped, said "stop," and as I withdrew my fingers, I saw a little pearl of semen had slipped from him, and I could not resist extending a single finger and delicately spreading it over the head with a single short swirling movement. He gasped again, but somehow controlled the urge to come completely, and as he kneeled before me with his face turned upwards and his eyes closed, his erection gradually faded and lowered, and he blinked and looked down at me with a contented smile.

"That was... close. Your timing is impeccable. You know me so well... but now, the car and the lunch." I had to grin at his boyish enthusiasm.

Later as we sat at Ann and Jeff's well-spread lunch table, sitting opposite each other, Jeff intercepted the looks which passed between us, and put down his knife and fork. "If you two need to go upstairs to use the spare bedroom, go for it!" he chuckled, looking from one to the other with affection. "I'll put on some loud music down here." We blushed, both of us. Then all four of us collapsed in laughter. We could no longer pretend that ours was a separate rooms relationship.

At the end of lunch, Jeff asked me about my business idea. We went into his study, while Petrus and Ann cleared the table. I showed him the designs I had been working on, and costings, and my initial research on how the fabrics could be marketed and at what kind of price.

"Well, Lila, that all looks promising. Firstly, without doubt, the designs are stunning. I do congratulate you. Secondly, I can see that there would be a market for them, but my concern is that it would be a rapidly saturating market. If you were predominantly thinking in terms of curtains and cushions and that kind of thing, people don't change them that often. You might find that you sold a lot to begin with, but then the market might almost disappear. It could be several years before repeat orders came in. Sure, you could bring out new designs, but people who bought the first designs won't be throwing money at new designs if the original fabrics themselves are still going well."

"I guess pricing becomes relevant. If I sell cheaply enough, people will regard the product as more disposable. But then I'd be selling into a reasonably upmarket group, and people like that think that anything cheap must be nasty."

"Lila, I think you may need to test market or additionally

market research the product. You said that you can get a fairly short run of fabric manufactured to begin with. Maybe do that, see what people think of it, how they would value it, then move into full scale production if it looks viable."

"That might indeed be the best idea. I should be able to finance that myself once my divorce settlement is sorted out. Then maybe we should talk again when I'm clear how to proceed. That's if you do want to get involved at all."

"I do want to keep in touch with the project, that much I'll say. But I have learned that I have to be very careful what I verbally imply to people. My only promises are those made by my lawyers, in writing, ok?"

"That's frank and very clear – thanks, Jeff. I will indeed keep you in touch."

"You're welcome. Now let's see what your… partner, and my wife, are getting up to in the kitchen."

Partner. I wasn't sure about that, but I didn't have another title prepared in my mind. Companion? Lover? Friend? Petrus had become all of these things, but 'partner' somehow implied promises and financial involvement and loss of independence. Our only promise remained that we would never leave the other one wondering. We wouldn't lose touch without explanation. Perhaps in our new situation, that would imply a degree of honesty and communication, particularly on matters affecting our relationship. No involvements with others without being upfront about it, I supposed. But then that started to imply the 'partners' title. I needed to think it through some more. Maybe even talk to Petrus about it. If I couldn't talk to him about it, then something must be amiss. Oh for the simple single life!

As I suspected, in the kitchen Petrus was up to no good. He was craftily helping himself to leftover trifle while my back was turned. Just for a minute I thought he was going to hide the spoon behind his back, but he realised he'd been caught red handed, and cream nosed. He was incapable of eating the wrong food without plastering it all over his face.

I growled at him under cover of the rumbling of the dishwasher. "I saw that. Just you wait till I get you home."

"Is that a threat or a promise?"

"Hmm. Maybe first one, then the other."

"I like the sound of that. Always liked a bit of the other."

"Get your mind out of the gutter and your spoon out of the trifle. And ask Jeff who did his garden landscaping."

We got home in the early evening, having been offered afternoon tea as well as lunch. Their generosity was exceeded only by their charm. They seemed to like us too, and said that before long they'd love us to spend a weekend at their inland retreat. At least now we wouldn't be imposing on them by using two bedrooms rather than one.

Chapter 25

The possibility of sharing my home, my life and my bed with Lila had never entered my head when first I got back in touch with her. But it happened. Even as the months drifted by, I found it hard to believe. I have always been insecure in relationships, probably as a result of adverse experience, and even so late in my life, the same happened to some degree with Lila.

In my head, I firmly believed that she should have her private space downstairs, and that it should be inviolate. If for some practical reason I needed to enter her space, I would knock on the door and await her invitation. Sometimes she would say, sweetly, that she was right in the middle of something and perhaps she would phone me when she was finished, or that she would come upstairs. That was understood and perfectly reasonable. I never asked to spend the night in her room. Once or twice she commented on that, and I told her I was scared of heights so her loft bed wouldn't suit me. Of course I was making that up.

But from time to time, Lila would spend a couple of days in her room, concentrating on her writing perhaps, and then I would begin to imagine all sorts of online infidelities taking place, or simply began to think that she had tired of my company, let alone my lovemaking. I didn't find it at all difficult to imagine why that might happen. I have never considered myself as a very sociable person. I am not really very good company. I have also never considered myself to be much of a lover. Perhaps writing about it has been a replacement for the real thing. On the page, I can imagine myself as the ultimate stud. On the bed, I am seventy years old, not in particularly good condition, with sexual organs which function at the barely adequate level, and that only if not used too often. I do not seem to be able to translate what I can imagine about two people naked on a bed into a lived experience. I am good at fantasy. I am useless at reality.

The lack of any formal commitment between us also played on my anxieties. When it came to it, neither could actually accuse the other of infidelity, as we had made no commitment which could thus be violated. We both emphasised our individual freedom. We had never discussed our individual expectations of each other. Everything was a matter of assumption, or common decency.

Still, the tension I felt within our relationship certainly avoided it becoming any kind of boring. I took nothing for granted. Each time we made love, part of me was wondering whether it was the last time. Sometimes that thought was stimulating, urging me to make the most of what might be my last sexual experience, but very infrequently it was, to put it bluntly, deflating, due to the anxiety of it. On such occasions Lila was always understanding, and I knew enough about giving a woman pleasure to know alternative means to do so other than through the use of my non-existent erection. But I did wonder whether I had any cause to expect our relationship to have any kind of long term status. One particular incident almost ended that speculation.

It was a pleasant enough day, a quite sunny late autumn morning. Lila needed to visit Launceston to browse around the fabric shops as part of her research into her fabric design project. She said that while you could see fabrics online, you needed to see them full size to really judge, and feel the fabric and the lie of it when handled. Also, I thought she probably needed a dose of the city shops and cafes. She loved our isolation, but did occasionally need to refresh her memory of crowds, traffic, and bustle. She left in the SUV immediately after morning coffee.

I settled at my desk after lunch, and tried to write. Lila had stayed with me the previous night, and it had been a night to remember. I was trying to write a story which would be built around some of the almost unbearably erotic techniques that Lila had deployed, using every shred of her imagination and her intimate knowledge of exactly what would take me to the most extreme heights of pleasure. But I always felt that my lovemaking with Lila should not be debased into some kind of research project for my writing. I would have to draw on the experience without relating it in detail. But my tiredness after so much loving and so little sleep inhibited my creativity, and I stared at the screen without making any progress at all, fighting sleep.

Mid afternoon, I heard the entrance door open, which surprised me as it was rather early for Lila to be back. But then I heard Colette calling my name. She rarely visited unannounced, so that was a different surprise. I called out to her, and she came into the study as I turned round in my office chair.

Colette stood in the doorway, eyeing my computer screen with suspicion. "Hi, Mr Stone," she said in a disconsolate voice, with only a half smile, not her usual high-voltage one.

I stood up to greet her. "I was about to ask whether you are well and whether you are happy, but you look like you would answer 'no' to both."

"I'm not at my best, I have to say. The twins have been passing a tummy bug between them for days and I feel like I'm getting no sleep at all."

"Isn't Ezra helping?" I asked, knowing the answer full well, but wondering whether just possibly I was about to be amazed.

"He's got morning surgery every day at the moment while Dr. Adams is away, so he has to get a good night's sleep."

"Ah, of course, I should have realised that it would be difficult for him to help with his children."

Colette looked at me a little sharply. She felt uncomfortable if any criticisms I made of Ezra were other than very indirect.

"Anyway, my mum is with them at the moment and I just needed to get out of the house, so here I am. But I'm probably keeping you from your work, I'd better go."

"Don't go. Let me make you some tea. I think there's even some fruit cake. Take a break for half an hour. Come, sit here, I'll bring it in."

Typically Colette would have insisted on making the tea but for once she simply sat down on the sofa, and just said "Thanks, Mr Stone."

Five minutes passed while I made the tea in the kitchen. I put everything on a tray and took it through to the study. Colette was sitting with her legs drawn up under her and her eyes closed. It was only after I had set down the tray on the coffee table in front of the sofa that I realised she was fast asleep.

I thought, Poor thing, she is simply exhausted. I sat down very gently beside her and poured my tea, adding my usual milk and sugar (my only vice), but then realised that stirring it might wake the sleeping beauty. I sipped a little and it was pretty revolting unstirred. I thought, I'll just sit quietly for a few minutes and she will probably wake. I sat back.

I have mentioned before the effect that sofa had on me. It did.

I slept like a baby, until startled awake by the light being turned on in the now almost dark room. Lila stood just inside the door. Colette lay with her head on my lap. I was frozen to the spot.

For about five seconds, Lila took in the sight on the sofa. Then she turned the light back off and almost ran out of the room and I heard the slam of the front door.

Colette stirred, then suddenly woke and sat up almost simultaneously. "Oh Mr Stone. I am so sorry! I must have gone fast asleep and toppled over on you. Please, I am so sorry!" she repeated.

"Don't worry, it's nothing, I fell asleep myself and didn't realise. I just hope you feel better for your sleep."

"I do. But I am sorry. I guess I needed that. And now the tea is cold. Perhaps I could make some more," she replied.

"Actually Colette, I have to make some personal phone calls right away – I really need the house to myself now – would you mind...?"

"Of course, I'd better get home anyway in case the twins have trashed my house. Thanks for tea, even though I didn't drink it!"

And off she went, at least smiling more like her usual self.

Shit, I thought. This won't go down well with Lila.

Chapter 26

The images were flipping in my head, one to another and back again. Brian with his schoolgirl. Petrus with his pharmacist. The one person I thought I could trust, the one person I felt safe with. Even he had betrayed me. Even he.

I felt sickened, almost faint with shock. At the bottom of the steps I gripped the handrail tightly for a moment, then decided which way I would turn. I needed air. I needed to get away from my supposed place of safety and refuge. I had to be somewhere else, not back in the downstairs room. I almost ran down to the beach.

Once again, I felt the urge to simply walk out into the sea, to let the waves close over my head, closing my book, closing my eyes. I wanted closure, not continuance. I remembered Petrus' theory of suicide. Don't do it, just walk out of your situation and start again. But I had already done that. And look where it had got me. Right back where I started.

Then I thought, I don't want to be even remembering Petrus' fucking theories. He had all those wonderful speeches and meanwhile he was getting involved with his neighbour's young wife, behind his lover's back. How tacky, how sleazy could that man be. The same as every other shitty man, I thought. Not one of them has his head above the gutter.

I heard a slight noise behind me, a step on the fine band of broken seashells on the shoreline. I screamed out at him. "Leave me alone, you fucking bastard, piss off and leave me alone!"

And as I half turned, there stood Ann and Jeff, hand in hand, on their evening walk in the twilight.

"Oh Christ. I thought you were Petrus."

"I'm glad for Petrus' sake it wasn't him," said Jeff, looking more than somewhat taken aback. And then his look turned to one of real sympathy as he saw my tears and the degree of my distress.

"Lila, please, if we can help…."

Nothing is worse than sympathy even when you really need it. My immediate instinct was to step towards him for the hug which he seemed more than ready to provide, but on that occasion the hug of a man was the last thing I wanted. But Ann got that instantly, stepped forward and put her arms round me, and said to Jeff over her shoulder, "I'll see you inside in a little while, don't worry."

After a moment she drew away from me and fished in her jacket pocket for a clean tissue for me.

"Here. One tissue, and lots of sympathy and concern. Want to talk? Something happened with Petrus?"

There was something so solid, so grounded about Ann. She always came across as the definition of sensible. Although I am normally quite reticent about private stuff, the whole story burst out of me, starting with what happened with Brian, and ending with what happened with Petrus, and my whole journey of wasted trust-rebuilding in between.

We walked up and down the stretch of beach opposite Ann and Jeff's house, and when I finally came to the end of my story, Ann said "Lila, would you like to come in with me, and you and I can continue this in a warm room with a glass of something?"

I nearly began crying again, but managed to say something reasonably grateful, and we walked up their path. At the house, Jeff came to the entrance hall when we went in, but quickly made himself scarce, and Ann took me into the library. Theirs was that sort of house.

She poured me a neat whisky at my request, and something for herself, sat me down in a comfortable chair, and settled herself in another opposite.

"Can I ask you some questions, and maybe make some suggestions?" Ann asked. Her voice was naturally gentle, and her manner was calm and affectionate.

"Go for it," I replied.

"Some of these might seem a bit personal or intrusive, but if you can, bear with me for a few moments."

"Ok, I trust you. I have to trust someone, don't I."

"First question. Your age and Petrus' age."

"I'm fifty-four and he's seventy."

"Don't be shocked at this one – when did you last have sex and was it good?"

I struggled to keep my eyebrows level, but I decided to treat her as if she was a qualified therapist. "Last night, and it was fantastic."

"How long have you been lovers?"

"First time was back in England in 1992. Then we lost touch, then we found each other again, and I think you know the rest."

"Ok. When you see Petrus, do you see a seventy year old man? Or are you really seeing a man in, let me see, his early forties?"

I thought carefully. "Well, no, I don't think of him as the age he really is."

"Now be honest. If you'd never met him before, would you even have begun to consider taking him as a lover? Wouldn't the thought simply not cross your mind? Isn't part of the attraction the fact that you've got a history, and then you became non-sexually intimate when you rediscovered him, and you fled down here when your husband betrayed you? And then it wasn't too hard to go back to sleeping together, based on the whole package including your history?"

"That all makes sense I guess."

"Next question. I know Colette is thirty seven. She is married to a well off, handsome doctor. She has three children. She has some pretty strong reasons not to have an affair with anyone, let alone with a man who from her perspective is positively ancient, and in financial terms has nothing whatever to offer her. So – how likely is it that what you saw was some kind of sexual encounter between that young woman and that elderly man? If you at fifty-four would be unlikely to fall for him if meeting him for the first time, Colette at thirty seven would be even less likely."

I thought hard. I could see very clearly what she was driving at. "But wouldn't it be different the other way round?" I said, trying not to draw the conclusion Ann was steering me towards.

"Yes, if Petrus was a total bastard he would no doubt be happy to seduce a pretty, no, beautiful young woman without regard to the consequences. But is that the man you made love with last night? And even if he did try his luck, wouldn't dear Colette just giggle at him?"

"I guess he's not like that, and I suspect she would. Giggle, I mean. It takes very little to get her going like that."

154

"And one last thing – a man of his age, having had great sex the night before, would be far more likely to doze off next to a beautiful woman than to try to mate with her. I'm right, yes?"

I thought about Petrus' overall sexual performance, and had to admit that even with the temptation of Colette, he might not actually be able to do much about it if he did decide to seduce her.

"Lastly, Lila, run the scenario again in your mind, painful though it might be. Where were her hands? Where were his? Anywhere inappropriate? Could it be that the poor old chap simply dozed off, and young Colette who is probably exhausted by the workload imposed on her by that husband of hers did the same, and without intending to, found a nice soft cushion on his lap – and not a lumpy one either?"

I sat in silence for a while. I had to admit that Ann's wise words made a lot of sense. My experience with Brian had twisted my imagination to the extent that I was at risk of tainting my perfectly good relationship with Petrus.

"Ann, I think you are right. But is there any way I can be sure?"

"Go home. Ask him what happened in as neutral a tone of voice as you can manage. Watch his eyes. If he tells a plausible story and can hold your gaze while he tells it, then I think you should believe him."

Ann walked with me to the property boundary. "One more thing," she said as she gave me a parting hug. "He's not my cup of tea age-wise either, but Lila – I can sure see the attraction. If you can trust him again, hold on to him. I think he's a good man who has found a good woman – you. That's pretty rare."

As I neared the yellow house, I could see Petrus sitting on the bottom step in the semi-darkness. He looked very cold, and not so much unhappy as frightened. I had to fight the desire to just take him in my arms. He looked up, stood up, and said "I didn't know where you had gone. I didn't know what to do. I wanted to give you space, but I wanted to explain."

"Petrus, I do want to hear what happened between you and Colette today. Now is your chance to explain."

"Nothing happened. It really was nothing, believe me."

"So tell me, in detail, precisely what took place."

155

And he told me everything, and I heard a loving man telling the truth.

"Petrus, I'm sorry I thought badly of you."

"Lila, I'm sorry that you had such an experience after all that happened to you in Brisbane."

"Can I sleep with you tonight? Just sleep. Just cuddle."

"That would be nice."

"Don't be so English about it."

"Perhaps I should be French."

And as we climbed the steps, he put on a dreadful mock French accent, and made seductive remarks all the way to the bedroom.

Chapter 27

A late autumn night, almost midnight. I had no idea whether Lila was asleep, but she tended to sleep deeply. If she heard the beep of a notification arriving on her phone, it would mean she would still be awake.

Hi Lila, are you asleep?

After about thirty seconds, my phone pinged.

Yes I am asleep.

What makes you think I'm awake?

I don't believe you.

Because you are messaging.

Easy. I can do that with my eyes shut.

What else can you do with your eyes shut?

Many things. I think I usually come with my eyes shut.

Eventually.

You do. I watch you. Then I shut my eyes and come too.

Don't mock the afflicted. Anyway, you once said you liked the way I take a long time.

True. Not complaining. As long as I've got a good book within reach.

Kama Sutra?

Don't need it. Memorised it.

And boy, do I know it.

Ask me any page number.

Seventy.

Any reason why you chose that number?

OK, on the page that matches your age, there's 'the tigress' position.

Sixty nine is a bit obvious.

We did it two weeks ago, before we moved on to page 71.

Which is...?

Ah yes. The one where you can pretend I've not got a beer belly.

But you get to watch my big bum.

No such thing. It's nicely rounded.

157

Like your tummy.

So you looked.

Only when we moved to page 71.

I thought for once I'd try my luck.

I don't suppose you fancy coming upstairs?

Nope. I'm not going down that bloody ladder again tonight.

Again?

Forgot my mobile.

So I'm lucky to be messaging you.

Yup.

So what are you wearing?

My reading glasses, so I can see this bloody phone.

Anything else?

A patient look.

What are you doing with your hands?

One is holding the phone, the other is typing.

Ah. Hadn't thought of that

Well you should have. Look at your own hands, idiot.

We could talk on the phone.
Proper phone sex.

Last time you took so long to come my phone battery went dead.

Your turn to have a nice time.
Pretend my hand is on your breast.

No thanks. I bet you didn't wash after you went to the toilet.

God, you're a spoilsport.

I know your dirty little habits when I'm not around.

Please?

No. I need to sleep well before that meeting in Launceston tomorrow.
Goodnight. xx

Lila?

Nothing came back.

I put aside the phone. I stared at the ceiling. The faint erection I had when messaging Lila faded.

I thought to myself, how much longer can this go on? Will it only last until the first time she comes across an available man more her own age? I can offer her unlimited love and care, but is that enough? She wants fun, adventure, challenge, late nights, physical pursuits, athletic sex, the great outdoors, travel, financial security. Let's think how many of those boxes I can tick. Er – none. Those are not things you get from someone of my age, unless they are a whole lot younger than their years, and I'm not. We are fine while we float in this temporary space, but is there anywhere to go from here? Any room for progression and development? Not that I can foresee.

If she loves me enough as a person, enough to forego all those things, enough to place our relationship above everything else, it could work.

A big ask. A very, very big ask.

I tried to sleep. A pre-sleep confused dream flashed through my mind. Lila meeting someone, Lila slipping away from me, Lila gone. And then nothing. No companionship, mutual support, care, love, bed-sharing, sex. Just me and that bloody ceiling.

I tried to sleep. I tried to believe. Failing in the latter, I finally succeeded in the former.

Chapter 28

"Ah, Mrs Moone. So glad to meet you. Welcome to Country Club Launceston. I'm Garrett O'Brien, General Manager."

"Mr O'Brien. I'm glad you were able to spare me a little of your time." We shook hands.

I had driven myself to Launceston that morning for an appointment to try to market my fabrics to a commercial enterprise in large quantities, which Jeff Leigh had suggested as an alternative to selling smaller amounts to multiple individuals. Through his restaurant and hotel contacts, Jeff had set up a meeting at one of Launceston's larger hospitality enterprises.

Mr O'Brien continued, "Mr Leigh, Jeff, was most insistent that I should have a look at your curtain fabrics for possible use in our restaurant. I can see you have your portfolio with you. But perhaps you would like to see the restaurant first."

"Thank you. I have seen photographs of course, and the designs I have with me are chosen on that basis, but indeed there's no substitute for seeing the room in real life."

"I did wonder if you have had the opportunity for lunch yet, because if not, I would be very happy to invite you to have some preliminary discussion over lunch in the room."

"That would be most kind, if you have the time."

"Mr Leigh suggested that to have lunch with you would be a pleasure, indeed a privilege."

"He is very generous with his support, and with his compliments."

"He and I often discuss hospitality projects over lunch, either here or at his restaurant out on the coast. Please, come this way. You can leave the portfolio in the care of my front desk staff. Eric – please would you take care of Mrs Moone's portfolio? We'll collect it after lunch."

I followed Mr O'Brien into the opulent Terrace Restaurant. The room was empty. We appeared to be the only diners. Only one table was set.

"Normally lunch is served in the Watergarden restaurant, but I have arranged for us to dine here so that you can absorb the atmosphere quietly, in the context of a meal."

Jeff had suggested that smart power dressing would be the thing, and now I could see why.

A waiter brought the menu from the Watergarden restaurant where lunch was normally served, and we made our selections.

"So Mrs Moone. What do you make of the room?"

"Please, call me Lila. The room is beautiful but perhaps slightly cold-looking. You'll see later that the fabrics I am suggesting are based on yellow tones, sand tones. They are inspired by the 'Painted Cliffs' on Maria Island. I thought that a little glow would improve the room, especially in the context of fine dining."

"And I would be glad if you would call me Garrett. Lila, I am most intrigued to see the designs. I think it a wonderful idea to use Tasmanian inspired themes. Actually, I can inform you that we are considering redecorating the whole room. Perhaps if we decide to accept your suggestions for the curtains, you could advise us on the rejuvenation of the rest of the décor. For a suitable fee, of course. I think that given the cachet your name carries, you might not object to a credit being given on the website and menu. You know, 'décor by Lila Moone' or the like."

I thought, either all my Christmases are coming true, or I'm delusional and in need of a straitjacket.

"Of course, that's down the track, but I'm sure we could reach agreement on such a credit. I would of course be more than happy to take on the entire project," I replied, trying not to let my voice waver.

After that, the conversation became more a matter of small talk. Garrett O'Brien was a very smooth talker, with an endless repertoire of inoffensive subjects. We seemed to have very similar tastes in movies, books, the countryside, and classical music. But I rather suspected that this was a conversational technique. I expressed admiration for the organ works of Bartholomew Spencer and he was in full agreement. This was surprising as I had just made up the name.

Eventually lunch was finished, and I suggested that perhaps one of his staff could bring through the portfolio. I was getting used to how things worked.

Garrett looked through my selected designs with genuine interest and asked some surprisingly good questions. I did withdraw one design from my suggestions, having seen the room, but the remainder seemed to me to be fitting, and I asked Garrett if he cared to make a selection for the curtains.

"Do you think one pattern for all, or slightly varying patterns for each of the bays?" he asked.

I was frank. "I think varying patterns could look, indeed would look, sensational, but the cost would increase somewhat due to a smaller production run for each pattern."

"Oh, my dear Lila, please have no concerns on that front. We will be happy to take your best suggestion, even if it happened to be your most expensive one."

I battled a strong desire to grin broadly, but managed to reduce it to a faint 'of course' smile and a little nod.

"Perhaps you would like me to submit a written proposal for your consideration?" I asked.

"Please do, Lila. I really look forward to receiving it." For a moment he hesitated. Then he added, "To be honest, there is a general need throughout the Club for curtains to be replaced, indeed fabrics generally. Perhaps if your work in this room is successful, we could discuss further projects elsewhere in the Club estate. We have suites, deluxe rooms, villas, all needing revision of the curtaining. I suspect you could make quite a mark on the place. Appearance is everything, Lila, everything. No matter how opulent the room, if the curtains are shabby, the room is shabby."

We parted on the best of terms. I tried to walk, rather than dance, out of the building, and only just succeeded.

I left the portfolio in the SUV and walked around the lake to calm down. I found a bench with a good view and sat down to think.

If this really took off, I'd be spending a lot of time here. Would I really be doing a daily commute from Dolphin Sands? What if this project lead to others in the town? Jeff was, of course, right. Marketing large amounts of fabrics to big clients would be a much better financial proposition compared with selling small amounts to many individuals. Maybe I'd need some sort of base here, then go back to Petrus at weekends? How would he take to that? Not well, I suspected. His relationship insecurity would go off the charts. Maybe nightly phone sex would keep him happy.

And what about me, I thought. Petrus and I had become quite a thing. We had some kind of weird but indescribable connection, despite all the differences between us. Ignoring what had happened in England, we had recommenced our relationship as friends, penfriends really, then developed that easy intimacy after I moved to his house, and then we had become lovers, not just for the sex, but for the love. I never told him that I loved him. I'm more one for showing it, proving it, rather than going on about it verbally. He on the other hand was one of the great romantics, and was constantly demonstrative in word and deed. We were good as a couple. We were good in bed, well, maybe a bit rusty and creaky, but we did ok. Would this career development wreck everything, or could I do both, follow the money and the fulfilment, and follow my crazy heart at the same time?

So many questions. I was getting bored with them myself. I walked back to the car, and put the whole thing out of my head until I had got that damn great SUV and myself back to Dolphin Sands in one piece. Or should that be two pieces?

When I reached the yellow house – safely, never mind how many pieces – it suddenly seemed less glamorous, smaller, more ordinary than before. I had spent my life torn between town and country, and it felt like the pendulum was starting to swing away from all this.

Petrus heard the car on the drive and came down the steps briskly to meet me as I climbed out.

"So? How did it go? I trust you totally slayed them in that outfit? Just as well I'm not into submissive sex, as you'd have no trouble dominating me wearing that."

"Petrus. Shut up for a minute. Make some late tea or something. I don't know what the supper plan was but I don't think I'll be ready to eat much before midnight." And I kissed him warmly, but there was also something sad, nostalgic about it. I prayed that he wouldn't notice.

We went upstairs and I stood by the kitchen counter while Petrus put together tea and his inevitable fruit cake. I gave him a detailed account of everything that had happened. There was no point in glossing over anything. He was as perceptive as any man. Some of the implications of things that I said would not escape him.

We sat with our tea facing each other at the dining table. When I finished speaking, Petrus looked at me with a strange mixture of affection and sadness. "Lila, that is amazing and I think this could be the start of a major new thread in your life. And you deserve it, and the recognition. You have a special eye and it should be recognised. It's not my place to feel proud of you, but... I do, sorry."

He said nothing of the possible future implications. But his eyes betrayed his thoughts. They were so glad for me, so sad for us, so scared for himself.

Chapter 29

When I am in bed with Lila, she often lies on her side so that I can snuggle up behind her, our bodies in full contact, my arm usually around her, perhaps gently resting my hand on her breast as she goes to sleep.

Then later in the night she may become restless, and she will stir and wake me, so I move a little away from her so that she can turn onto her back, or even onto her other side so that she faces me. Then I can see her face in total repose if there is enough moonlight in the room. There is no more wondrous sight. The years seem to fall away and we might almost be in my tiny apartment in London back in the early nineties, when I could barely believe that so beautiful a creature was asleep beside me in my bed, at home in my home, her skin intimately in contact with mine.

So it was on the night of her first visit to the Country Club. She was too tired from the drive and from the stresses and excitements of the day for lovemaking, but she had asked if she could just sleep with me. We spent minutes just kissing and intimately caressing, and then settled down to let our sleep float us away to dreams. But when she became restless later, she seemed to be unable to settle, and must have been dreaming, although she did not speak in her sleep nor wake from any nightmare. Eventually, as she lay on her back and I on my side, I stroked my hand over her breast with a feather-light touch, her nipple under my palm, and this seemed to soothe her and comfort her. Finally we were both asleep again till the dawn.

In the first light Lila turned to me with a gentle smile, and we kissed, and I said I would get up and bring her breakfast. I left it with her while I showered and dressed, and sat with my toast and coffee while she took her turn in the bathroom. She emerged wrapped in my bathrobe, made herself another coffee, and sat down next to me at the table, facing the sea. I could not resist slipping my hand into her robe and lightly stroking her thigh, and after a moment she turned to me and kissed me with such warmth. I thought, we are being very loving towards each other because something is wrong.

"This guy O'Brien. Garrett, is that really his name?"

"He said so. Irish background I suppose."

"Tall?"

"Quite. Ok, you want the full detail. He is not quite as tall as you, particularly when you stand up straight. He must be early sixties. Quite good looking in a pampered, well groomed kind of way. Very neat hair cut. Very smooth operator."

"You're making me sound jealous."

"Knowing you, you probably are, but you don't have to be. He's not my type. I told you about the fictitious composer that he said he liked. He's a nice guy because that's what he gets paid to be."

We looked out at the sea in companionable silence.

"So what next with this project? You submit a quote?"

"Yup. But I'll need to talk to Jeff about it first. Basically I'll have to find out what it will cost me, and hopefully Jeff will invest the money to cover that until the Club pays me, and he'll take some slice of the profits. Or, he'll invest a larger sum and leave it in place to cover the possible expansion of the project. I know our visit to their other house is supposed to be a social thing, but the timing makes me think it's partly going to be a business weekend."

"They pick us up after teatime tomorrow, Friday?"

"Yup, about four thirty. He said to pack reasonably warm clothes for country walks and stuff, but also swimwear for their indoor pool. Sounds like we are really going to be slumming it."

Lila finished her coffee and pushed back her chair. "I'd better get working on the quote," she said, kissed my cheek, and sauntered out of the front door.

I thought, this is strange, I have no role in what is developing here. Jeff has a role, O'Brien has a role, the people at the fabric printing plant have a role, but my job is just to make the coffee. Then I thought, what role does Lila have in writing my erotic literature? None, apart from being an inspiration. So, snap out of it, Petrus.

The following afternoon Lila and I walked across our property to our neighbours' house carrying our weekend bags, and arrived just as Ann and Jeff were following their driver to their car. He loaded the bags into the boot, shook hands with Jeff, and went back to the house.

"Yes, I can actually drive myself," said Jeff, having followed my gaze. "Eddie is going to be looking after the house while we are away. And I took the liberty of asking him to keep an eye on yours too. It's rare to have any problems round here but you never know."

There was a round of handshaking and cheek kissing, and then Jeff ushered us into the spacious back seats, and he and Ann settled in the front. We swished on our way.

"I'm afraid this Chrysler doesn't quite compete with your other neighbour's Tesla, but it will get us there. And I think there's more room in the back."

"After our humble SUV, anything is pretty luxurious to us," Lila replied. I thought, the SUV is a perfectly adequate vehicle, and it's not ours, it's mine. Still, we have to be nice to our hosts.

"So where is your country estate, Jeff?" I asked, then realised my question might have been better worded.

"It's more of a house than an estate," Jeff responded, taking my question literally. "We only have one chap there to look after the house and ourselves, with a little help outside from a local gardening enthusiast, so we sold the original land apart from the bit round the house itself. Actually we ended up effectively paying next to nothing for the house due to the way planning laws work up there."

It seemed like the actual location was not going to be revealed, so I let the matter drop.

We drove for about an hour and a half, the last few tens of kilometres being distinctly uphill. Finally we turned off the road into an unpaved drive, and pulled up outside a spectacularly modern house, hidden by trees and bushes from the road. "Here we are, journey's end," announced Jeff happily.

From the front door emerged a dignified-looking chap who opened both the front passenger door and the rear with one well-practised gesture. Jeff came around and assisted Lila from the car in gentlemanly fashion.

"Lila, this is Butler. Butler, Lila. Petrus, Butler. Butler, Petrus."

Hands were shaken. I was too much of a socialist to accept the notion of being introduced to someone by his function rather than his name, so I said perhaps a little pointedly, "Pleased to meet you – and your name is…?"

"Butler. Butler Spantiri. My Italian father had a sense of humour, but it didn't deter me from taking up the profession after which I was named."

"Ah, I see. Mine shared that sense of humour by naming me Petrus Stone. So we have something in common."

"Indeed, indeed. Perhaps if you would all care to go inside, I will bring in the luggage."

With something like a flourish he pointed us to the front door and we trooped inside. A vestibule larger than the lounge in the yellow house led to a lounge larger than our whole home. Floor to ceiling windows faced the front garden on one side of the room, and similar windows faced the indoor lap pool on the other side. It was at once evident that the house was built around the pool in the centre.

Lila's face took on the look of a hunter in hot pursuit of prey. She stalked around the room examining the detail of the décor, then as Jeff and Butler brought in drinks trays, she asked Jeff if she might look around the house at once.

"Of course, of course. Just ensure that if you steal any of our ideas for your magazine, you give us credit," he replied with a grin.

"To be honest, I feel a multi-page article coming on," Lila assured him.

"No," Jeff said at once. "Sorry, this place is a sort of a secret. We even had stuff in the builder's contract to prevent any photos being published, and to date I've not found anything that's leaked onto the internet. It might seem odd, but we have a bit of a thing about our privacy."

"Jeff, please forgive me, I'm sorry I even let the thought cross my mind."

"No, no, not a problem. I know many well-off people only build houses for publicity. I just happen to take a different view. But do please take your time to look round all you please. Friends are different from internet stickybeaks. I'll get Butler to go with you so he can explain things and show you your room in passing."

Ann and I settled into the most comfortable of armchairs, followed by Jeff when he had poured drinks of our choice. "This is a life I could easily be persuaded to live," I said.

"I guess it has its compensations," chuckled Jeff, "but in fact we don't get up here nearly as often as we would like. I suppose if we had decided to sit back and enjoy the fruits of our original good fortune things would be different, but we decided that we'd be more proactive with those fruits, and as a consequence we never seem to have a spare minute, a lot of the time."

"And indeed, Lila tells me you and she may be closeted for a while this weekend to discuss her restaurant fabrics project. I gather the meeting in Launceston went very well."

"To be honest, Petrus, I've not had an opportunity to hear about it from her side, but my acquaintance at the Club rang me to express his enthusiasm. I think Lila impressed him no end – as I rather expected."

Ann had been following the conversation without joining in so far, but now she quietly said, "I do wonder whether Lila will be able to tear herself away from the peace of Dolphin Sands to spend the required time on the project in Launceston."

"Of course she will have to consider that aspect," I responded. "But she has always been torn between town and country. She loves sitting in our yard just watching the ants going about their business, and she equally loves sitting in a city coffee shop watching her fellow humans bustling past attending to their business too. Personally though, I couldn't bear to return to a city life now. Give me the sound of the sea and a beach view and I'm happy."

Ann exchanged a quick glance with Jeff, but not too quick for me to spot it. "I'm sure she will at least spend weekends at the Sands, and the project won't last forever," she said in a manner of one who deems it wise to drop the subject. "But Petrus, let me show you to your room, as it looks like Lila is still on the grand tour, then I will find Butler so he and I can dish up some dinner. I asked him to prepare one of his specials. He's a rather good cook, so I think you will be in for a treat."

The bedrooms were accessed from a corridor which had windows onto the pool on one side, and the bedroom doors on the other. Our room was remarkably large, with an ensuite bathroom and a walk-in closet. And it boasted a very comfortable looking king-sized bed of a contemporary four-poster design. The modern fabrics and furnishings only just helped avoid the look of a room intended for honeymoon couples on Valentine's night.

After tidying myself up I went back to the lounge where Lila was now sitting and talking with great animation to Jeff about the house. She seemed to like it. Well, that was the impression I received when she told Jeff she thought it was the most beautiful house she had ever seen.

"But what about our yellow house at the Sands?" I protested in mock jealousy. Well, mainly mock.

"Sweetheart, that's beautiful too, but in a different way," she responded, using the term 'sweetheart' for the first time ever. I thought perhaps the sight of the four poster bed had given her ideas. In fact, I very much hoped so.

Ann came through from the adjacent dining room and asked us to take our places at the table. The dining table was clearly intended for larger gatherings, indeed the room itself would have been adaptable for use as an aircraft hanger.

The meal was, as predicted, superb. While we waited for the starters, Butler brought in two large flatbreads, with spinach, pear and gorgonzola, topped with a balsamic glaze. These were followed by arancini balls filled with mushroom, pumpkin and cheese with a lemon mayo dip, and also sweet potato and zucchini fritters with tomato salsa and cumin yoghurt. Finally, after a decent interval to allow our appetites to recover, Butler brought in a Middle Eastern lamb salad. The precise ingredients he declined to reveal, but it was stunning. It was in fact a vegetarian dish apart from the lamb, so for Lila he brought a version with tofu prepared in the same marinade recipe that the lamb had been soaked in, and she declared that it was a culinary triumph.

Much later, Ann confessed that only one dessert was on offer, namely a raspberry semifreddo, but she received no complaints at this news. In fact, we would have been largely incapable of any speech at all at this point, were it not for the plentiful fine wines which accompanied the meal, and which helped us each to recall anecdotes which brought tears of laughter to the eyes of all at the table. It was an excellent evening.

After liqueurs in the lounge, Lila looked as if she might doze off any minute, and I suggested that perhaps we should head for bed. "Now is there anything I can get you?" asked Ann. "Do you have everything you need for the night?"

Lila grinned cheerfully and I braced myself for what might follow. "Don't worry," she said in a slightly slurred voice. "We came fully equipped."   Jeff spluttered. His liqueur must have gone down the wrong way.

In our room, I had hardly closed the door before Lila pinned me up against it.

"Hey, slow down Lila. I am seriously in need of a shower before you start to get any ideas."

I turned on the light in the ensuite. The shower was enormous. There was a little engraved sign on the wall. 'We use tank water – we suggest showers of less than 20 minutes to conserve it.' Good grief, I thought, they must have a tank as big as a lake.

When I returned to the room, Lila had already totally undressed. I narrowly avoided her embrace and stripped too, by which time Lila had navigated her way along the wall and had stepped into the shower. I hoped the water would have a sobering effect.

Tipsy or not, Lila looked as unimaginably beautiful as ever even from behind as I followed her into the bathroom. She clearly wanted to do the right thing and save water. "Let's share, come in with me," she said in a persuasive voice. I didn't need persuasion. I stepped in, standing behind her, the water already running warm and strong.

Lila found herb-scented shampoo on a little shelf on the shower wall, and handed it to me. Gently I worked it into her already-wet and so richly coloured hair.   I spread it all the way through, then massaged it into her scalp with fingertips that knew just how she wanted them to stimulate her there, such was our familiarity with each others' bodies.

She stepped forward into the strong warm flow and together we rinsed her cascading hair, our hands overflowing each other, touching and briefly interlocking.

I slipped more shampoo not only through her hair, but tipped it all down her whole sweet body. After a little while I brought my soapy hands down to her shoulders and massaged her there, both sides at once, with firm movements which smoothed away the tension in her neck and back. But then I felt her shiver a little despite the warmth of the water, so I moved my hands down her sides, with gentle circling movements, till they were at her waist, and for a moment I drew her against me, holding her body against mine all the way.

Now my hands moved forwards to her tummy as I still stood behind her, circling, circling soapily, moving upwards until they rested beneath her breasts. I feel her breathe more deeply as I cupped my hands beneath them, then stroked above, and finally dwelt just momentarily on her nipples, which did not hide her desire. She turned her face to her shoulder, and our lips met and locked and opened, and our tongues flickered together as the water ran across our faces, a long kiss of equal parts love and desire.

Then my hands slipped across her tummy again, and found their way down the outside of her thighs as I bent and leaned forward a little, and before long they moved with that same circulating stroking motion back upwards along her inner thighs, until finally they reach the place where she most yearned for them to be. One hand returned to play at her breast, and the other stayed between her legs. There it caressed, and caressed, and caressed, and gently separated, and found the place where the moistness came not from the warm water still sliding down her, but from the longing within her. Then with the most delicate strokes, she felt my gentle but insistent finger finally slip inside her, just a little, to find the core of her desire, and in a little while she came softly, unstoppably, in waves like a sea remembered in the distance, and she made those little cries and gasps that I remembered from so long ago.

Then at last Lila turned to me, and we were face to face, body to body, my hardness unashamedly against her, and we embraced each other for what seemed an eternity, neither wanting to let the other slip away.

And a little later, wrapped in towels, she led me back to the four-poster bed, and made love to me in ways, so many ways, that words have no power to begin to describe.

Later as I drifted into sleep with my arms wrapped around Lila, I thought, how could I have believed that something was wrong?

Chapter 30

I sat in Jeff's study on Saturday afternoon, going through the breakdown of the quote I was intending to send to Garrett O'Brien. Through the window I could see Petrus and Ann deep in conversation in the garden, occasionally pulling up the few weeds they spotted. I very much hoped that Petrus wasn't pulling up any rare plants too. His gardening skills were legendary for all the wrong reasons.

When I had finished my presentation to him, Jeff leaned back in his leather office chair and regarded me with a gentle smile.

"You are a fine businesswoman," he said, "though saying that sounds somehow both sexist and condescending. I'm simply saying that your sales pitch to me has been most persuasive, and your analysis of the business case has been meticulous."

"Well, that sounds encouraging anyway. Should I be encouraged? Or was it a great pitch but a negative outcome?"

"Positive. I'd like to back you on the assumption that you will be asked to oversee the complete refurbishment of not just the restaurant but the rest of their premises too."

"But taking on board what you said before, no champagne till I hear from your lawyers."

"Exactly. One problem with doing business with friends is that you have to have tacky conversations about money. I will leave that to the lawyers. They will outline the financial terms and conditions, and then if you are not happy with what they say, you may make a counterproposal to them. If that requires them to consult with me, they will do that and come back to you. In other words, it should not be necessary for you and I to discuss the matter again. And we can carry on being friends – or so I very much hope."

I gathered up my papers, returned them to my briefcase, and closed my laptop. "Perhaps we can at least shake on it?" I suggested.

"No. That can have contractual implications. I am like a virgin who does not even pat her boyfriend on the arm. You can never tell where it might lead."

We laughed, and I arrested the movement of my hand which had been about to pat him on the arm.

"Let's see what the gardeners are up to," said Jeff. "I imagine that Petrus is a good gardener with seriously green fingers?"

"Not exactly. Not everyone over seventy is a good gardener, you know."

"There, you have caught me being ageist." Jeff paused at the study door, his hand on the door handle, not yet opening it. "Lila – I do hope this business development will not be a source of inhibition to your relationship with Petrus, given the amount of time you will need to be away? I realise that's an almost unforgivable intrusion into your privacy, but please believe that I – I and Ann – would hate to be the cause of any strains for you both."

"And you would hate to see your investment endangered by me underperforming in the business due to any choice I might make about being away from him?" I kept my tone even but with difficulty. It seemed that Jeff was trying to make his concern over his investment look like concern for Petrus and I.

He looked very directly at me for a long moment. I returned his look. Then he smiled, and said "Lila, I accept that there is a small grain of truth in what you said. But I would ask you to believe me that 90% of my concern is personal. And 100% of Ann's. She really doesn't give a toss about the business aspect. We are very fond of you both, and you two seem to have a special connection that transcends your age difference. There, I'm being personal again, sorry, but you can't expect people not to notice. But at the same time, I am aware that you have other qualities, not least your abilities as a designer and as a businesswoman, and I am hoping that you will be able to fulfil your potential with the understanding and support of Petrus."

"I accept what you say, Jeff. I know from past experience that Petrus would rather lose me altogether than to stand in the way of my life's path as I chose to take it. That, he says, is what love is all about. But I'm very confident I can take him with me on this path. His support is of considerable importance to me."

"Ok, enough intrusion from me. Let me just say that if down the track there is something you need to talk about in that area, I think you would find Ann to be a very good counsellor. She has some qualifications and experience in that area."

"I rather wondered whether she did," I said. "She is very clear thinking, and an excellent listener. What was her training?"

"I think we know each other well enough that I can tell you in confidence a little background about Ann, though it is known to very few of our friends. I used to be the Chief Executive of a large Australian company. I took the company in a direction which proved to be a disaster commercially, and the only way to save the company was to resign my position and forgo my benefits and pension, in order to restore investor confidence. In essence I lost everything. But the company survived."

"I became suicidal," continued Jeff. "One night I was in total despair, but had the sense to phone Griefline before doing something stupid. The lady I spoke to kept me talking for more than two hours. That got me through that night. We talked again on subsequent nights and she gradually turned me around. It became clear I was talking to a very special person. I asked her if we could meet. She explained that it was completely against the Griefline rules to do that. The matter was dropped. We then spoke more or less weekly for some time, until one evening she asked if I was still interested in meeting her. I said I was, and she said that she was about to resign from Griefline due to the stress of talking to desperate people night after night. She was burnt out."

"I think you can guess the rest," said Jeff. I nodded. "That's how Ann and I met," he confirmed. "We had little money when we got married, but treated ourselves to a honeymoon in Dolphin Sands. And that's where our luck changed, as you already know."

"Hence Ann's counselling skills, and hence some of your attitudes to your fellow man. Or woman."

"Well..." Jeff shrugged modestly. "Anyway, perhaps we really should get out in the garden and rescue Petrus from Ann."

"Or the other way round," I said.

When we reached them, Petrus was looking with embarrassment at a rather nice plant in his hand that he appeared to have just wrenched from its bed. Ann was looking like a saint who was currently being severely tested.

"Petrus, just put it gently back where it came from, and come indoors before you do any further 'weeding'," I said. "I think if you ask nicely, Jeff will arrange some pre-dinner drinks."

Chapter 31

It was a long Sunday night drive home from Ann and Jeff Leigh's place up in the hills.

During our stay Lila and I had done our best to dispel the notion that we were other than young and fit. In her case, this was not too difficult a task - she had kept her body lithe and supple. She probably dressed a little younger than her age and did not embarrass herself by doing so. I on the other hand was somewhat out of shape, and I needed to remind myself to keep my back straight and my tummy in, but this was not too hard so long as I had no need to breathe.

So, we had joined in the younger couple's vigorous morning swims in the warm lap pool, climbed to the top of the hill with them, and stayed up late at night to sample the pleasures of Jeff's well stocked wine cellar, after further remarkable meals prepared by Butler. Jeff and Lila had spent some hours on Saturday afternoon going through her quote for the fabrics for the Club restaurant, and had reached an informal agreement on Jeff's investment in the project, which he said would be formalised by his lawyers in a couple of days. Meanwhile I had spent an agreeable time in the garden with Ann, weeding and talking. She was very glad of my help.

As a result we were pretty exhausted, and on the journey home we were dozing almost before the car had left the drive, both seated as before in the rear of the saloon. I just had time to unfold the light blanket that I found on the back window-ledge and cover all of Lila and most of myself with it, before sleep overtook us as the car hummed into the night.

I dreamed a delicious dream. A naked young woman was pirouetting in front of me as if performing the dance of the seven veils. But I must have missed most of the dance, as she seemed to be making do now with a single veil, failing dismally to keep any part of her beautiful body hidden. The flimsy cloth revealed first one breast, then the other, and then a blur of black pubic hair. My dream-self grinned a guilty grin as the hair was flashed a second time - heh, not Lila, I thought. Then the dance was over, and the young woman was beside me, trying to undo the top button of my jeans. My dream-self said, I'll help, and reaching beneath the blanket, undid the button and lowered the zip, and a hand, not mine, slid inside.

For some seconds I hovered between dream and reality, and then firmly chose reality and woke fully, as I recognised the unmistakable touch of Lila's hand gently teasing my erection. I would know her hand anywhere, even beneath a blanket in a darkened car; it was always gentle, but had become oh so knowing, now so experienced at arousing me under any circumstances, so insistent on bringing me to a climax whenever she chose to do so. And, I thought, let's face it, there's nobody else in the back of this car anyway.

I quickly glanced at Ann and Jeff in the front. Jeff was wide awake, well primed on black coffee. I was glad of this as Jeff was driving. Ann, in the front passenger seat, was clearly dozing, with her head swaying gently at each bend in the road. Neither could be aware of what was happening beneath the blanket in the back.

Lila turned her head a little at the same time as I turned to look at her. She had a beatific half-smile on her face, and glanced meaningfully at her lap. Clearly her favour was to be returned.

I again checked our hosts in the front, and then moved my hand from my side and found the hem of her skirt under the blanket. Lila looked ahead again, then closed her eyes as my hand slid its way up her inner thigh, and her smile became even more content. Now I used four fingers to stroke the very top of her thigh, and she shuffled on the seat a bit and moved her knees a little wider to improve my access. Moving her panties aside, my little finger was now against her outer lips, and I could feel her being drawn remorselessly into arousal. Gently I brought my middle finger to the place, as those either side made the necessary parting movement, and she stifled a gasp as she opened to me and my finger slipped within.

Lila's hand on my erection had ceased to move for some moments while her attention had been fully occupied with her own pleasure, but now she toyed and caressed and stroked and circled it, drawing up my foreskin a little and twisting it lightly against the head. She knew all about the place there. She knew all my secret

179

places. Meanwhile my finger was moving across her, barely penetrating, now straight across, now circling a little, tenderly priming her for a deeper entry. At last I changed the angle of my finger, and with the most gentle but irresistible movement, slipped it fully inside her, identifying where most she longed to be caressed. And thus we sat as the car sped into the night, each toying with the other's delight, movements which in our own bed would have been not nearly so prolonged, being only the preamble to the centrepiece of our lovemaking, but here there was but the one course on our sexual menu.

The kilometres fell away behind us, and I knew that Lila, like me, had caught sight of the legend on a passing sign. We realised that we would soon be discovered by the Swansea town lights. Lila began to push rhythmically and insistently downwards with her fingertips on my full erection, the constraints of the limited space in my underwear not inhibiting her. She was, I suppose, never one to be greatly inhibited in any situation. I recognised her intent, and made my own movements mirror hers, my finger pressing a little more firmly against the upper side of her, my strokes becoming longer, to the full length of my finger. Later, Lila told me that for a moment she reconsidered the wisdom of making me come, but decided that our sexual adventures in the comfortable bed in the Leigh's house would have left me drained, and in any event, if she stopped I might stop too, and that was the last thing she wanted at that point. As she realised I was tipping her over the edge into the rush of her climax, she did that little movement at that special place on me that she knew so much about, and felt the pulse of my coming. We both clamped our mouths shut with gritted teeth. My finger came to rest within her - her fingers pressed down firmly on me just once more, to assure my satisfaction, and she felt the little moistness there, and moved her hand to gently massage it onto me. We stayed in intimate contact until the first of the town lights rushed towards us, then reluctantly separated ourselves. Our hands met and briefly caressed.

We pretended that the lights had awakened us and rearranged our clothing beneath the blanket as inconspicuously as we could. Ann also awoke, and turned round in her seat with a sleepy smile, as the car turned into their drive.

"Dear Lila, Petrus - we've had such a good weekend - you really must come again soon!" I smiled at her and thought, probably not for a couple of hours.

Having parked, Jeff went to the back of the car and brought our weekend bags from the boot. Lila said, "Thank you so much, we really enjoyed ourselves."

"So I noticed," replied Jeff, kissing her cheek while squeezing her hand. "I'll get the blanket dry-cleaned."

Chapter 32

After our hedonistic weekend with Ann and Jeff, we came back to earth with something of a bump. I received documents from Jeff's lawyers within a couple of days, which were fine, I submitted my quotation for the restaurant curtains, which was immediately accepted, and I was able to place orders for the fabrics and for the making-up right away, backed by Jeff's investment in a newly set-up business account.

Seeing to all these matters kept me largely in my own downstairs room for much of the week. I made occasional visits upstairs, but not overnight. I rather suspected Petrus' appetite for any more lovemaking was going to be minimal for a good while anyway. I knew he loved us just sleeping together, but I've never been able to sleep in someone else's bed nearly as well as in my own, and I needed to be fresh for each day's challenges.

I could foresee one practical problem, which was related to Petrus and I sharing the SUV. If I needed to spend more time in Launceston, I wouldn't be able to simply drive there, park the car for a few days, and drive back. Petrus would meanwhile be stranded.

At the end of that week I climbed the steps late in the afternoon and quietly made tea for Petrus and myself, assuming he was busy in his study. Having set his favourite cake beside his tea mug on the table, I tapped very gently on his study door, but was surprised that he wasn't in fact there. I looked in at his bedroom door, which was ajar, and there he was on the bed, just waking.

"Sorry Petrus, I didn't mean to disturb you."

"You can disturb me anytime, Lila," he said in a slightly groggy voice. "In fact, you are disturbing even when you are asleep."

"Do you ever stop being amorous, Petrus? Anyway, are you ok? Not feeling ill?"

"No, I'm just overtired. Ever since we got back from Jeff's place I've felt dozy in the afternoons and I've been coming in here for a snooze."

"Perhaps we overdid it at the weekend."

"No, we didn't. I should be perfectly capable of taking plenty of physical exercise for a weekend, both in and out of the bedroom, without needing extra naps like a ninety-year-old for the rest of the week. I'm just seventy. I'm not incapable on any front." He actually sounded quite annoyed at me.

"I'm just making sure you are ok," I said, starting to get annoyed myself. "Anyway, your tea is on the table and I want to have a word with you about something."

Petrus expression softened at the sound of the word 'tea'. "And is there cake?" he asked expectantly.

"Yes, there's cake. Not that you should be having any after we both, repeat, both, over-ate while we were away."

"Ok. Give me a hand here. No, not there, I mean a hand to get up. No, not that sort of getting up, I mean, assistance in arising gracefully from my bed."

When Petrus was in schoolboy mode, there was no stopping him. The innuendo always came thick and fast. As usual I tried to set my face into a disapproving look, but failed.

I knew that as soon as I took his hand to pull him up, he would try to do the opposite and drag me onto the bed, so I was ready for it, and something of a tug of war developed. I won, but found myself being a bit irritated at the game, for no obvious reason. Normally Petrus' idiocy amused me, or even aroused me, but today he was just annoying.

We sat at the table for tea. He faced the sea, I faced him.

"So what do you need to talk about?" Petrus asked with more than a degree of suspicion.

"Transport."

"As in transports of delight? You want to come back to the bedroom?"

"Petrus, can you for once get your mind out of the bed? I'm talking about how we are going to get around the problem of me getting regularly to Launceston, or for a period of some days or whatever, when we share a car. And while we're at it, I really should be contributing more than the odd tank of petrol."

"Maybe you should get your own car, but that would be a relatively expensive solution. If you are going for more than a day, I guess I could simply drive you there and then come back. It's not really that far. But I don't recall us discussing you being away in the first place."

"You mean, I haven't asked your permission?"

"You know that's not what I mean. Hitherto we've kept each other in touch with stuff like that. I keep you in touch with my movements and you have kindly done likewise. It's what... friends do."

I could understand Petrus' hesitation in giving our relationship a title. What were we? Housemates with benefits? Just very good friends? Partners? Significant Others? 'Lovers' actually described it best, but wasn't socially acceptable when performing introductions. "Hello Mrs Smith, this is my lover Petrus. No, he's not too old for it. Nor am I. Yes, I'm a lot younger. So what? Before we became lovers he went to the doctor and the doctor gave him a health warning about going to bed with me. 'If she dies, she dies' replied Petrus. Yes, it's an old joke. Good day, Mrs Smith."

I dragged my mind back to the topic.

"Well, we haven't quite got there yet. I'm just thinking ahead about how I'll travel there if it works out that way."

Petrus was silent for a moment. Then he took a big bite of cake and was silent for several more moments. Then he looked up at me and I could see his eyes were brimming with tears.

"I'm sorry, Lila. I'm just getting a bit scared about how things are changing. Yes, probably being seventy makes me insecure, but never mind why, I just am. You know that 'Cream' song, 'We're going wrong'? Possibly the saddest song ever recorded. Right now it keeps playing in my head 'cos it feels like the sound track for this part of our story."

"Petrus, don't be dramatic. I'm just going to be spending a bit of time in town, a few nights, then I'm coming back. It's not a big deal. You know you have issues with this sort of stuff, and you really need to grapple with them a bit." Then I thought, shit, that sounded like precisely the wrong thing to say.

"Sure, you're right," Petrus replied abruptly. "Anyway, end of problem, I'll be the taxi driver when you need to get there, and you can get a real taxi for any journeys in town." He pushed back his chair, stood up, and began to clear away the tea things. But then he came back from the kitchen and added, "Hey Lila. Thanks for tea.

I really appreciated it. And when you have a clearer idea of your plans and movements, we'll talk again, ok?"

As I went back downstairs, we hugged briefly as we passed. We both hated any bad feeling between us. But the hug felt like a small sticking plaster on a surgical incision. I had to agree, something was going wrong.

Over the next couple of weeks we continued as before, but we seemed to lack commitment to each other. We were more polite, we backed away from arguments, we tried to make love as before, but nothing came close to the abandonment we had relished at Ann and Jeff's place in the country. And Petrus' sexual appetite was markedly reduced, which not surprisingly made him more anxious and therefore more unable to produce much of an erection. It was a task for which even my skills, which I considered pretty effective, seemed inadequate. Because he was convinced he was starting to lose me, there was a real danger that it would become a self fulfilling prophecy.

From my point of view, I just felt preoccupied with the new horizons opening in front of me. I spent a lot of time researching ideas for the possible overall redecoration of the Club. If the initial job was the success I hoped for, then I needed to be ready to pounce on any extension offered to me. My thinking was turning to a design theme based on images obtained in and around Launceston. This would require me to capture original photographs, and then to render them somewhat abstract, but still identifiable, and finally to produce designs that would work on large expanses of fabric such as bedcovers and curtains and suchlike. I would need to spend time in the town with my camera, there was no way around it.

I had arranged for the restaurant curtains to be delivered direct to the Club, and I had contracted a local firm to install them. This would be no great task, but did require a couple of experienced guys, or girls, with a ladder or two, as the windows and therefore the curtains were large. I decided that I would go to Launceston to see the result for myself, and to spend a couple of days with my camera around the town and a little beyond. The fabric supplier gave me four days' notice of delivery, so I could not put off a discussion with Petrus any longer. I went straight upstairs.

Petrus was in the lounge, reading what looked like a novel. He looked up with a happy expression but then his face clouded as he realised I was there for a particular reason. I sat down opposite him. He closed the book.

"Petrus, I've just had notice that the restaurant curtains will be delivered on Friday. I'd like to be there to see them go up. Then I'd like to stay on in Launceston for a few days to take photographs for the next phase of the job, if it happens. Would you be able to drive me there?"

Petrus looked at me, searching my face with his gaze, and then stood up, with a gentle smile. "Come with me," he said. He took me through to the bedroom, holding my hand. I trusted him and did not resist. He reached down to the bed and threw aside the doona. Then he sat down on the edge of the bed, and patted the space beside him, inviting me to sit with him.

"I'd like to lie down with you for a moment, please," he said.

I shuffled across the bed, he turned, and we lay down on our sides, facing each other.

"Cuddle?" asked Petrus.

I moved closer to him and he took both my hands in his.

"Lila, I think this will be a key time for you. I want you to know that I am totally behind you, even though you will be away from me and perhaps not able to think much about me, with your commitments. Of course I will drive you. And of course I will miss you every minute of the time you are away. It would make a mockery of everything I have said to you if I didn't help you make the most of this chance. So don't worry about me, I shall be fine with it, and I am more than confident that you will totally shine and be a wonderful success. And then, if you can, come home to me and tell me everything about it."

I moved towards him, and we teased each others lips, mouth to mouth, until we kissed with infinite tenderness.

After several minutes in a close embrace, we separated. Petrus' smile became a little wicked. "But you can pay for the petrol," he said.

We drove to Launceston on the Thursday afternoon, to ensure I would be there for the installation on Friday. We split the driving, Petrus taking the first shift, with me taking over somewhat beyond half way in order to drive into town the best way to arrive at the small hotel I had chosen. This would also mean that Petrus wouldn't have driven all the way there and back in one go.

At the hotel, Petrus extracted my small suitcase from the back of the SUV, but held on to it instead of passing it to me.

"I'll take it, thanks," I said, reaching to retrieve it from him.

"It's ok, I'll carry it in for you. Not a problem."

"Petrus, I'd like to say goodbye to you here. It's been fantastic of you to drive me so far, but now I need to take things from here. Including my case. And I'm not good at long goodbyes."

"I'm just wanting to be sure everything is ok with your booking – you know, just checking."

"Petrus, you may be just about old enough to be my father, but for god's sake don't behave like it."

"Ouch," said Petrus.

"Don't forget that for years I was completely in control of everything that I did professionally. Brian never had anything to do with my work. I did my thing, and he did his."

"And look how that turned out."

Without thinking, I slapped Petrus' face. Not hard enough to leave a mark, but hard enough to make it very clear that he had crossed a line. I grabbed the case and strode into the hotel without looking back. I booked in at the small reception area and went up to my first floor room. The window looked out onto the street. I could see that Petrus and the car had gone.

For a few moments my anger burned bright. Then, almost as suddenly as I had lost my temper, I regretted what I had done more than I could say. But I had to say something, somehow. I pulled my phone from my pocket and brought up the messenger app.

I typed 'Petrus, I'm sorry. Please drive home safely. I love you xx'

I had never put those three words in writing to him before. Despite everything, I meant what I said.

Chapter 33

I drove straight back to Swansea. My stinging face helped my concentration. My anger with myself over my behaviour seemed to add to the stinging. The slap itself had not been so hard as to cause this much discomfort. If I hadn't inadvertently left my phone on the kitchen bench, I would have phoned Lila or at least left her a message of some sort. I felt an apology would probably be in order. At the one moment when I should have made sure things were good between us, I had derailed things altogether.

I stopped to get some groceries at Morris's just before closing time. I had a cold bag in the back of the car, and I packed the perishables into that. It was a cool evening anyway. I didn't plan on going straight home to an empty house.

The pharmacy was opposite Morris's. I thought, I need company. It's Colette's late shift, and she should be about to finish when they close. I walked round the back to the rear parking lot, and the Tesla was there. I leaned up against it and waited for Colette to emerge from the back door of the pharmacy. Then I thought, This is like going into a church and leaning on the altar. So I detached myself from the car and paced up and down a bit.

Colette came out. She looked surprised to see me hanging around, but pleased. "Hi Mr Stone, I'll be with you when I've locked up."

"No rush."

She locked the door with two different keys. "Ok, that's all good. Even out here in sleepy Swansea we have to make sure the alarm works and all that. So what brings you here?"

"Well, basically, you. I wondered whether you have to go straight home, or whether you have time for a quick bite at The Saltshaker."

"That's a nice idea. Are we celebrating something? Is Mrs Moone joining us?"

"No celebration, no Mrs Moone. She's in Launceston."

"That's a coincidence, so is Ezra. He's at a get-together of GP's overnight. He tells me that it's work, but I rather doubt it when there's a slap up meal at Country Club Launceston involved."

"Well there's another coincidence, I'll explain later. So your mother is with the kids? I rather hope so, else you'll find the house in small pieces when you get back."

"Yeah, she's in charge. I'll just phone her and let her know I'll be late. Why don't you walk over to the restaurant and grab a table, and I'll join you in a couple of minutes. My mother is never brief on the phone."

I strolled across, feeling brighter already. Around Colette it was never possible to feel depressed. I managed to get a table at the window looking out over the jetty to the great arc of Nine Mile Beach beyond. There were in fact only a couple of other diners there at that time. They would normally be pretty full later on.

I ordered a bottle of Pinot Grigio in the hope that Colette would enjoy at least a glass too. I was about half way through my first glass when she arrived, and I stood up and seated her like an English gentleman. By which I mean, I was the gentleman, and she was seated.

"Order away," I encouraged her. "Whatever you like. I'm going to have a starter to start. That's what they're for. Tomato Bruschetta looks reasonably healthy. Then I'm having the fish and chips because I'm English. We eat a lot of fish and chips. And anything else on a menu tends to confuse me. The English are a confused race. Take Brexit for example." I was already running off at the mouth and only half a glass in.

"Bruschetta for me too, thanks," said Colette. "Then the Shaker Scallop Pie, which I've had here before. It's pretty good."

"So do you come here often?" I asked, as I more or less had to, after Colette had fed me the line.

"Occasionally. Sometimes we bring the kids and sit outside. I suspect the staff are glad to see me here without them."

"They need to remember that we were all young once."

"But I bet they weren't like my three. The twins in particular can be diabolical. I have to distract them to get them to stop fighting all the time. They have a thing about garbage collection vehicles. I found a YouTube video where all you see is a garbage truck going up a street lifting the bins one by one and emptying them. It hypnotises them or something. Anyway, anything to keep them quiet."

I poured her a glass of the wine, which she said she was happy to have, but only a little as she was driving home.

"Roll on the day when the car drives you home on its own," I said. "I guess your car is closer to that than most?"

"Ezra did tell me about some of the tech stuff, but I prefer to stick to normal controls. The trouble is, if you start to rely on the automation, then you drive another car which doesn't have it, you'd get a surprise when it doesn't drive itself round a corner."

"And the guy coming the other way gets an even bigger surprise."

Colette giggled. I relaxed another notch. Her giggles were so much better than too much to drink. But I finished my glass anyway.

I ordered our meals and the bruschetta arrived promptly, quick service tending to be the reward of all who dine early in restaurants.

"So tell me more about you and your car being here, and Mrs Moone being in Launceston. You said there was a coincidence related to Ezra."

I explained the reason for Lila's trip. It had been a while since I had spent any time with Colette so it took me a little time to bring her up to date with developments. Needless to say I didn't include the slap in the story.

"So Mrs Moone will be spending some time there, I guess?" asked Colette.

"We don't know yet. If the larger project goes ahead, Lila will have to spend extended periods away from here."

Colette looked at me quizzically. "You'll miss her." As usual, she went straight to the heart of the matter.

"Yes. But I guess it's all part of life's rich pattern. Lila came to me completely out of the blue, because she had nowhere else to go. Now she has recovered from her situation, and she's moving onwards and upwards, and maybe my role in her life will be different now. And that's as it should be. I can't visualise myself as representing her future. Though I guess for a while it was a dream I did have. Time for realism. Farewell fantasy."

Colette said nothing but her look said it all. She momentarily extended her hand across the table, but then drew it back, almost with an effort.

"Thanks, Colette." Even though she could not complete the gesture, the fact that she had instinctively begun it meant a lot to me. But warning bells in my head reminded me not to let it mean too much.

"Hey, let's talk about happy things. You said Ezra is there, but unless Lila decides to go to the Country Club tonight, their paths won't actually cross. As I understand it, meals there are not that cheap, so she may decide not to eat her profits in a single night."

"I guess so. It would be funny if they did see each other. Ezra wouldn't expect her to be there at all. Anyway, he'd probably be tied up with his medical colleagues so might not notice her."

The main course arrived and we spoke little while we ate. I had refilled our glasses, or rather my glass, as Colette wouldn't have a second one. I realised I'd emptied that too. I filled it again.

In due course the waitress cleared our plates and asked if we wanted a dessert. Desserts consisted entirely of cakes with cream and ice cream. Colette declined immediately, and for once so did I. Despite my affection for Colette, there was only one person in the world who I would allow to wipe cream from my nose.

"I'd better be getting back," said Colette, checking her phone for messages and for the time. "My mum is supposed to have the kids in bed by now, but I bet they are rampaging around still."

I quickly drained my third glass. I paid the bill and we made our way out. I walked with Colette across the road to the pharmacy to see her safely to her car, parked in darkness at the rear.

"Mr Stone…." began Colette, tentatively.

"Yes, Mrs Cheung," I said.

"Not that I was counting, or anything, but I think you've had too much to drink to be driving."

"Really? I wasn't counting either," I lied.

"Could I suggest that you should go back in my car, and we'll collect yours in the morning?"

I thought for a moment, then agreed. It would not only be a pleasant way to end the evening, it would also be the means by which I might preserve my rather vital driving licence.

"Your concern is touching," I said, and without really thinking, I put my arm around her shoulders and gave her a little hug as we walked.

"Talking of touching," Colette said immediately, "please don't. You know you shouldn't."

"Sorry, I forgot myself."

"Simple rule, Mr Stone. Don't do anything you wouldn't do in front of Ezra or Mrs Moone. It's as easy as that."

Colette thought for a moment as we arrived at her car in the dark. Then she added, "Think of it as a kind of compliment. If we meant nothing to each other, and if they thought we meant nothing to each other, then a gesture like that would probably not be noticed. But I just happen to think you are the nicest guy on the planet, and I get the impression you quite like me too. So it's necessary to observe the lines that are thereby created."

Colette made her way round to the driver's side while I waited by the passenger door. Before she unlocked the car, she spoke again.

"I'll say one more thing, while we're speaking frankly. Being the nicest guy on the planet doesn't make you a suitable candidate for some kind of affair with me. There's more to it than that. All in all you're not my type, but I am more than pleased that Mrs Moone feels differently from me. As a woman, I can tell that she simply loves you to bits. Don't take risks where she's concerned. It's simply not worth it."

I got in the car and said nothing. Colette had left me little scope for comment. At the gate to the yellow house, she wished me goodnight, said she would run me back to my car at 11.00am in the morning, and gave me one of her grade one smiles. In Hobart they probably thought they saw lightning on the horizon. It was enough to see me walking down the rough path to the house in complete silence, as my feet didn't quite touch the ground.

I turned on the kitchen lights as soon as I got in. I turned on my phone, and a notification popped up that there was a message from Lila. I thought, that can wait till the morning now. I turned it off and went to bed.

Chapter 34

I got no response to my message to Petrus. Nothing worse than telling someone you love them, and getting not a word of a reply. I sat in my rather small hotel room for a couple of hours, waiting for him to respond, so we could talk it over by text or on the phone. But nothing. Ok, I thought, whatever, I shall do my own thing. I shall have something for me. Fuck the expense, I'm eating at the Country Club tonight. Anyway, it will be a good before-and-after exercise. Soak up the atmosphere as it is tonight, then see how it feels after the new curtains are up tomorrow.

I walked there in about half an hour. It felt good to be out in the town. Different sounds, smells, sights. I love countryside (particularly if it involves outdoor sex), I love to be on a beach, (particularly if it involves outdoor sex), but I equally love the bustle and life of a town (and there's always the parks if I need... anything). I thought, this is part of my dilemma. Petrus needs the beach now. The sea has taken root in his soul. But I don't need it. I just like it. I could move to the town and I wouldn't grieve.

I arrived at about 7pm, and didn't recognise the staff on duty from the previous occasion, which was good. I wanted to be undisturbed. The reception waiter wanted to know if I had a booking. No. No problem. Does madam expect other guests? No. Not a problem. Please step this way.

I declined the first table and asked instead for one with a good view of the whole room. No problem. Would madam prefer this table? Yes. Not a problem.

In this Terrace Restaurant, there are no problems.

Would madam like to see the wine list? Yes, so long as it's not a problem. That stopped him.

I chose a Chardonnay, a whole bottle. I would either walk back to the hotel or take a cab, so driving was not an issue. The entrées were not suitable for a vegetarian so I asked for some good bread with some olive oil to begin, and the Stilton Risotto to follow. I glared at the waiter and he said, That's... fine.

The bread with oil was actually rather good, simple but effective. And the Chardonnay went well with it. The room was more than half full. I noted that I was the only lone diner. I tried to remember when last I had dined alone, and failed.

The existing curtains, half closed, were bland and contributed nothing. Nobody would notice that they had gone, but I hoped that regular diners there would notice that the new ones had arrived. They would make a statement.

The risotto arrived. And so did Ezra Cheung, of all people. He walked briskly into the room and did not notice me, but I spotted him at once, though it took me a few seconds fully to recognise him. He was in the wrong context, and that can play tricks with memory. He sat down alone at a table for two across the room, with his back to me.

I ate the risotto slowly. I did not like Ezra, especially his attitude to young Colette, who seemed to be a combination of trophy wife and household slave. I did not wish to be recognised, and I made a plan to hold the voluminous dinner napkin up to my face if he turned my way. It wasn't long before I needed to do so, when an elegant, tall blonde woman walked into the room as if expecting a round of applause, and made her way to Ezra's table. He stood up quickly, and kissed her on the lips with a degree of passion that was only just passable in a refined restaurant. He helped her to her chair, and at that point I used the napkin again to maintain my anonymity. But Ezra only had eyes for his companion anyway.

I was more than somewhat intrigued, needless to say. There was clearly a significant degree of intimacy between them. When the woman perused the wine list, Ezra left his chair, stood behind her with his hand on her shoulder, and pointed to his suggested choice on the list. Before he returned to his chair, the woman turned her head and kissed his hand where it rested.

I finished the risotto as slowly as I could, not wishing to leave the room before Ezra and his guest had finished their meal. This was much better than watching Netflix in my hotel room. I hadn't planned on a dessert, but a further course would help draw things out. A dish called 'Signature Apple' looked worth a try, although I wasn't sure it would be worth the cost.

Ezra and the blonde actually held hands across the table between each of their three courses. Even Petrus and I when feeling at our most randy didn't do that. I could not escape the conclusion that this was a mistress.

I have a natural disinclination to judge others or cast the first stone. I am myself guilty of many sins. But Ezra's behaviour with this woman, in the light of his treatment of his wife, turned me into judge, jury, and for that matter, executioner. I could not suppress the thought that Colette's earnings might in essence be funding this liaison. What a bastard.

Having started my meal somewhat before them, although I ate slowly I finished before them, and asked for my bill as I sipped a third glass of wine. Despite the meal, the wine was going a little to my head. Perhaps it made me braver than I might otherwise have been. I paid the bill, but stayed in my seat, still sipping the wine. At last I saw Ezra ask for and pay his bill too. His manner was becoming as one who is keen to leave the restaurant and go elsewhere. Whatever he was saying to his mistress was making her look downwards and blush.

Feeling like some kind of spy, I followed the couple as they left the restaurant, and moved into the foyer where I paid a great deal of attention to a watercolour hanging there, with my back to passers by, but keeping watch in the glass of the picture frame. To my intense satisfaction, they were heading for the hotel itself.

Ezra took his mistress to the reception desk to collect his key. Meanwhile I waited by the lift. But I could not help hearing the desk clerk say, "Goodnight Mr Cheung, Mrs Cheung" as they left the desk. Bingo. Guilty as charged.

I turned just as they arrived at the lift. Ezra looked at me, then again, and looked somewhat more than surprised and shocked. "Mrs Moone! What a surprise to see you here!"

"And you, Dr Cheung. And this must be…?"

"Er, my colleague Dr Anderson. We are here with other G.P's for a little get together we have occasionally to compare notes. We've just dined. The others left the table a little ahead of us. Dr Anderson, don't let me keep you from your room."

The so called Dr Anderson exchanged meaningful glances with Ezra, but got into the lift alone and was whisked away.

"Perhaps I could offer you a coffee or something?" Ezra asked, returning his attention to me. "But I must have an early night, I have a very busy time ahead of me."

I thought, I bet you do. And then I said it aloud. "I bet you do, Ezra."

"I beg your pardon?"

"It's Colette's pardon you should be begging. I've been watching you in the restaurant for the last hour. Nearly put me right off my risotto. This is going to cost you, Ezra."

"I really don't understand..."

"Oh yes you do. I think you would be very glad if I didn't mention this to Colette."

His tone suddenly changed and his manner became significantly less pompous.

"Lila, please, this was just an isolated indiscretion. I really don't think you need to involve yourself in the matter. But if there's anything I can do to ensure that you keep it to yourself..."

"There is. When did Colette last have a holiday?"

"I don't follow. We have an annual holiday with the children."

"That's not a holiday for a mother. She needs a couple of weeks, probably back in Malaysia with her friends and the rest of her family, on her own. You can look after the kids. Or get Dr Anderson to help, I don't care, so long as they are properly cared for. When I get back to Dolphin Sands, I will expect Colette to tell me about it right away with much excitement, ok? As for the supposed Dr Anderson, I don't care what you two get up to, but from now on, Colette chooses her own jobs, if she wants to work at all, right? No more getting her to fund your mistress."

"I'll think about what you say, Lila."

"Sure. You have ten seconds to do so. Yes or no?"

"You will say nothing to Colette, nor Petrus, nor anyone?"

"My lips will be sealed all round. You have my word, which is probably worth more than yours."

Ezra capitulated.

I walked back to my hotel feeling more than satisfied with my evening. Whether Ezra ended up more than satisfied, I neither knew nor cared. I checked my phone. Nothing from Petrus. Damn. Now he's getting me worried. I resolved to simply tackle things head on, and phone him in the morning.

Chapter 35

I slept in. I slept until Colette was tapping on my bedroom door at the appointed hour of 11am.

"Mr Stone! Time to wake up and collect your car!"

Grunt.

"Mr Stone!"

I called through the door, struggling with the doona. "Colette, sorry, I overslept. Can you make a quick coffee for me?"

I decided to skip anything to do with cleanliness and godliness and threw on my clothes. I dragged myself to the toilet, but at least had the decency to wash my hands after. I made my wrecked appearance in the kitchen.

"Colette, I am so sorry. The drive yesterday and the meal and the wine made me sleep right through the alarm. Or maybe I didn't set it. Anyway, here I am, and you've made me a coffee, and I will drink it right away and we can go. I know Friday is a busy day for you."

Colette was giggling at my dishevelled appearance. She'd seen it before on many a morning but it still made her giggle every time.

"Don't worry, I've got half an hour. But I need to be back to welcome Ezra home. So we'd better get going as soon as - oh, it's all gone. Off we go."

I had the presence of mind to grab my phone and my car keys, and I collapsed into her car. It was so low on the ground that there was little option but to collapse into it, unless you were young and fit and still able to spring in and out.

Colette sprang into her side.

As we turned into the road, my phone rang. Shit. Lila. I dithered for a moment, then answered.

"Hi, Lila, sorry about not calling, can I ring you back in about half an hour?"

"Where are you? What's happening?"

"I'm with Colette. Give me half an hour."

"I guess that's how long it takes you these days."

"In her car, Lila."

"Even worse."

"We're driving."

"Really? I hear nothing."

"You wouldn't. It's silent. Colette, say hi to Lila."

"Hello Mrs Moone!" called Colette, brightly.

"Say hello from me to her," said Lila, "and say goodbye from me to you." The phone went dead.

I hoped that was goodbye for half an hour, not goodbye forever.

"I wonder whether she bumped into Ezra at the restaurant last night," said Colette.

"Like I said, I don't suppose Lila actually went there. But I'll ask her if I talk to her later."

Colette dropped me at the supermarket car park. I drove back. I went upstairs and almost poured myself a stiff drink. But at 11.30am, that would be the start of a slippery slope. I called Lila. There was no answer. I looked at the message from the night before. I read it a second time. My head reeled. For the first time she had said she loved me. And I'd stuffed that up too. Shit, shit, shit.

Ok, think. Reply to the message.

I typed, "Lila, I'm sorry too. More sorry than you were. All my fault. I'm a shit. But you love me, and I love you, so everything will be ok. Please?"

I sent it. Then I sent another one. "Lila, what's happening there? Is it all going well? Maybe we'll talk. I care about what's happening there. I care about you. I care about us. I'll take the phone in the toilet and everywhere, so call me."

The message app said 'sent' but it didn't say 'read'. This was not going well. I thought, maybe I should drive back there and try to find her. No, that would be totally counter-productive. She's doing her own thing in her own way. Back off, Petrus. Back off.

There was only one thing to do at a time like this, so I went into the study and tried to write an erotic story about make-up sex. It came out quite well, given that make-up sex after our row was getting uppermost on my mind. Hopefully Lila was thinking about it too. But if she was, she was too busy thinking to ring.

Chapter 36

I rang Petrus at about the time I thought he would be conscious. He was. He was consciously with Colette, rather than returning my message which I had left him a whole day before. Well, almost a whole day. There could be no possible excuse. I was not only being ignored, I was being dumped for another woman. And one half his age. Well, not dumped, because the very idea of him actually getting up to no good with Colette had now become laughable, but it certainly looked like his mind was elsewhere from the minute he had driven off.

I thought, shall I send a message saying 'I don't love you anymore'? But that would be the shortest love on record. And I had no real idea what I thought at this stage.

My deliberations were brought to an abrupt end by the arrival of the curtains and the installers. I had arrived at the Country Club at 10.00am and I had consumed three coffees already, partly because I needed the stimulus and partly because Mr O'Brien has told the staff I was on the free list. I muted my phone, and went to greet the incoming team.

About an hour later, I was in the best of moods. The curtains were well made, correctly sized, and the installers got the old ones down and the new ones up with no mishaps. And they looked spectacular. The work I had done on the images from Maria Island had left the Painted Cliffs looking recognisable, but as if painted in water colours. But denser than that. Hard to put into words. I once knew an artist who was commissioned to create a very large contemporary stained glass window for a church. He laboured lovingly and long, and finally it was all installed. The priest came to take his first look at it, and said to the artist, "It looks fantastic, but what does it mean?" To which the artist tersely replied, "If I could put it into words, I wouldn't have bothered to do it in stained glass." Moral, don't try to describe art.

When he saw the installers leave, Garrett O'Brien came in to examine the result. I had asked the installers to leave the curtains fully open. Garrett looked impressed. Then I turned on the room lights, and starting at one end, pulled the cords which closed the curtains one by one. As the last one closed, so he could see the full effect, he actually clapped. I'd scored.

"Mrs Moone, Lila, I congratulate you. They are magnificent. They raise the look of the room to new heights. I have half a mind to leave them closed at all times and never mind the daytime view of the lake. Well, perhaps that would be a little eccentric, but really, they would merit it. Perhaps you could come to my office and we can discuss some matters of mutual interest?"

I followed him to his inner sanctum in the private part of the building. He waved me into a comfortable chair in front of his imposing desk, and pressed an intercom button.

"Miss Steel, would you be so kind as to ask Mr Pyke to join us as soon as he can? Thank you. And may I be permitted to compliment you on that most fetching blue dress you are favouring us with today? Good, good. Don't forget to contact Mr Pyke."

I thought, I would call him a creep except he's simply living in the wrong century.

I declined the offer of further coffee, lest I should start walking across the ceiling, and Garrett began the discussion without waiting for Mr Pyke. In essence, he said that he would now want to go right ahead with the whole refurbishment project he had mentioned before. I tried to stop myself from shouting "Yee-haa" and fortunately succeeded.

Mr Pyke arrived. He was a rather different kind of man from Garrett O'Brien. Slightly taller than myself, and perhaps fifty-five, he was rather handsome and a little tanned, with the general air of a man used to physical effort and who would be eminently capable of it. He also had a mischievous smile, which when he was introduced to me he deployed in an almost conspiratorial look, apparently commenting on Garrett O'Brien's mannerisms without saying a word.

He was introduced to me as Tony Pyke, the Building Manager for the complex. It was explained that his responsibility was for all the practicalities of operating and maintaining the Club buildings under the overall direction of Garrett O'Brien.

"Have you seen the new curtains in the Terrace, Tony?" asked Garrett. "I have told Lila that I am quite delighted with them, and I hope you agree."

"I saw them as I came through," he replied, "and indeed, they quite transform the room." He looked at me and this time the unspoken message was, actually I really mean that, not just agreeing with the boss.

"I have told Lila about our plans to progressively refurbish the Club decorations, and I have asked her to take on the role of designer for the project. I hope you and she will be able to work closely on the matter, and that you will be able as a team to make an early start. As usual, I will expect a weekly update on plans and progress, but other than that, I am turning the project over to your joint expertise."

Tony stood up and stepped over to my chair, and shook my hand in a manner that was both formal and light-hearted. "I look forward to our partnership, Lila. I heard great things about you from my late wife, and it will be an honour to work alongside you."

As he was smiling broadly I made no comment about his loss but thanked him and left it at that. I turned to Garrett.

"We will need to agree terms of business, Garrett, but perhaps that is best approached by a formal exchange of letters. I would be minded to simply quote an hourly rate, and present you with a weekly itemised bill, and if you are happy with that in principle, I'll get the letter to you as soon as I return home."

"Good, good, yes, that sounds splendid. Talking of home, given the scale of the project, you might care to avail yourself of one of our one-bedroom apartments as a combined home and office during the week, or full time, whatever you wish. In quoting your hourly rate, you might care to make a modest adjustment to offset the accommodation, but something along the lines of half the cost of a cheap hotel would be acceptable. If necessary we can haggle but I'm sure any such negotiation will be easily completed."

All I could think was, on the one hand, this is a life changing opportunity, and on the other hand, how the hell am I going to break this to Petrus?

Garrett O'Brien closed the meeting, remarking that he had to leave the premises for another meeting off-site, but he suggested that Tony and I might care to start kicking some ideas around over

201

lunch. I was more than happy to accept and he and I walked through to the Watergarden room.

"Well, this is very exciting," said Tony as we sat ourselves down at a table by the tall windows overlooking the fountains outside.

"Terrifying actually," I said, surprising myself with my openness. "Are you ok with the division of labour? I guess I will design and specify and you will do all the hard work of making it happen?"

"Seems reasonable. I'm happy to deal with all the ordering side and payments to contractors. Garrett seems to like the idea of starting with the Terrace restaurant first, then moving outwards from there. I think if we approach that flexibly, and discover on that relatively small job how well we work together and where our strengths and weaknesses lie, then we'll be able to tackle the rest with confidence."

"I'll second that."

When the wine we ordered arrived, we toasted each other and our project.

While we ate lunch, Tony confessed that he knew little about me, and invited me to tell him the story of my life. "That's a long story," I said.

"How long?"

"I'm guessing about as long as your story."

"Fifty-six."

"Mine's slightly shorter then."

"Married, I guess?"

"In mid divorce." I should have added "but I have a partner," but for some reason didn't. Maybe right at that moment I was unsure what I had. And with a jolt I remembered my phone was still muted, so if Petrus had been trying to contact me, he'd have drawn a blank. God knows what he would be thinking. But tough.

"And you are a widower? I was sorry to hear that."

"Happened about four years ago. Accident at home. I don't talk about it."

"I'm sorry, I shouldn't have gone there."

"Oh, that's fine, I just don't talk about the details. If you knew the details, you wouldn't expect me to talk about it."

"I don't expect you to. Your choice, your grief. Sometimes people treat others who have had losses as if they were some kind of public property. That's not my way."

"So you don't live in Launceston?"

"No, I'm based in Dolphin Sands actually. I'm kind of conflicted over how I'm going to play the commuting thing. Staying here during the week makes a lot of sense."

"As time goes on you might need to stay weekends too. Hard to predict at this point."

"And you're locally based?"

"I have one of the little apartments too, but I've retained my own house about half an hour away. So I go there at the weekends, but if there's a problem here, I can be back quite quickly. But I'm not so close that they keep calling me out all the time. It's pretty ideal."

As we finished our lunch, Tony said, "Would you like to see the apartment they've put aside for you? Maybe you could move in there right away and scrap your hotel booking. I'm assuming you're in a hotel?"

"Sure, I'll at least look at it."

We walked across to the apartment block and Tony showed me the way to the one I was to occupy. He pulled out a large bunch of keys from a shoulder bag he carried. I had thought that a bit effeminate but now I saw its purpose. You wouldn't want that bunch in your trouser pocket, nor even on your belt.

"Here we go, apartment master key, I can go anywhere!"

The apartment was more functional than luxurious, but would serve the purpose very well. There was a bedroom, a living area, a kitchenette and a bathroom.

"Internet?" I asked.

"Free wifi provided. TV, parking, everything you need."

"Great, done. Perhaps you could arrange for me to pick up a key before I leave?"

"Sure. Actually I have to deal with some plumbers in a short while, but if we go back via reception, I'll get them to fix everything. Oh, my apartment is next door but one, that one there. Of course I'd be happy to help sort out any problems once you move in. If anything needs fixing, I'm your man."

He grinned his mischievous grin, but his manner was not in the slightest suggestive. I felt perfectly at ease with him. He was, in fact, the icing on a pretty fantastic cake that had been served up to me almost out of the blue.

After Tony had left me at reception, I took the key he'd arranged for me to have and returned to the apartment. I sat at the small table and unmuted my phone. I checked for messages and missed calls. There were two messages from Petrus.

I read the first one. "Lila, I'm sorry too. More sorry than you were. All my fault. I'm a shit. But you love me, and I love you, so everything will be ok. Please?"

I read the second one. "Lila, what's happening there? Is it all going well? Maybe we'll talk. I care about what's happening there. I care about you. I care about us. I'll take the phone in the toilet and everywhere, so call me."

I felt a bewildering mix of desperately wanting to talk to him, and at the same time, wanting a holiday from him. It was all too intense. There wasn't enough fun. Sure, we had laughs, but the humour was becoming repetitive. The sex was faltering - I could tell that there were many pages of the Kama Sutra which we'd never attempt. But there was no avoiding ringing him, if only out of common decency, if only because I'd promised not to leave him wondering. And right now, wondering would be just what he'd be doing.

And so was I.

Chapter 37

Fortunately I wasn't in the toilet when the phone rang. It being tea-time, I was sitting at the dining table consoling myself with tea and fruit cake. And then some more fruit cake.

"Hi Lila."

"Hi Petrus."

"Lila, I'm sorry, I've stuffed everything up, that remark was way out of line."

"Well, Petrus, I shouldn't have slapped you."

"I think I deserved it."

"You did. But I shouldn't have. Anyway, let's move on. Tell me what's been happening. What were you doing this morning in the car with Colette?"

"Collecting mine from Swansea. I treated her to dinner at the Saltshaker last night, and I had too much to drink. Then I overslept this morning, then she woke me up and took me back to my car, then I drove home, then I finally saw your message on the phone."

"Sounds like you've somehow been managing without me. Unlike you, I dined alone, at the Terrace."

"Apparently Ezra was there. Did you see him?"

"Ezra? No. Maybe he was there at a different time. Anyway, to cut a long story short, the Terrace Restaurant curtains have been very well received and I've got the big contract for everything else."

"Wow, Lila, that's fantastic. I really mean it. But I'm not surprised. You're good, very, very good at this stuff."

"Thanks. By the way, they've provided me with a little apartment to stay in when I'm here."

A knot tightened in my stomach.

"That's great," I lied. "So when does all this start?"

"Right away. Petrus, there's no point in me coming back on Monday. That's when I need to be here. And over the weekend I've got to start getting more local images for the Terrace Restaurant. Basically I guess I won't be coming back till a week today."

The knot in my stomach gripped hard. I suddenly felt completely deflated. It felt like I was being left. My abandonment issues, which I thought I had long ago curbed, burst to the fore.

"Petrus? Are you there?"

"Yes, sorry, just absorbing that. Will you manage with just the stuff you took with you? Should I bring some things you need up there? I don't mind, honest."

"I'll be ok. Look, give yourself a holiday from me. We got caught up in this whole thing totally out of the blue, you were just starting your new peaceful life, and along I came and ruined everything. For a week or so, just be the person you would have been before. As far as I'm aware, that was a happy person. You'll be fine. Maybe I'll phone in a few days or something."

There was so much I wanted to say. Yes, I'd started a new peaceful life on my own, but that was force of circumstance, and once Lila had burst into my little self-imposed hermitage, there was no going back. Except that going back was all that was on offer, right now.

"Ok. Take care, Lila. And..."

"What?"

"Oh, nothing. Just take care."

"You too. Eat the right food and not too much. Bye."

And she was gone. I couldn't tell her that I loved her because I was too scared of the silence from her that might follow. I didn't want to push my luck.

I went into the study, sat down at the PC, and deleted the make-up sex story. And the backup.

Sometimes over the years, when I have been hit by something hard to deal with, I've simply sat in a chair and let it all wash over me until the pain naturally subsides. It always does. Nothing hurts forever. There's usually a dull throb at the site of the wound, but that's all. The world continues to turn.

I sat in the easy chair in the lounge, the one that Lila used to sit in when she was in my little flat in London. I just stayed still, giving my thoughts free rein, not suppressing any of the emotions, even the totally selfish ones, which most of them were. The woman I loved was being very successful, was achieving long-deserved recognition, was finding real fulfilment for the first time in years probably. And I begrudged it, and I didn't stop myself thinking that until I was really ready to restore the nobler side of love. I sat for a couple of hours.

It was going to be a long night, a long week, a long week of long nights.

Finally I got myself to my feet, and went through to the kitchen to look for something for supper. I had a nasty feeling that beans on toast might be the only option.

The phone rang again. Colette. She rarely rang, so I picked it up.

"Hi Mr Stone, it's Colette."

"Hi Colette, everything ok?"

"Yes, all's fine, Ezra came home, and I just thought I'd ring to say he saw Mrs Moone at the Terrace Restaurant, and she seemed to be just fine. I know you worry about her."

"Thanks, Colette. Did she see him? Did they talk?"

"Yes, they just had a little chat. Apparently she told him I'd been looking super tired when she last saw me, and she asked if I'd had a holiday recently, and when he said no, she suggested I should have a couple of weeks back home without the kids. Well, normally when I've raised that possibility he's said that a good mother wouldn't ask such a thing, but this time he seems to have changed his mind, and so I'll be off in a few weeks when I've arranged everything."

"Colette, that's fantastic news. You deserve it. Did he mention if Lila was with a friend or anything?"

"Not that night, but he did say he saw her from a distance just before he drove home, going into the apartments, and he did mention that she was with some guy."

"Oh, that was probably someone from the hotel or something. Anyway, thanks for letting me know. I may need some help here later in the week, would you have some time? I guess I'll ring you when I know and we can work something out."

"Sure, Mr Stone, just let me know. Bye!"

Something was very, very odd. Lila had denied seeing Ezra. Ezra had said he'd seen her with a man going into one of the apartments. Well, she'd mentioned the apartment, but not the man. Why might that be? This was all the kind of stuff that really nourished my issues. I knew that. But I didn't know what to do about it. Maybe Ann would know how I could fix myself, stop this maelstrom of emotions battering the inside of my brain. Maybe I'd try and see her tomorrow. Meanwhile, I needed food and then I needed sleep.

The beans were ok but the toast was a bit burned. After a meal like that, sleeping alone was probably a good plan.

The week, the days and the nights, dragged by. I didn't see Ann. I didn't see Colette. Seeing either of them might have cheered me up, and frankly I preferred to wallow in my depression, amplify my suspicions, feel unwanted and unloved, and generally flop around in a morass of self pity. I was really, really good at self pity.

But the end of the week was approaching, and on Thursday my mood was lifting, and once again I was taking the phone in the toilet, anticipating Lila's call any minute.

What I didn't anticipate was what she told me when her call finally came through.

Chapter 38

Petrus didn't seem too bothered about me staying on for another week. He said something like "take care" and that was more or less it. Oh, and he said some supportive stuff about my work, which was nice of him.

I walked back to my original hotel, checked out, and hailed a taxi to take me and my bag across to the Country Club. Once again I was in the little apartment, and I unpacked my stuff, such that it was, and set up my laptop. Now I needed to come up with some inspiration for the rest of the Terrace Restaurant redecoration.

I hadn't sat down for more than about five minutes when the necessary inspiration arrived. I would make the outer walls, the ones into which the newly-curtained windows were set, effectively transparent. What I would do would be to simply stand out on the terrace with my camera, lean against each of the sections of wall between the windows, deliberately defocus the picture, and take an impressionistic shot of what you'd see if the wall wasn't there. Then, I'd get a company offering photo printing on wallpaper to print the images very large, then paper the relevant walls with the result, so when the curtains were open, the view through the windows would be echoed by the wallpaper between the windows. The pelmets above the curtains would echo the images on the curtains themselves. The end walls could also echo the curtains, the Painted Cliff designs, and the ceilings could also be photo wallpaper, from photos taken on a sunny day with some interesting clouds. Thus the ceiling would look like the sky. The whole room would be covered in natural imagery, as if the walls and ceiling were simply not there.

I thought, wow, I'd love to run this past Tony right away but I guess he's gone home for the weekend by now. But I felt really tempted to knock on his apartment door, just in case.

I deliberated for about five seconds, and stepped out of the door to my apartment, only to see Tony leaving the door to his.

"Hi Lila!" he called. He walked over. "All settled in now?"

"Yes, and thank you for arranging everything. I've actually

been brainstorming ideas for the Terrace right away. I'm not one to let grass grow under my feet."

Tony pretended to try to see beneath my shoes, and said with his impish grin, "No, no grass to be seen. I'm actually on my way out to drive home for the weekend, but if you want me to I'm happy to listen to your ideas. I know what it's like to be bursting to tell someone your idea, and then you find there's nobody there."

He didn't set out to make himself sound wifeless and lonely, but even so, that's the impression I got. His exterior manner was robust, but I got the feeling that there was a much more sensitive man lurking within.

I had nothing to show him, but I did have some photos of the Terrace as it was that I'd found online, and we sat side by side at the little table in my apartment in front of the laptop while I took him through my idea, pointing out what I meant on the screen.

He listened, then was silent for a moment. Then he turned to me and said, "Lila, that's pretty radical, and the Country Club doesn't do radical. But having said that, it's a fantastic idea and I would love to see it happen. Do you think your Photoshop skills would be up to preparing a mock-up that we could present to Garrett O'Brien later in the week? I think it goes beyond what I feel I could approve on my own, but I will certainly endorse it at a meeting. And I don't think it would need to be particularly expensive to implement, which will help recommend it."

"That sounds like we have a plan then. Thanks for your support! So over the weekend, particularly if the weather is kind, I'll do the photography and create a mock-up we could submit on about Thursday."

"I shall feel guilty lounging around my house over the weekend while you are slaving over a hot laptop, but please be assured that my thoughts will be with you."

He stood up to leave, and I went with him the few steps to the door.

"Lila, I am really excited about this. I can't wait to see you on Monday. Take care." And perfectly naturally, he bent a little and kissed me on the cheek. I wasn't really aware that he'd done it until he was several steps away from the door.

For a moment I stood still, trying to decide whether it had been a polite gesture, albeit one that wasn't much in tune with the times, or whether it had been more meaningful than that. What helped me make up my mind was when I saw him turn part way across the car park, and wave to me, as if he was going on a flight and wouldn't see me again for weeks. I waved back before I could check the impulse.

I decided that I needed to relax and turn things over in my mind away from the Club. I remembered that I had passed a small Spanish restaurant while walking back to my original hotel, and I thought that would be a good place to eat. In about ten minutes I was there and seated, and as usual I had to put up with the slightly odd looks I got as a woman dining alone. The waiter brought the food menu but I waved it away. "Bring me your choice of food," I said, "but make it vegetarian. No egg, and nothing derived from anything that had eyes."

"My sister is a vegetarian," said the waiter, who looked young, good looking, possibly of Spanish heritage, and completely uninterested in a woman of my age. "I understand your needs."

"If only," I muttered as he walked away with an easy stride.

Having a selection of tapas and other dishes brought to the table one by one helped extend the meal. One of the downsides of dining alone is that the meal tends to be over in minutes, without conversation to slow things down. So by the time I had paid the bill with a generous tip for the young bullfighter, or whatever he did in his spare time, and walked back to my apartment, it wasn't at all too early for bed. In short order, I was asleep and dreaming a complex fantasy involving Petrus, the bullfighter, a well-hung bull, and Tony. Tony? Hmm. Never dream about your work colleagues.

Saturday dawned damp and photographically unpromising. I decided that a little retail therapy was in order, and until mid afternoon I wandered the streets of Launceston, buying a few clothes to supplement the meagre collection I had brought with me, and having coffee at coffee time and lunch at lunchtime. I mentally catalogued a few locations for future photography to make myself feel that I was working, but I had decided that I wouldn't be billing any time for today. I couldn't be bothered to make the necessary records. I had tea in my apartment, and wondered whether Petrus would be doing the same, and if so what the state of his nose might be. No matter how exasperating he could be, there was something haunting about him. I wondered whether, regardless of our future, I might still be thinking of him at least with affection in ten years' time. Of course he would be eighty by then. I'd be in my mid sixties. Heaven only knew what the nature of my thoughts of him would be by then. Probably not too erotic.

After tea, I collapsed on the small sofa in front of the small TV and had a small nap while attempting to watch Netflix. I hadn't thought of it before, but I noticed on the coffee table there was an in-room dining menu. That seemed to be the easy option. Nothing much vegetarian but the Potato Gnocchi dish seemed to qualify, with a seriously overpriced tub of ice cream to follow. And that was another day gone.

Appropriately, on Sunday the sun was much more in evidence and I managed to do more or less all the photography I had planned. Even the sky shots were successful. I decided to leave the Photoshop work till Monday. I ate in the room again, went to bed early, and slept very well.

On Monday morning I breakfasted first, showered second, and I was wrapped in a towel when I heard a tap at the door, and I realised I hadn't put out the tray for collection after my meal the night before. I assumed that anyone working in a hotel would be used to the sight of a betowelled lady, so I took the tray to the door, and held it out.

"Well, good morning to you!" said Tony, his smile no less impish than before.

"Shit! I thought you were collecting last night's tray!"

"Well, now I'm here, I'll put that down by your door for you. If you tried to do it right now, I think there could be a major wardrobe malfunction."

"Well, I'm sure you've seen it all before," I said, and then realised that was a pretty crass remark to make to a man who had quite recently lost his wife. "Oh god," I said, bringing both my now-empty hands to my mouth, "that was a very insensitive thing to say, I am so sorry."

Tony straightened up, having placed the tray on the ground,

and gave me a wry smile. "It's ok. Hey, don't worry, I didn't read anything into it." And he took both my hands in his, looking me in the eye, and gave them a little squeeze. I thought, if this towel comes loose now, I won't have a spare hand to grab it with.

Although I moved away from him, our hands only slowly parted. Was that him, or me, or both? I thought, this is ridiculous, I've only just met this guy, he's supposed to be a working colleague, and yet he's crossing lines left right and centre, but without me noticing. Time to put the brakes on.

"Tony, perhaps you'd give me a few minutes to get dressed and put my makeup on – not that I wear much – and I'll come and knock on your door when I'm ready to talk about progress, ok?"

I thought, why am I telling him I don't wear much makeup?

After I closed the door behind Tony, and went through to the little bathroom, I took off the towel and looked at myself in the mirror. All in all, I thought, I'm not in bad shape for my age. I still have a good figure, my tummy is reasonably flat despite having carried a baby, and my bum doesn't sag. And my breasts are to die for, beautifully shaped and full of promise. And then I thought, admiring myself in the mirror is in no way useful for getting ready for a meeting with Tony. So why am I doing it?

The meeting with Tony was quite brief, requiring me only to bring him up to date with my progress over the weekend, and to set out my plan for the next few days. The plan was pretty simple – work on the photos to extract the kind of images I wanted printed on wallpaper and ceiling paper, and then to superimpose the designs onto an existing photo of the room, ready for the meeting with Garrett O'Brien. I might need to do some revision on some of the Photoshop techniques I would need to employ, but I was very confident of being ready by Thursday.

"What's your plan for lunch today?" asked Tony.

"I'll probably just eat on the fly," I replied. I would have much preferred Tony's company but that's exactly why I thought I'd eat alone.

"Well, if you need anything or have any queries, I'll give you my mobile number, as I could be anywhere on the estate," Tony said with no particular sign of disappointment. I was slightly disappointed with his lack of disappointment.

I jotted down the number, returned to my apartment, and began work on the photos. Then I thought, huh, he didn't ask for my number in return.

I didn't see Tony other than waving at a distance until Wednesday, when I capitulated at around coffee time, phoned him, and asked if he'd like to meet for lunch somewhere, simply so that we could talk about Thursday's meeting with Garrett O'Brien. I said I'd not been impressed by the vegetarian options at the Club, and could he suggest somewhere else.

"I think I could come up with a suggestion, in fact, a strong recommendation," he said. "My wife was a vegetarian and she liked the cafe I have in mind. I'll pick you up at 12.30."

I dressed midway between smart and casual and when Tony collected me, I could say he'd done the same. He'd certainly gone to the trouble of changing out of his tradies trousers and t-shirt. We walked round the corner to the apartment car park, and he opened the passenger door of his car, which revealed itself to be a BMW coupé, a more expensive-looking car than I would have expected. But then there was something slightly raffish about Tony, so perhaps it was unsurprising that he didn't have a pedestrian saloon.

We drove towards the town centre, but stopped in a residential street a little way out. On the street corner was a very elegantly converted corner shop, now proclaiming itself to be a restaurant by the name of "Green and Bean", which did indeed sound as if they might know a vegetable from a steak.

Tony strode in confidently and held the door for me, and we were shown to an evidently pre-booked table by the side window. "It's actually quite a while since I've been back here," said Tony, his matter-of-fact delivery concealing what must have been a fair bit of emotion.

"You said you wife liked it here – if you wanted to tell me a bit about her, I'd be happy to hear it, but if that's intrusive, forget I asked."

"No, it's kind of you to ask. We actually met at the Club, when she was staying there to participate in a high powered conference of senior staff from investment companies. She was a high flyer, in her mid forties at the time – I was a couple of years older – no kids, totally career minded until she met me. Heck, that sounds vain, I guess I'm describing the timeline rather than claiming to be some kind of Lothario. Anyway, there was an unfortunate episode with the lock to her room, such that she couldn't get out just before she was due to deliver the conference keynote speech. So I called our usual locksmith, who promised to be there in an hour or two, which clearly wasn't going to soon enough, so I told her to stand well clear of the door, and shouldered it from a run across the corridor. And bang, practically off its hinges. I used to be a rugby forward when I was younger. Anyway, she asked to see me when the conference day was over, and offered to buy me a meal for my trouble – I did have a sore shoulder for a week – and we came here, and, well, hit it off. How she'd never been married I don't know, as she was a lovely person and very elegant, but as I say, men and marriage just hadn't been on her horizon."

We ordered our meal, with a glass of wine each. It was good to eat somewhere where they understood that not every dish has to include generous quantities of deceased animals.

"So was she a Launceston lady, or from elsewhere?"

"Sydney. But she loved Tassie and was happy to buy us a nice property here for weekends and longer breaks, while I carried on working here. No way would I have moved to Sydney, nor would she have asked me to. So we had a weird kind of marriage, lots of time apart, but for anyone not wanting things to get stale, I highly recommend it as an arrangement. But I don't recommend the widower thing."

This would have been the moment for me to mention Petrus and how we had just begun a similar arrangement, without the marriage bit of course, but for reasons I couldn't quite analyse, I said nothing about it. Or him. At least, I kept it vague when he asked about me being in mid divorce.

"My marriage fell apart rather suddenly. I should have seen it coming and didn't, or maybe I just looked the other way when I should have had my eyes on the road ahead. Anyway, I took refuge at an old friend's house at Dolphin Sands, but I don't think I'll be there for much longer, it was just a stopgap till I get set up on my own two feet again. Living within striking distance of Launceston might be a good option, as that's where the opportunities are. Well, here and Hobart."

"You don't want to go to Hobart. Housing costs are going through the roof there. Launceston is still quite reasonable. I'd say it's got more going for it for someone like you, someone with design skills and experience. And when it comes to writing, you can do that almost anywhere these days and liaise with the magazines online. If you want help finding somewhere here once this project is over, I'd be happy to assist. And I have quite a few contacts in the hotel business and others who might be glad of your services, especially once you can show them the Country Club as your portfolio."

"Thanks, Tony, I might well take you up on that in due course."

"Tell you what, if you want a taste of what it's like near here but not too near, why don't you come down to my place for the weekend? I have a live-in housekeeper lady who would ensure that the arrangements were decent and proper."

I was completely taken by surprise. But Tony had such an open and straightforward manner that I immediately said "I'd love that, it's very kind of you to invite me," whereas had it been almost any other man, I would have thought 'You have to be joking' even though I would have said something marginally more polite out loud.

When I accepted, it helped that he had a knife in one hand and a fork in the other, as did I, so when I glanced down to see if he was going to do some classic move like taking my hand across the table, I was pleased to note that no such move was forthcoming. At least, I think I was pleased.

The conversation then moved on to the project. I asked him to trust me to be ready on time, and suggested that he should call on me on Thursday morning, maybe coffee time, and we'd run through the informal presentation I would give Garrett O'Brien in the afternoon.

Later, he drove me back to the Club and parked behind the apartment block. He was fit enough to quickly hop out of the car, and gentleman enough to open the passenger door before I could do it myself, and he gave me a hand to exit from the lowish vehicle with some degree of grace and decorum. He did give my hand a little squeeze before relinquishing it, but simply said, "See you tomorrow then," before striding off across the courtyard to the main buildings where he had his office.

He was so hard to make out. Elements of his behaviour could be regarded as qualifying for the old-fashioned word 'forward', while at the same time he was a total gentleman and made me feel completely at ease – at ease enough to agree to spend a weekend with him and his housekeeper.

Perhaps I should have phoned Petrus right away when it was clear that I would be staying in the Launceston area for another full week. But I didn't, not until Thursday evening, when he had probably already cleared his diary in order to drive down to collect me on Friday afternoon. And even when I spoke to him, the conversation was filled more with white lies than truth.

Chapter 39

As I was due to collect Lila from Launceston on the Friday afternoon, I was more than glad when she phoned on Thursday evening to make arrangements, and to bring me up to date with her news. But my gladness was short lived.

"I don't understand, you say you are not coming back for the weekend?"

"Sorry Petrus, you have to realise I'm making my way into new circles here and I have to be able to be flexible about things."

"So who is this guy you are going off with?"

"Don't put it like that, Petrus, you are trying to make it sound like some kind of assignation. I'm staying with the Building Manager and his lady, he's in effect my boss. They live in a place in the country about 30 minutes away from here. It will be partly a working weekend. We had a great meeting with the Club manager today, and he's accepted my designs for the rest of the restaurant, which is just as well as they had taken me a fair bit of effort, and they were bloody good too."

"Well I'm glad things are going well for you. But next time you get an invite, maybe you could ask if your partner could come along too."

"Partner? I'm not sure whether that's how I'd describe you."

"Thanks a million, Lila, have a nice weekend."

"Petrus, don't cut me off. When I get back, we're going to have to do some serious talking. We've drifted into some comfortable assumptions which may not reflect reality. If we're not open with each other, someone's going to get hurt, maybe both of us. And apart from me not wanting to get hurt, I don't want that happening to you either."

"Sure. I'll strap on a parachute ready for a big fall."

"If you think you're in for a fall, then you've got yourself up in a hot air balloon of your own creation. We've promised each other one thing, and that's not to leave the other wondering. Now I'm not saying I'm leaving, but I don't want to go on staying with you doing the wondering thing all the time. It's all getting out of hand."

"Ok, let's drop it for now. Ask me how I am."

"How are you?"

"I thought you'd never ask. Tired, lonely, depressed, malnourished, self-centred, stupid, too old, and I may have cream on my nose."

"That's my man. But you're not my man, don't take that remark seriously."

"Would I ever."

"Probably. Have you seen Colette?"

"Not since we last spoke. But she rang. Lila, she said Ezra not only saw you at the hotel, but that you had a nice chat with him which resulted in him letting Colette off the leash for a proper holiday. You said you hadn't seen him. What's that about?"

There was silence for a few moments at the other end.

"I see. Did she say whether Ezra said anything else involving me?"

"Apparently he saw you going into your apartment at the Club with a man."

"Cunning bastard, trying to get his own back. Petrus, you'll have to wait till I see you in the flesh for some explanations. Or you may have to wait forever. I'm not obliged to tell you about every last thing I do."

"Sure, Lila, sure. Just leave me to think the worst for the rest of my life."

"Why do you have to think the worst? You'd live a more healthy inner life if you started assuming the best about people instead."

"Like you thought about Brian." Oh god, I've done it again. No point in trying to take that back, it's out there.

The silence that followed wasn't prolonged. But it just felt like an eternity. Eventually Lila responded.

"Petrus. It's so unlike you to take these low shots, even if you did have a point there. Before we speak again, I'd be glad if you would raise your game a bit. Look, I have to go. I'll call you after the weekend, as early in the week as I can. Maybe I'll even message you a photo from my trip. Just don't get into a grumpy mood, so that when I come back I wish I hadn't."

"Yes, Lila, that was best unsaid, I'm sorry. And I'll try to be full of sunshine till we speak again. You know me, that's what I always do."

"Bye Petrus. Have a good weekend."

"I'll try. And I'm sure you'll succeed. Bye."

Chapter 40

I felt a bit of a shit telling Petrus I was going to stay with Tony and his lady, without making it clear it was his housekeeper lady. But if I'd explained the detail, there would have been a fuss. And I couldn't stand any more fuss from Petrus. Even if it was justified. But hey, why justified? I'm not married to Petrus. I'm not having an affair with Tony. But then sometimes I do feel married to Petrus, and it's not such a bad feeling most of the time when he's not having his issues. And I might have an affair with Tony. Damn, where did that come from? I was starting to get almost as confused as Petrus, and he got confused for Australia.

It was, as he had said, about half an hour to Tony's house. It was on a hillside with woods behind, an open grassy paddock in the front, and a fantastic view across the valley. It also was a six bedroom house, not as spiky modern as Jeff and Ann's place, but certainly contemporary and certainly luxurious. I supposed all this wealth came from his late wife. It certainly wouldn't have come from his employment at the Country Club.

To my slight relief we were, as promised, greeted at the front door by Alice Capper, the housekeeper. She seemed to have the same sort of multifaceted role as Butler Spantiri had at the Leigh's place. She showed me to my room as protocol demanded, rather than Tony, and asked if the vegetarian meal she had prepared would be to my liking. It sounded great, and yes, I would like a glass of Chardonnay before sitting down.

The room was very well appointed, with a wardrobe about five times bigger than was required for my weekend clothes, and an ensuite bathroom almost as big as the bedroom itself. I was getting used to this luxury life. It wasn't becoming any kind of a problem.

Tony showed me around the principal rooms downstairs, which included a home theatre which would have made an impressive suburban cinema, and having sat in the lounge for a few minutes with our drinks, he escorted me to the dining room. He didn't just show me the way, he escorted me. There's a difference. He too seemed to have no problem with the luxury life and had modified his tradesman manner to suit. Having thought that, I unthought it as unbelievably snobby. But it was true.

The meal was perhaps less ostentatiously good than one of Butler's, but radically better than I could have prepared, indeed better than anything on offer at the Terrace Restaurant. Butler had never eaten with us when we stayed at the Leigh's, but here things seemed less formal, and Alice actually sat at the head of the overlarge table, with Tony and I facing each other at the sides. I did wonder whether this was a special arrangement to put me at my ease, but then I recalled that Tony hadn't been born to this life and was probably perfectly accustomed to Alice's presence.

After the meal, Tony said with uncharacteristic hesitancy that he'd love it if we could sit and watch a movie together, as that was his regular habit on a Friday night, to unwind after work. I was happy with the idea of course, and so we sat side by side in the theatre room, watching Keira Knightly in "Begin Again", which I had seen before but I didn't mention that. I'd forgotten most of it anyway. I wondered whether the title was supposed to convey any message but I put the thought out of my head almost as soon as it popped in.

Alice didn't join us for the movie but she did appear the moment it finished. Perhaps she had a feed from it in her own room. Or perhaps she sat in front of a bank of video monitors watching everything that happened in the house transmitted by hidden cameras. I have problems watching movies because they send my imagination wild afterwards. Anyway, appear she did, and asked if there was any nightcap I would like before retiring. I actually asked for hot chocolate, which I drink about once every ten years, and in no time she brought a straightforward mug containing the richest hot chocolate I have ever consumed. Tony and I sat in the lounge while I sipped it, exchanging anecdotes about things that happened in hotels, of which he inevitably had a rich fund. And then I stood and said I'd like to get to sleep, and Tony stood and wished me goodnight, and his sole demonstrative move was to give me a little half-bow.

His behaviour was entirely proper and respectful at all times. Perhaps he was the last such man on the planet. Or perhaps he and Petrus were the last two. Or was it something to do with me? Did men think I might break every bone in their bodies if they made a false move? Or perhaps I seemed frigid and unapproachable? To some extent that might be the kind of signal I was currently putting out, being involved with Petrus on the one hand, and my traumatic experience with Brian wasn't so long ago on the other hand.

There was something about the bedroom which invited me to sleep naked, which I didn't always do even with Petrus. Poor Petrus, sometimes I would come to him clad in a shirt and pants as a sign that I just wanted company in bed, and sometimes it was a sign that I wanted to be slowly stripped and ravished. He never knew which to choose, and more often than not he got it wrong. Not his fault. Dear Petrus. And with that thought I fell asleep.

In the morning Alice was up before me, and an excellent breakfast awaited me, even though I was up earlier than might have been expected. I had almost finished before Tony appeared, dressed in smart casual to match my own outfit. His intuition was impressive. I asked him what he had in mind for the day.

"It looks like a reasonable day out there. I wondered whether you might be up for a walk to the top of the hill? Trouble is, at the top of our hill there's a taller one behind. But if you get daunted, we can turn round at any point. Alice can throw together some sandwiches to take with us, I'm sure.

"I'm sure too," she said with a smile, and slipped away to the kitchen.

We donned our jackets and left via the back door, from which a narrow path led towards the woods. Tony was clearly fitter than I, perhaps not surprisingly as most of my walking in recent months had been along the flat beach back at Dolphin Sands. But he adapted his pace to mine as we followed the path up the hill between the trees, and we talked of little things, likes and dislikes, places we'd visited on holiday, musical tastes, books, and all manner of things which taken together consists of a human being's particular character.

Eventually we reached a partly clear area at the top of the hill. From there the view extended in three directions downwards, and in one direction upwards to the top of the next hill. Tony stood behind me pointing out various points of interest near and far, and it was a perfectly natural thing to have rested the hand that wasn't doing the pointing on my shoulder. But he didn't. The thought occurred to me that perhaps this was tantric non-contact. Constantly not touching me would get me into such a fever of anticipation that when he did touch me, I'd be all his. Or, of course, I could simply slap his face. Petrus had given me some useful target practice in that respect.

"So," Tony said, still standing behind me. "Shall we do the next hill or have you had enough?"

I turned to face him and cocked my head a little to one side.

"I suspect I have just been issued with a challenge," I replied. "Game on. Last one to the top avoids the cardiac arrest."

Tony made as if to run off towards the hill, and in fact did so for about half a minute, then stood and waited for me to catch up. This I did fairly easily, as it was necessary to walk a little downhill before recommencing the ascent. As I neared him, he held out his hand to me as if to pull me along up the impending slope, and as ever, the gesture was so natural that my response was unthinking, and before I knew it we were walking hand in hand along the track. But if the initial impulse was natural, within seconds I was swamped by inner turmoil. Should I withdraw my hand? Should I encourage him with a little gesture of a squeeze? Should I think of something inconsequential to say? What's the protocol here?

Tony didn't help, because he just continued to hold my hand as we'd been holding hands for years, but he seemed content to walk in silence, a silence which grew more pregnant by the minute. Heck, I thought, this silence is going to have twins.

At last I was rescued by a force of nature. "Excuse me!" said Tony suddenly, withdrew his hand abruptly, and thrust it into his pocket. The hand emerged immediately clutching a large hanky, and Tony sneezed with a such gusto that I actually detected an echo bouncing off the hillside ahead of us.

"Bless you!" I said, blessing Tony at the same time as blessing the guardian angel who had caused him to release me and sneeze. He stood for a moment recovering, then gave me his broad, impish grin, and set off again up the slope. My hand remained spurned. At least that complication had been dealt with.

At the top of the second hill, which thankfully was not the precursor of a third, we found a flattish rock on which to sit and eat our lunch. I was more than glad of a rest. It wasn't possible to see the house below us due to the first hill obstructing it, but I thought we must have climbed quite a way up.

Tony seemed to read my thoughts. "We've climbed quite a few hundred metres," he said. "When we get back, I could probably work out how many from the map. But the good news is, it's basically downhill all the way home."

"I have to admit I'm not used to this much exercise," I confessed. "I hope you don't mind if I sit here for a little while before we return. But it's a beautiful place to stop, with this all-round vista. And it's so quiet. Do you often meet other people up here?"

"Never have," replied Tony. "I don't think there's an easy way up unless you come through my property to reach the path, and people don't do that."

"Great spot for outdoor sex," I said. And then I thought, Christ, for a moment I forgot I wasn't with Petrus. If I was, we'd be at it like rabbits on this flat stone. But it was Tony who was with me, and it was Tony who was smiling very broadly.

"I thought you'd never ask," he said.

Looking back later, I tried to analyse what went through my mind. Partly I was horrified at what I'd said, and the response I'd elicited. But more than that, I was suddenly lit up from within at the thought of outdoor sex on top of a hill with a man I barely knew. To say I was turned on would be to say that the Eddystone lighthouse glowed. I felt my face flush, and saw Tony turning towards me on the rock, and then I felt our lips lock together with more lust than I would have dreamed possible. We had climbed the hill both wearing jeans. In a moment, here on the hilltop, both of us were trying to rip them off. Tony was more successful. My zip jammed. And that was enough. Something in my head said "Not meant to be!" I tugged at it vainly a couple more times. I thought, I'm sure I could get these off anyway. But the head voice came back again, slamming the brakes on, while at the same time I heard Tony say, "Here, let me help."

I blurted it out. "Tony, I have a partner, I can't do this."

Tony looked completely confused. He also looked seriously aroused. He'd pulled down his jeans and his underpants to his knees, revealing a physique which was impressive enough to counter the absurd look of any man in that state of semi-undress, and by physique, I'm not even beginning to refer to his erection. That was beyond impressive, bordering on downright frightening.

"Hell, Lila, this is no time to spring that on me."

"I'm sorry, I'm sorry. Look, I'll do what I can. Come here. Come on. I'll sort it out, I can do that much."

I had to fight myself all the way not to take him in my mouth. It would have been a significant experience for both of us. But something, someone in my head had drawn a line. Bloody Petrus. Get your lines out of my head. I want to give this poor widowed man something to remember for the rest of his life, help him to forget all his grief in an unbridled explosion of sexuality. And all you are letting me do, Petrus, is to walk round behind him, take his erection in both my hands, and bring him to a climax that he could have managed himself in the shower. But as he almost immediately came, his groans and cries made anything in a shower surely pale into insignificance. He collapsed onto his knees, and I went down with him, and used every manual trick I knew to keep him pulsing in my hands, with his semen wetting the grass in front of him as if he hadn't come since the day he had lost his wife.

At last I felt the pulses weaken and stop, and his erection began to fade. I reached into my jacket pocket and found the packet of tissues there that I always carry just in case on such walks, not that this was a case I had envisaged. As he knelt there with his head back, still gasping, I cleaned him up, which only encouraged his erection to rebuild, and I wondered for a moment if he was going to need a second orgasm before he was done. But as if answering my thought, he shook his head, and I buried the tissues under a clod of earth, while Tony eventually rearranged his clothing.

He was, as ever, enigmatic. In a little while we walked back down the hill, not talking so much as before, but holding hands, yet he made no comment about what had happened. From another man I might have heard recriminations, or words of persuasion, but Tony made the whole business entirely unregrettable. When we reached the house, he gave me one of his impish smiles.

"I think I'll go and have a shower and a lie down after all that exercise," he said. He left me to extract the double meaning. He did not say the words pointedly. "Alice will make you some afternoon tea. Do make what use of the house you wish. I'll see you in a little while."

But Tony did not reappear for the evening meal. Alice and I ate alone. At one point she left the room and I assumed she was quietly taking Tony his meal in his room. Alice was pleasant company, but I was sorry Tony wasn't there. I couldn't take him as a lover, not right now anyway, but he seemed to have the potential to be a good friend.

Later I found a novel on the bookcase that I didn't think I had read, and I settled down in the lounge with it, expecting Tony to join me in due course, but after about half an hour, as the words on the page began to lose the battle to fight off my sleepiness, Alice came in and said that Tony had been kept in his study by a work related matter, and he wished me goodnight.

I slowly undressed in my room with some regret. Tony should have seen me like this. I was proud of how good I looked at a time of life when looking good didn't come so easy. I slept well and dreamed of what might have happened on the hilltop were it not for Petrus' imaginary intervention. If Tony's skills had matched his equipment, it would have been an afternoon to remember. Yet sometimes the best wine comes in older bottles.

On the Sunday morning, once again Alice had prepared breakfast for me, and Tony was nowhere to be seen. I was about to start in on the novel again, even though I now recalled I had indeed read it before, some years back, when he came into the lounge looking a little preoccupied.

"Lila, I can't apologise enough for my rudeness, but I've had a number of phone calls relating to the Country Club and I'm having to return there this afternoon, instead of Monday morning. But I would like to show you the Hope Springs waterfall if you've never seen it. It's about twenty minutes' drive and about five minutes walk from the car park. It's a very popular place, but worth a look."

I noted the reference to it being popular. He was reassuring me.

As we drove, Tony still seemed preoccupied but I didn't interpret it as anything to do with what happened on the hilltop. Even so, it was a little concerning, so I took my courage in my hands.

"Tony, you seem a bit preoccupied – is it the problems at the Club? Nothing to do with our project? The new curtains haven't fallen down or anything?"

As he drove, he patted my knee briefly. It wasn't a pass, it was a straightforward gesture of reassurance.

"No, it's a generalised problem that some business associates have drawn to my attention. Our project isn't involved. And Lila, my manner is in no way whatsoever related to our walk yesterday. Even though we didn't quite reach the destination I had hoped for, it was a very special time for me, thank you."

We arrived at the car park from which the path to the waterfall wound up a steep slope. As Tony had said, it was a popular place. In fact, we took the last available place in the car park. Two young men in a black saloon pulled in just after us and had to stay idling in between the lines of cars, presumably in the hope that someone would shortly leave. One of them must have decided to go on to the waterfall, as he got out of the car just after we did, and followed us up a little way behind.

When we reached the waterfall, I could see the reason for its popularity. It looked perhaps like a girl's long braided hair. It was not notable for its width, but its narrowness and the twisting of the water as it fell off the cliff from which it emerged gave a wonderful sparkling effect, the light shattering everywhere at its foot where it gurgled into the pool below.

We stood for some minutes. I took Tony's hand and gave it a squeeze, and thanked him for taking the trouble to show it to me. He smiled his mischievous smile, squeezed my hand in return, and we headed back down the path.

At the car park, I noticed that the saloon car had now found a space, but it pulled out just after us, with the passenger having resumed his seat. I supposed that there's a limit to the amount of time anyone cares to look at a waterfall, and the young man had reached that limit at the same time as us. As we turned in to Tony's drive, the black saloon passed us and disappeared down the road.

Tony was more his usual self over lunch with Alice, and seemed more relaxed. But he did look at his watch a couple of times as inconspicuously as he could, and as soon as lunch was over, he suggested we should make a move and get back to the Club.

I was in one way disappointed to find myself back in my apartment somewhat earlier than planned, but took the opportunity to do some more preliminary work on the photographs for the Terrace Restaurant. Garrett O'Brien had in fact suggested some minor changes to my proposal which I felt did no harm to the overall scheme, and so there was some more Photoshopping to be done. I half wondered whether Tony would suggest eating together in the evening, but when I looked out of the apartment window which overlooked the car park, his car had gone. Perhaps he was seeing one of the 'business associates' he had mentioned. I ate alone in my room, watched some TV, and went to bed early, feeling a little deflated. I almost rang Petrus, but having told him I'd be away until Monday I couldn't face making the explanations about what had happened. But there were some aspects of the weekend's events that I would never tell him.

On Monday mid morning, I wanted to double check with Tony that I had correctly carried out Garrett's alterations, and as usual phoned his mobile, but there was no reply, which was unusual. I asked at reception and they said he hadn't been seen all morning. It hadn't occurred to me to check the car park, but when I did so, the car was still not there. It did not appear for the rest of the day, and it still wasn't there on Tuesday.

I was now both worried and mystified, and was starting to run out of things to do, as the next stage would be to order the wallpaper printing, which Tony had planned to do in consultation with myself, given that he would be responsible for the installation. I was sufficiently worried that I got up early on Wednesday, and as I had done on the previous two days, enquired at reception whether Tony had been seen. They said he hadn't, but now I was there, could I wait a few moments as Mr O'Brien had asked to see me once he had dealt with some visitors.

Eventually I was ushered into his office by young Miss Steel, who having been praised for the look of her blue dress, was wearing it again. Garrett's visitors were still there, two of them. One of them was wearing a police uniform. And Garrett was looking glum to say the least.

"Ah, Mrs Moone. Most kind of you to attend. May I introduce Chief Inspector Arnold, and Detective Constable Baxter. Gentlemen, I imagine you will recognise Mrs Moone."

"Good morning, Mrs Moone," said the Chief Inspector.

I sat down without invitation, sufficiently suddenly that it was as well that one of the comfortable chairs was right behind me.

"Tony! Is this about Tony? Is he ok?" Suddenly I was panicked.

"It is about Mr Pyke, but I can assure you he is in good health. He has been under arrest since Sunday evening. It seemed he was doing a runner after a tip-off, and it was unfortunately necessary for our officers to force him to stop his car, but despite the ramming, he was uninjured," said the Chief Inspector solemnly.

"Unlike our car," said the detective with some annoyance.

"Why? What has he done? There must be some mistake."

"Well, Mrs Moone," continued the Chief Inspector, "it appears that he has been involved in some serious corruption involving contracts for the maintenance and improvement of these premises. He may have also been diverting funds belonging to the Country Club for his own purposes. Furthermore, we have commenced an enquiry into the suspicious death of his wife, possibly involving a motive of financial gain, and lastly there may be charges related to secret cameras installed in his home. It's from those cameras that we have recognised you, and also from surveillance taking place at the weekend."

"You mean, he was recording me when I was in the house? In the bedroom? No wonder he knew what clothes to put on to match my style."

"Yes, madam. Recordings showing yourself, and a number of other women in recent months, have been seized. In your case, no offences appear to have been committed in relation to your person, and those images have been deleted. In the case of other women, I'm afraid some serious offences may be involved. We are also interviewing under caution one Alice Capper who was acting as housemaid for Mr Pyke, but from the recordings we have seen, she was somewhat more involved with him than most housekeepers are. She may also have been involved in elements of the fraud, we're not sure at present."

My mind was in a complete whirl. Everything was suddenly upside down. I now realised who the young men in the dark saloon car must have been. Hopefully they didn't follow us to the top of the hill. But bloody hell, these policemen had been watching me undress on the video. Probably gathering their colleagues around to watch. But then I thought, maybe they weren't the least bit interested, and maybe the other stuff on those tapes would have revolted them. Maybe some of these guys need counselling at the end of their shifts, after what they see and hear.

The detective, Baxter, cleared his throat. "Mrs Moone, you will understand that we would like you to assist us in our enquiries, and with that in mind, perhaps you would agree to provide a statement. We're happy to interview you here, no need to come to the station. In a moment, you might care to take us across to your apartment, and tell us everything you heard and saw during the time you knew Mr Pyke, and especially over the weekend."

"Of course, but I still can't believe he's done these things. It's just impossible. He seemed a perfectly nice guy."

"That's so often the case, madam. Villains make it harder for us by refusing to behave like villains. Keeps us guessing. Not very fair of them."

I had the uncomfortable feeling that the detective was being perfectly serious.

"Also, madam, we'd like to check your apartment for hidden cameras. It's possible that Mr Pyke was monitoring you there too." I could hardly believe my ears, but thinking back to one or two odd coincidences, perhaps that was the explanation.

It was Garrett O'Brien's turn to speak. "Mrs Moone, Lila, I regret that there's one more thing. While I accept you had no knowledge of the matters that the police are investigating, it is clear that the hotel has suffered a significant financial loss. We have also lost a senior staff member, who was performing an important role, as well as ripping us off. I regret that the refurbishment project will have to be terminated immediately, and although we are happy to accept your bill for time spent and expenses in accordance with our agreement, as of this moment, no further work is to be done and no further expenses incurred. As soon as your interview with these officers is concluded, I would be glad if you would vacate the premises."

A few hours later, I was standing in the street outside the main entrance to the Country Club complex, with my bags beside me. A light drizzle fell. I rang Petrus. By some miracle he had his phone with him.

"Petrus, it's Lila, everything has fallen apart."

"I know. I had some local police at the house checking your identity and background first thing this morning."

"Oh god. Petrus, I want to come home. Can you pick me up? Please?"

"Sure. I'm parked right opposite."

I looked up, and there was the SUV which I hadn't looked at twice when I walked out of the gates. I could see Petrus at the wheel with his mobile in his hand.

"I figured you'd need a lift, so I drove straight up here."

With friends like Petrus, who needed a Tony?

I ran across the road to him. He took me home.

Chapter 41

Lila held it together till we got home. When we arrived, she headed towards the house while I got her bags out of the back of the car. She walked past the door to the downstairs room and trudged up the steps. I followed a little after with the bags.

When I got into the house, I saw her sitting at the dining table with her head on her arms on the table, sobbing. I had some inkling that once again, as when she had first arrived, the hug that I wanted to give her would not be welcome. So I sat down opposite her. As soon as I did so, without lifting her head she extended her hands towards me, and I took them in mine and held them tightly.

We sat like that for several minutes. Her sobbing gradually died down, and she lifted her tear-stained face to look at me.

"Petrus, I have been such a fool. But he seemed so genuine. Just a nice guy. And yet they are saying he was a monster, a fraudster, a pervert, maybe even a wife murderer. How could I have known?"

"Lila, don't blame yourself. You have a wonderful way of taking people at face value, trusting people, and sometimes there's a price to pay for that. On the other hand, I'm constantly suspicious of even my nearest and dearest, and I too pay a price."

"But meanwhile I've been such a shit to you since this whole Country Club thing started. I can't believe I did that. You've done nothing but love me, and I've done nothing but leave you. You deserve more, so much more."

"Lila, you've been following your path. That's fine, it's what you have to do. But it was a wrong turn. Yet I've experienced so often a wrong turn leading me to something much better than I first envisaged. Don't give up. There's more to come. Now, let's have a little bit of lunch, then we'll sit comfortably in the lounge and if you want, you can tell me the whole story. I only got a top level summary from the rather indiscreet young cop who called here."

So after lunch, Lila described all that had happened. I really did get the impression that she had seriously fallen for this Tony guy, to the extent of kissing him at the hilltop. But she seemed resolved to be a lot more cautious next time. Still, knowing my own inclination to fall head over heels in love at the slightest and earliest provocation, I took her resolution with a grain of salt. To err is human, but to love is divine. Or something.

Finally, Lila said, "Petrus, I am totally shattered and I really need to have an afternoon nap – any chance of borrowing your bed, alone, for the purpose? I want to be with you up here, but alone at the same time. You know what I mean."

I did, very well. I made sure she was settled comfortably, and closed the door to ensure she was not disturbed. I went through to my office, sat myself down on the sofa, and was probably asleep before Lila was.

We rebuilt our relationship gradually over the next few days. After sleeping in my bed until almost dinner time that first day, Lila spent the night in her own bed, apologising to me for making me sleep alone for yet another night, but as always I made it clear that she was under no obligation. To make a woman feel duty bound to share one's bed seemed to me to be completely counterproductive if a meaningful relationship was the objective. Increasingly I felt less and less pressured by sexual drives anyway. I felt resigned to that, taking it as part of the same process that made the floor feel further and further away when I went to pick something up.

About three nights later, Lila asked if she could sleep upstairs with me, without making it clear (as she sometimes did) whether this was sleeping only, or sleeping with benefits. We had spent the afternoon having tea with Ann and Jeff, followed by Jeff and Lila having a long talk alone in his study, while I unburdened myself a bit with Ann. She gave me little direct advice, but later I realised that her small promptings and short questions led me towards finding my own answers.

The conclusion was that the time was coming when Lila and I would have to make some kind of plan about our future. Just stumbling along and hoping things would work out without any meaningful discussion just wouldn't cut it. I dreaded that process because I could not foresee the outcome. But Ann helped me to realise that unless I was careful, I could be wasting Lila's time, and my own, in pursuing a relationship which might, or might not, have nowhere to go. Ann was careful not to express an opinion as to our future. But she did point out to me that I had less time to waste, statistically, than Lila. She didn't need to tell me. That thought was growing in my mind every day.

I fiddled with things in the kitchen while Lila showered. She called out "your turn" as she went through to the bedroom. I didn't spend any more time in the shower than necessary, and I was probably a bit damp still when I padded along the corridor wrapped in a towel.

Lila held aside the doona and I dropped the towel and slid onto the bed beside her. "This is nice," I said in my English understated way.

"English twit," said Lila in her straightforward Australian way. "Help me get these off."

I was glad of a clear message about benefits. She sat up a little and between us we peeled off her tee shirt. The sight of her breasts coming free was beyond unbelievable. Keeping my eyes off them was tricky, keeping my hands off them was an insurmountable task. Then she arched her back to lift her hips off the bed, which was a blindingly obvious signal to me to slip off her pants. I complied without delay.

"While you were away I wrote a story about makeup sex," I said as best I could as I nuzzled her nipples.

"Mmmm," replied Lila. "Mmmm," she repeated. "So what did the makeup sex involve?"

"I deleted the story in a fit of pique," I admitted, "but as I recall it, it involved a ring doughnut and one of those canisters of whipped cream, amongst other props."

"Whipped, huh. Mmmm. Your tongue seems to have grown since I last felt it."

"That's not all."

"I think you might be right. Let me check. Can I still get my hand round? Wow, only just."

"Mmmm. Dammit, that word is catching. Oh. Oh god. Lila, I don't know how you do that, but I'm sure glad you know. Hey, don't stop..."

Lila had suddenly stopped her magic, and rolled onto her tummy, burying her face in the pillow. She lifted her head enough to speak and said, "Petrus, I told you a white lie about what happened on the hill."

Suddenly, nobody was saying 'Mmmm'.

"Tell me," I said.

"Petrus, maybe it was more than a white lie."

"Ok, still tell me. I can see that we're at a standstill until you do."

"Petrus, he wanted to go all the way. I didn't let him. I promise faithfully I thought of you and stopped him." She paused for a moment, then said, "And also my zip jammed and I couldn't get my jeans off."

"So... conscience or wardrobe malfunction?"

"Total honesty? First the latter, followed immediately by the former."

"And then?"

"You can guess. You know what I'm like."

"You jerked him off, a sympathy jerk."

"Yup."

"Just that?"

"And cleaned up afterwards. Then we just walked back down the hill."

"With him whistling as he went."

"Petrus, don't."

"Turn over again." Lila did so with a degree of uncertainty and lay on her back.

"What do you think he wanted to do?"

"I don't know. He was pretty desperate. I don't think much finesse would have been involved."

"He'd be like this?"

"I guess so."

"You would probably have helped him a bit."

"You mean like this?"

"Yup. That would have helped."

"More help?"

"Just a little."

"And then you would have drawn him towards you?"

"I think I would, around now."

"You would have been pretty ready. Just as well with nothing to help."

"I would. So ready. He would slip in pretty smoothly. I'd be guiding him like this."

"And you'd be there on the hilltop, with that hard rock under you, which wouldn't give beneath you at all when he got to work."

"I'd be looking up at that open sky, and I think I'd be hearing the rustle of the trees in the woods, and his gasping as he worked above me."

"I think… he would indeed be… gasping by now."

"He would be very near to coming... and so would I."

"Do you think… someone might come… up the path?"

"Maybe. I only care about your coming, that's all I care about."

"And you…. coming… yes?"

"Yes. Yes. Oh god."

Lila's climax exploded within her, as did mine. I didn't let up though. I was acting about fifteen years younger than now, and hard as a rock, and giving a woman I barely knew the orgasm of a lifetime. Well, that's what I hoped she felt. She certainly didn't do anything to make me think otherwise.

And then I stopped, and held myself right there, and we both opened our eyes. I think I said 'god' and she said 'wow', but it could have been the other way round.

We never played that game again, but just that once it was pretty damn good.

Chapter 42

After tea, I had a long talk with Jeff, while Petrus had a long talk with Ann. I didn't ask Petrus what about. Sessions with Ann stayed in the vault. Nor for that matter did Petrus ask about my talk with Jeff. I think he regarded my business relationship with Jeff as something outside his friendship with them, and for that matter, outside my friendship with himself.

Jeff was mortified about what had happened in Launceston. He wanted to take some responsibility for it, but I wouldn't have that. His contact was Garrett O'Brien, and Jeff knew nothing about Tony. I told him frankly that I'd been stupid to mix business with pleasure, let alone agreeing to a weekend away with a man I had only just met. Overall, I'd been stupid and gullible, and that didn't sit well with being a businesswoman with an investor behind her.

Jeff suggested that I simply needed to regroup, and see where I could go from where I now was. He said that I should be proud of the reactions I had been getting to my work, and that I'd got some good creative experience in the last few weeks regardless of this outcome.

"Lila, did you retain your rights to the designs you created, or did you assign those to the Club?" he asked lastly.

"I retained the rights. While I was losing my mind in every other direction, in that respect I had the presence of mind to be specific in the exchange of letters."

"Good. Paper products," he said.

"I beg your pardon?"

"Paper products. Various ways to approach it, but basically, think of anything made of card or paper that could incorporate your designs. Writing paper. Envelopes. Wrapping paper. Greetings cards. Notebooks. All that kind of thing. Or even tea towels. I remember seeing a shop in Hobart selling nothing but that stuff. Work for them. Or set up a rival business. Sell online. Whatever. Step one, go to Hobart and sniff around that shop. Come back and we'll talk about it again."

I thought, there speaks a man with business vision. No wonder he lives very comfortably.

I was going to talk about it with Petrus that night, but instead we got otherwise diverted. I had to confess to Petrus about what really happened on the hilltop. I couldn't put it off any longer. But instead of being angry about it, which I wouldn't have been surprised about, Petrus just absorbed it into his sex game and that was that. I assumed he'd taken me seriously. Maybe he thought it was a sex game I was starting myself. Anyway, it brought me closure, and a damned good orgasm, and left Petrus and I on an even keel again. It was a shame I now had to raise the whole spectre of going away again. Sure, it might even be just a day trip, or a one nighter, to begin. But I knew Petrus would immediately be looking for the thin end of a wedge in the plan.

Yet I also knew that we simply couldn't keep drifting on like this. We had to have some agreed basis for our relationship. Were we free agents, open to whatever opportunities came along? Or were we committed to each other, happy to describe ourselves as partners, passing up chances in favour of a stable love life, even if the grass sometimes looked somewhat greener elsewhere. And that consideration took me to the other side of the hill. How long would it be till Petrus was indeed over that hill? Was I ready to support him through his old age, thereby likely to become celibate well before my time? Was loving and being loved more important, or equally important, or less important, than having a reasonable sex life?

For days I turned these thoughts over in my mind. Jeff had spoken of Hobart almost as if it was taken as read that I'd burned my boats in Launceston at least for the time being. But Hobart was a longer journey. Still, it was the largest city in Tasmania, and there would lie the biggest opportunities. A bricks-and-mortar paper goods shop would hardly be viable in Swansea. Once again, the choice seemed to be to spend the week in Hobart and weekends at Dolphin Sands, or just manage everything online from Dolphin Sands and make occasional trips to Hobart, or to move myself lock stock and barrel to Hobart, and say goodbye to Petrus altogether. Well, we'd still be friends online like we had been before my marriage exploded, but I couldn't imagine Petrus being happy about that, even if he lied about it, which would tend to be his way.

Right now, staying with Petrus and operating online seemed to be the 'right' thing to do. Moving to Hobart totally would be the logical thing to do. The middle option would probably see Petrus and I gradually, or even rapidly, drifting apart.

Of course Petrus and I could move to Hobart together. But could I ask him to tear up his roots again and leave his beloved yellow house? He'd often said how this was the house he would be carried out of in a box. He'd said that he couldn't face the upheaval of a further move.

The whole thing was impossible. I decided that talking it through with Petrus calmly and logically would help the best plan to emerge.

Silly me.

Chapter 43

It was about three weeks after Lila's return that she sat me down at the dining table at coffee time for what she billed as a serious talk. Serious talks always worried me. In fact they terrified me. I was therefore on the defensive before we even started talking. It didn't help that I was feeling somewhat off colour and hadn't slept well. Or maybe I was off colour because of the lack of sleep. Instinct was telling me that I should get checked out by Ezra. Anyway, Lila didn't pick the best moment for the talk.

She began by revealing what she and Jeff had discussed, on that day we had the makeup sex. That was a bad start to the conversation, because my immediate reaction was to wonder why she hadn't come clean about it at the time. I just felt right away that she and Jeff had been talking, plotting even, behind my back.

Then she said how she had been thinking about various options for our future. That too went down like a lead balloon. She'd thought, and come to a conclusion, and was now presenting me with a fait accompli about 'our' future.

No, she denied that. She said there seemed to be three options. She wrapped up the first option very prettily, but basically she said it would involve her in staying on in the yellow house indefinitely, developing her business online, and meanwhile nursing me through my declining years, becoming an old maid in the process. She clearly didn't like that option.

Second option, spend the week in Hobart and weekends here. I think that brought the Launceston experiment to mind for both of us. It might work to begin with, but there was a lot of scope for it to go pear shaped in short order.

Third option, she'd move to Hobart without me, assuming I wouldn't go there too. She knew I wouldn't. Perhaps 'couldn't' would be a better word. I was in my last home, I had no doubt. I'd be carried out of here, either in a coffin or on my way to a nursing home, hopefully the former.

She tried to wrap it up nicely, but the bottom line was that the third option was the plan. She was leaving me.

She said, no, she wasn't leaving me, I could visit her, she could visit me, we'd be able to use the messenger service just like before, we could phone, use Skype, whatever. We could do everything except touch each other, cuddle, hug, kiss, make love, dry each other's tears, wipe cream from my nose. She didn't enumerate that list, I did. I was angry, hurt, and just for once, I came out fighting. I had no option. I felt my heart was being broken, one last time.

Chapter 44

For some moments, Petrus and Lila sat at the dining table in silence. Lila stared at her coffee cup. Petrus stared at Lila, while trying somehow to translate his anger and hurt into words. The pain in his heart was almost physical.

Finally Petrus said, "Remember the last time we had this conversation, back in London? I bet I trotted out the old line about how if you really love someone, you'll love them enough to lose them, enough to say goodbye? That if they think it's best to go, the loving thing is not to stand in their way?"

Lila thought back, and indeed she remembered that phrase. In fact, she remembered thinking that he'd used it to make himself look good, but from where she stood today, she realised he'd probably just meant it to be taken at face value. It was what he believed. It was what had defined his relationships for the whole of his adult life.

Petrus stood up, turned to the window, and looked out at the sea. Then he turned back to her, looking pale, almost as if in pain. He said, "Lila, I don't love you that much. I love you enough to fight for you, but not enough to lose you. The time has come to have something for me. I don't want you to go off to Hobart. I'm not going to just nobly let you go. I am begging you not to just think of yourself, I want you to think of me. Or think of us. For once, I want someone to love me more than I love them. Or at least to love me the same. I can't out-love someone again. I just can't do it. Go and walk by the sea, and maybe you will come back without the need to break my heart. But if you have to do that, please don't come back and say goodbye. Just go. I do love you enough that I wouldn't want you to see my face when you tell me."

Lila looked at him, shocked by the anger in his words. She shook her head as if trying to free her ears from the sound of his voice. Then she snatched up her jacket and walked out of the house, and down the steps, and strode towards the sea.

In the yellow house, Petrus stood very still. He gripped the back of one of the dining chairs and his knuckles were white. He stood there for several minutes. Then he thought, I have said something unworthy. Those words do not represent who I am, even if they represent who I might wish I could be. I must tell Lila. I must unsay it all. How could I say that I do not love her enough? If I have to prove it by hearing her say goodbye, and offering her my love to take with her wherever she now goes, then so be it. If I had to, I would lovingly lose her. I would lovingly die for her. I will follow her quickly, he thought.

Lila reached the sea, too devastated even to cry. The Petrus she had known all these years would never have made such a speech, full of wounding and emotional blackmail. How could he think they could have an ongoing relationship on that basis? What had happened to him? What was he thinking? And why?

Then she thought, for the moment I will put aside what he said. I will make my own decision, weigh up the merits of each side of the argument one last time. And if I decide to stay, I will tell him why, and I will tell him I am doing so of my own free will, not as a result of his bullying and manipulation. And if I decide to go, I will go back and tell him to his face, even though it will be the most awful moment of my life. At the outset, I promised only to not leave him wondering. So I will do that. If I leave him, I will tell him.

But Lila did not know what to do.

She faced the waves. They broke across the sand. They were drawn back to the beach every day. They retreated, they came back. It was the way it had always been, a force of nature at work. They had no choice but to return, for all eternity.

The tide goes out, the tide comes in.

At last she made her decision.

As she turned back towards the house, she could see a young woman coming across the yard. Today Colette was leaving for her first real holiday in years. She was coming to say goodbye to them. She was wearing a long multicoloured scarf, its colours almost as bright as her eternal smile. Bad timing, Colette, Lila thought.

Then she heard a metallic clang, maybe two. It sounded like something falling on the metal steps of the house.

Almost at once she heard Colette scream, and Lila's blood ran cold at the young woman's words.

"Petrus! Oh God, Petrus, no!"

Lila had never heard Colette use his first name, never.

She saw her run to the steps. Lila ran too. When she got there, she could see Petrus crumpled, doll-like, at the foot of the steps, face up. She could see blood spreading on the ground. She froze.

Colette said out loud, but to herself, "I have been trained for this, I know what to do, I know what to do." She turned to Lila and said, "Do what I say. Don't move him. He may have injured his back, or broken something. Just keep him calm and comforted. I'll get help."

Colette was on her mobile. She was speaking to someone to whom she used words of authority and command. Lila heard her say "heart attack" and "head injury" and "possible spinal injury" and "immediate response." Lila heard her say "Yes, air ambulance, now."

Lila fought the urge to straighten him, to cradle him in her arms. He was deadly pale, and blood was oozing plentifully from a wound which seemed to be at the back of his head. She said, "Petrus, I'm here. You'll be ok. They're coming for you now, the air ambulance. Colette called them. You'll be ok."

He repeated the name, almost as if trying to remember who she was. "Colette."

He was silent for some moments as Lila knelt beside him, his eyes searching her face. Then he almost whispered, "Lila, can we walk down to the beach?"

Lila reached for Petrus' hand as he lay immobile before her.

"Of course Petrus, we'll walk. Here's my hand. Now we're walking by the sea, just us."

Petrus struggled to say something more. She bent her head to him. "Lila, it was madness. I love you. Enough to lose you."

"I know, Petrus. I know. I love you too."

More moments passed. She could not hear help coming. It wasn't moments, it was eternity.

His eyes closed. She said firmly, "Petrus, don't sleep." He slowly reopened them.

He said, "I want to float on the water now. I just want to float."

"No Petrus. Hold my hand because we are walking along the

beach, you and me, and we mustn't go too near the water. Stay on the soft sand. Stay with me."

At last she could hear the sound of engines and rotors in the sky. Colette was across the yard, waving her glowing scarf to them.

Lila looked down at Petrus, at an elderly and broken man, holding onto her hand and to his life as best he could. But after all the years, he was still Petrus. She knew what she had to say, what she wanted to say.

"Petrus, they are almost here. And then you will be safe. And when you come home, I will be here."

He smiled so weakly, but he smiled. "And the next day?"

"And the next day."

"And the day after?"

"We'll see."

He still smiled. Then he paused, gathering the strength to speak again. He said, "The kids used to ask, We'll see 'yes', or we'll see 'no'?."

Lila smiled back, blinking away the tears. "Don't push your luck, Petrus."

But she didn't think he heard her against the sound of the helicopter landing in the yard.

- The End -

246

Acknowledgements

My thanks are due to my faraway friend

who proof-read the book as it was being written,

gave me unstinting encouragement,

made some excellent suggestions,

and in particular,

introduced me to Maria Island.

I am also indebted to 'Barb'

who gave me wise counsel and advice,

and spotted some howlers.

Printed in Great Britain
by Amazon

61518822R00149